To my sister Carolita
who has found summer again

CAST OF CHARACTERS

in order of appearance

SIMONA GRIFFO
Transplanted Italian ad exec. Runs hot and cold.

BUD WARREN
Grieving advertising legend. Hates losing.

POLLY PYNES
Former owner of The Pynes Cottages and
Bud's ex-wife. Died a year ago.

DMITRI K.
Simona's Russian partner. Plays detective
and Dear Abby.

LAURIE WARREN
Bud and Polly's daughter. Holds back on trust.

STAN GREENHOUSE
Simona's lover, an NYPD homicide detective.
Hesitates to commit.

WILLY GREENHOUSE
Stan's fifteen-year-old son. Mishears a nightmare.

REBECCA BARNES
Hamptons' artist. Specializes in still lifes.

DODO PARSONS
Local eccentric. Communes with Jackson Pollock,
Lewis Carroll, and the bottle.

JIM MOLTON
Ex-corporate trader. Offers seafood and
a salty romance.

LESTER KENNELLY
Bud's advertising partner. Dreams of California.

CHARLENE SOBEL
Lester's assistant. Knows where the butter is.

RAF GARCIA
Greenhouse's partner. Worries about a code name.

DICK KNIGHT
Bud's P.I. Thinks the money's in his file.

STEVE KING
Local bayman. Grapples with a net
full of mixed emotions.

CAPTAIN COMELLI
Cop in charge. Sticks to his own theories.

AMANDA KENNELLY
Lester's lawyer wife. Puts people together.

GREGORY PRICE
Works with Simona at HH&H.
Makes the right phone call.

Plus a summer assortment of fire fighters, policemen,
dogs, birds, fish, and the eclectic residents of that
wonderland known as the Hamptons.

ONE

Thas magical light that enticed countless artists was gone. Gardiners Bay, twenty feet ahead, had disappeared during the night like Brigadoon. The white windmill of Gardiners Island across the bay had turned into a memory. It was an August Sunday in Springs, a hamlet just north of East Hampton on Long Island, New York. At 6:03 A.M. the temperature was seventy-four degrees. The sun a white blister wrapped in gray gauze. Depending on your mood, the fog was dreary, romantic, or scary.

Bud Warren was unusually talkative. "The ugly cliché. Greed and vanity destroying nature's beauty." He wiped his forehead with a tanned, gnarled hand. "When I first came out here in '56, the place was still unspoiled." Bud poured coffee. "This heat we've been getting? Man-made. Ozone layer's thinner than a Park Avenue wife."

The temperature in the Hamptons was expected to reach ninety-three for the fourth day in a row.

New York City, one hundred again. This was the third morning Bud and I met at this hour. We'd mostly stared at the water's edge and the fog beyond.

Bud Warren had joined me with a red thermos full of iced coffee with plenty of skim milk and too much sugar. I accepted the coffee and recalled the view I couldn't see. "This is an incredibly serene spot."

"If you look at the map of the East End, it's like a lobster claw," Bud said. "The place grabs you. The Millers, the Parsons, the Kings, Talmages, Mulfords, Bennetts. They're still here, the same families, three centuries later. They found their home and they stayed. I admire that loyalty. I just wish it got applied to people instead of places." He took a long sip, then peered inside his cup as if it held something he needed. Water lapped loudly, like a thirsty dog. It was high tide.

"After more than forty years of marriage," he said, "my wife divorced me."

"My marriage lasted six years."

"In the old days when the winters got bad around here, everyone thanked God for the clams. Maybe that's what I should do. Go clamming."

"If you do, bring over your catch and I'll cook up some spaghetti. Guaranteed to clear the fog."

"Divorce is not the worst of it." A drop of sweat dangled from Bud's chin. The humidity was tropical. "A year ago today Polly was killed. Murdered."

I leaned forward, surprised. "I'd heard it was suicide."

"That note they found? My wife didn't know the word sorry. And she sure wouldn't apologize for killing herself. Hell, most people around here would be relieved, including our daughter."

"Is the case still open?"

"It will be soon." Bud poured some more coffee into his thermos cup.

I unstuck the shirt from my back. "Why do you think she was murdered?" A perfect conversation for a gray, muffled dawn.

"I have my reasons," Bud said. "And it wasn't some psycho who'd come out here for a fast kill either. Someone close. Someone she trusted."

A woman slipped out between peeling trunks of red cedars. Bud raised his cup in a wave. The drop of sweat left his chin and hit his bare knee. The woman turned and threaded her way back through the trees.

Bud offered me more coffee. I declined. "The Russian said you're detectives."

"I don't have a license," I said.

"One license is enough. I like a woman being in on this. I'm not going to demean you by talking about intuitive sense, but you've got your way of thinking, a man's got another. It makes a more complete picture. I've already negotiated the money part with the Russian. His English is poor, but he understands dollars."

A seagull cawed. Others joined in. "When was this great negotiation?" I asked.

Bud turned to look at me, surprised that I didn't know. Strong nose, jutting cheekbones and chin, topped by an Einstein mass of white hair that repeated on his chest. His gray-blue eyes matched the color of the bay as I remembered it. So did his swim shorts. "We talked last night at the barbecue. Look, I know you're neophytes, but I've already gone through three PIs from the city."

"Today's my last day in the Hamptons."

"Call it the South Fork or the East End, that'll win you points with the locals. I've already given your partner a retainer."

"Then your agreement is with Dmitri."

"I'm paying for both." Bud lifted himself up from the sling chair. His body was in sharp contrast to his leonine head—narrow shoulders, a thin, worn-out frame. He was somewhere in his sixties. "The Russian says he doesn't work without you."

So now Dmitri would blame me for loss of income. He's a jack-of-all-trades. Cab driver, bodyguard, hair importer. Always in debt.

"Our place is rented as of tomorrow." I finished off my coffee. It tasted lousy that morning.

"I'll talk to my daughter," Bud offered. "Maybe Laurie will let you stay in her cottage. She's moving up to the big house today." He lifted his chin in the direction of a gray-shingled house barely visible at the bay's far end, behind the oaks, cedars, and black cherries that covered the sixteen-acre plot of The Pynes. Polly Pynes's castle.

"Some anniversary," Bud said. "See you tonight, at eight. Here." He walked toward the water's edge where he'd beached his scull. I toyed with my glass, wondering what I should do. I was curious, tempted.

Bud had forgotten his thermos. I screwed the top back on, noticing that the plastic cup was chipped, and waded through the wet air after him.

"I don't know about this job," I said. I had one more week of vacation. "A year-old trail is hard to pick up."

"I've got some ideas, but I need hard evidence. Join me in the water tonight, after your family's gone."

"Why not now?"

He looked at his watch. "I've got to go. Tonight I'll fill you in on my hunch. Eight o'clock. We'll cool off." He took his thermos and stooped off toward the water with a slow gait.

He didn't get far. "Simone!" My name's Simona, but I forgave Bud. In that humidity, pronouncing another vowel was too much effort.

I followed Bud to where his contraption was waiting. A scull with a rowing machine attached on top. "Are you going to be all right in this fog?"

"I know this coastline like the arteries of my heart." Bud dropped the thermos in the scull and strapped his life vest on. Red like his thermos. "Simone, three things you should know."

"What?"

"The cottage Laurie is vacating is air-conditioned."

"Tempting."

"If that doesn't work out, you can stay with me. I'm too worn out to be a threat to any woman."

"What's the third?"

"One of the New York detectives came up with something." His jaw set.

"You didn't like it."

"You and the Russian will have to do better."

"How?"

"That's what I'm paying you for."

Bud Warren rowed into the fog. It was a morning and evening exercise you could set your watch to. A response to the heart attack that struck him four days after his wife committed suicide. Or was murdered.

TWO

A N HOUR LATER DMITRI met me for breakfast at Dreesen's in nearby East Hampton. The sun was slowly burning the fog off the water. Inland it was clear. The temperature had risen three degrees. It felt like twenty.

The store was cool, air-conditioned, with a ceiling fan for an extra boost. "You should have consulted me first," I said, using the counter for support. I needed a nap.

"No time." Dmitri raised four fingers and pointed to the Donut Robot in the window that was dropping perfect rounds of dough into simmering oil. Cinnamon filled the air like dust. I moved toward the bananas. They didn't smell.

"Why the rush?" I asked. "Last I saw you, you were grunting through your fifth ear of corn. I gave up counting the hot dogs." A fire engine howled nearby. The counterman looked through the storefront window.

"The pines are burning," he announced in a low voice. His nose paralleled the bill of his baseball cap.

"The Pynes cottages?" I asked. "In Springs?" It hadn't rained on the Island in twenty-two days.

"Up Island. Pine Barrens on central Long Island. Near Rocky Point. It's a five-thousand-acre state forest. Fire started last night. It's bad."

"How bad?" asked a man with dripping, slicked-back hair. He grabbed the Sunday *New York Times* as if it might disappear. "I gotta get back to the city today. Am I gonna be able to get back?"

The counterman gave him his change, which did not include answers. The New Yorker slammed the door shut.

"What can we do?" I had a sleepy vision of setting up a pasta kitchen for the troops.

"Don't throw out cigarette butts and pray the wind stays down. Every able-bodied firefighter's working this one. Used to be a firefighter myself in younger days. Volunteers, every last one of them." The counterman cast a disapproving eye Dmitri's way. For not being a firefighter, for buying four artery-clogging donuts, for his looks, for being from the city—I didn't know. Maybe his clothes. Dmitri had on one of his FizzEd gym outfits, ready for an hour of intense aerobics: sand-covered black Reeboks, one of which was held together by silver duct tape; a wrinkled black T-shirt dribbled with last year's borscht, and pin-striped charcoal wool trousers cut off below the knee by nail clippers.

Dmitri gathered his four donuts and hot tea. I paid.

"I still say you should have asked me first before accepting Bud's offer. I mean, what's the rush? She's been dead a year."

"I lose job."

"Perelman fired you?" Dmitri had spent the summer at The Creeks, Revlon mogul Ron Perelman's fifty-seven-acre estate facing Georgica Pond, *the* place to be in the East End. He'd been hired as resident goon, along with his friends Ivan and Igor, known in the U.S.A. as Mike and Phil. "Why?"

"At party I ask tall lady with long hair if she like to cut? I buy hair at good price. She laugh so long Ron get jealous. Turns up lady is Julia Roberts, which I know of course. What's big deal, I ask? Lady stays. I go. No loyalty. After I get in trouble with police for him." Earlier in the season he'd brandished a pistol at two canoeists for rowing too close to Perelman's shoreline, a shoreline that is public property. Ron prizes his privacy. Dmitri prizes being fearsome.

"I'm sorry about the job." I patted his shoulder, large enough on its own to have brought down the Berlin Wall. Dmitri could also pass as Stalin's clone, complete with hairbrush mustache. Except for his height. Dmitri claims he's six feet and three quarters inches; Stalin was five-four. Yakov is his real name, but he likes Dmitri better, introducing himself as "Violent, proud, sensual, and cruel, but generous. Like Karamazov brodder." He is mostly sweet.

"I have no home in Hamptons now," Dmitri said, "but it's okay. One thousand dollar Mr. Warren give us for commitment. I stay and live with you."

"We are not licensed detectives."

"I show him detective gold shield, he plenty impressed. Tell him I am ex-cop." After walking the perimeters of the store to check out the goodies, Dmitri headed for the door. There was no place to sit inside. I picked up the last big bottle of Pellegrino. In the past three days the A&P had sold 450 cases.

"That shield's a fake," I said, "and you can land in jail for using it." A detective had lost his shield in a nightclub brawl in Brighton Beach. Dmitri had picked it up, had it copied, and then mailed it back. He'd even gotten an IOU from the grateful detective.

"I have to give up the cottage tomorrow morning," I said, walking out to the street. "So we both don't have a place to stay." In August, in the Hamptons, that's a problem akin to America's national debt.

"One hundred dollar a day for each, plus expenses," Dmitri said.

My eyebrows shot up.

"We sleep in car."

We sat on the bench on Newtown Lane, the shopping street of East Hampton. Across the way was the Barefoot Contessa that sells food and flowers at premium prices. Dmitri's vintage Cadillac, which doubled as his office, was parked in front of Sam's Bar, at a fire hydrant. Vintage cars are common in the Hamptons, but Dmitri's didn't make the grade. The car was 1950s pink and a pothole shy of the junk heap. It was, however, large enough to comfortably accommodate two sleepers.

"There is more to deal," Dmitri said. "Two thousand dollar bonus if killer arrested." He topped his hot tea with vodka from a flask.

I took a long drink of my ice-cold Pellegrino, leaned back, and imagined myself sitting in the shade of green money. "I could buy myself a real Armani suit."

"The skirt maybe."

"It's a start."

"I could finish to pay my cousin's wife for Caddie." Dmitri sipped thoughtfully, then wiped his mustache. "Bud in advertising. You in advertising. You know him?"

I'm an art buyer in a small agency that is heavy into cosmetics and fashion. The art I buy is photographers, models, stylists, sets, everything that is needed for a print shoot. It's a crazy, hectic job with kooks and egos. Most of the time I love it.

"What I know is that his check won't bounce." I took a long swig of my water bottle. The sweating process was in full swing. "Bud earns a lot of money."

"Why he not live south of highway like rest of rich people?"

"He gave me a little lecture on greed, so maybe he's not into the ostentatious display of money. As for his bio, Bud is the creative head of Warren, Shepard, Kennelly. *Advertising Age* just did an article on the agency. It's private, established in the seventies. Nine hundred million in billings in the late eighties, it now hovers around five hundred million. Last year there were rumors of a merger with

Chass\Dayton, the international agency based in California." Merger was a polite way of saying acquisition. Chass\Dayton was a much larger agency with more than a billion in billings. "The merger fell through, but the rumors are on again."

I slid down, resting my head on the back of the bench. "Bud made his name at Doyle Dane Bernbach back in the late fifties, early sixties. Worked with Bill Bernbach on Volkswagen—'Think small'—and Avis—'We try harder.' 'You don't have to be Jewish to love Levy's real Jewish rye.'"

"But you better have tight tooths. Seed gets stuck."

I propped the cold bottle under my jaw. The world around me was wobbling. "At WSK he's shown jeeps leaping across the Grand Canyon—'We handle rough.' He's put a large-women clothing manufacturer on the map with his 'The More the Merrier' campaign. He's done more pro bono work for charities and humane causes than all New York art directors put together. His partner, Lester Kennelly, is into greed. He lives south of the highway and docks his sailboat in Three Mile Harbor. I'll bet you a quarter you can't guess the name."

"Okay." Dmitri smirked. "*Eighteen Percent!*"

That's the percentage above cost that the agency bills its clients. "You've seen the boat."

"Seventy-foot Hinkley, sleeps eight. I wish to crew but I get seasick." Dmitri held out his hand. "Bet is bet."

I fished into my shirt pocket. In the breadth of

his palm, the quarter looked like a piece of confetti.

"What you know of ex-wife Polly?"

"You're going to have to tell Bud the truth," I said. A police siren started up. More fire engines. A boy ran out of Dreesen's, mother on his tail.

"If I tell truth, Bud fire us. Where is American capitalistic spirit?"

"'I can never tell a lie.' That's what George Washington said. Father of this country."

"We take case," Dmitri said. "I need money now. What you know of this Polly Pynes?"

"I never agreed to being part of a detective team."

He reached into his improvised pedal pushers and extracted a silver-on-white card. Russian on one side; English on the other. DimSim, Dmitri-Simona Detective Agency. His car-phone number. No address. "Last year you like."

"I thought it was a joke. And you were going to change the name."

"You want to come first?"

"I want to not sound like Chinese hors d'oeuvres. I'm sorry, if you're not going to tell Bud Warren we're amateurs, I can't help you."

"You speak English good."

"I speak English well. Look, Bud Warren can get me fired if the mood strikes him. Let me see that check. Come on." I wiggled fingers at him.

Dmitri had to stand up to reach in his pocket. Reluctantly he handed over the check.

It was made out to me. I handed it back. "So that's your need."

"My last name impossible to spell. Even I don't know."

"What's your social security number?"

"Numbers bad for me."

He didn't have one. Or a green card. The cab driving and hair import business dealt mostly in cash. His pals Mike and Phil had been cashing Perelman's paychecks for him. "The police declared Polly Pynes's death a suicide. There's probably no case. After lunch I'm going back to the city." I shut my eyes. Sugar in hot water, that's how I felt.

The bench creaked. Dmitri must have moved. "So why Bud pay money to find murderer?"

"Suicide is hard to accept. It involves guilt, blame. This heat is killing me."

"You look like scrambled eggs. Now I tell you what I know." Another creak. "At FizzEd, woman instructor is friend of daughter Laurie. Instructor has long hair so I become friend." Dmitri went to the hot local gym every day, ostensibly to lose some of his two hundred and fifty pounds. He soon made a deal with a local hairdresser. After an hour of serious sweating, he'd sweet-talk some long-haired ladies to go short. The hairdresser would cut at a discount, and Dmitri would swim in hair, which he then sold to wig makers.

"Polly move out here to East Hampton permanent five years ago," Dmitri said, "and Bud—"

"—used to commute from Manhattan until the

divorce. Then he moved out here too. According to him, Polly wasn't too popular with people, including their daughter."

"And"—Dmitri poked a finger into my arm. I nearly fell over.—"Polly found in Accabonac Creek, behind Jackson Pollock house. Dead drowned. Full of Valium."

I sat up, eyes open, and took a long breath. "You know, you really have to learn to use articles." Russian didn't seem to have any. "When Polly decided to kill herself she gobbled lots of pills so that, even if she chickened out at the last minute, she wouldn't be able to swim." I hate it when he knows more than I do.

"Suicide note they find three days late. After police check. This make many rumors. I get curious. I hear Bud pooh-pooh suicide. At barbecue last night, I spot man at the grill. I smell barbecue sauce and possibility of remunerative enterprise." Dmitri paused for a long sniff.

I took the hint. "Bravo. Good vocabulary. Go on."

"I tell Bud we are detectives. He bites into hamburger and my story."

"You're on your own." More fire sirens howled. The fire station was just off North Main Street, not far away.

Behind us, Dreesen's screen door slammed open and the counterman came out. "They're headin' in the wrong direction. Something else is goin' on."

"An accident?" I pushed myself up. Last week there'd been a three-car collision right by Hook Mill.

Dmitri sat me down again. "Stan and Willy are okay." He offered me his last donut.

I took it. Food soothes. "They were sleeping when I left."

People started running toward Main Street, voices rising with the shimmer of the sidewalk: "It's a fire. Nearby." "I don't smell smoke." "It's another accident." "Someone drunk again. Six accidents just this week." "I can't wait to have my town back." "Fireplace Road, that's where they headed." "It's gotta be terrible."

Fireplace Road, where Jackson Pollock had lost his life ramming into a tree. Fireplace Road, at the end of which the first settlers lit fires to send signals to Gardiners Island. The road I had just driven on. Which I needed to take to get back. To Stan. And Willy.

"I'm going." I broke into a fast trot toward my car. Dmitri barreled after me.

"You drive." I threw him the keys and got in the passenger's seat. The way I was feeling I would have crashed into the nearest tree.

THREE

AIR-CONDITIONING AT FULL BLAST, we drove past Hook Mill, which had been standing there since 1806, past the police car parked on the side of the road, with Manny in the driver's seat. Everyone but the day-trippers knew he was a dummy. The pace was snail with sore feet. That wasn't unusual, even at eight o'clock on a Sunday morning. August in the Hamptons.

The police were setting up a roadblock at School Street. Cars were backing out, U-turning, taking the side streets. I got out of the car and asked the nearest officer, "Is it an accident? A fire? I'm staying at The Pynes. Is everything okay over there?"

"Fire. Closer in."

I looked for smoke and saw none. The land in Springs is thick with trees.

"Which house?"

He shook his head.

Others had joined in, asking questions: Whose

house? How many firefighters were on the job? Hadn't they all gone to the Pine Barrens? Was there enough water? Whose house? Again and again.

The officer raised both hands. "Look, I don't know which house." He looked old enough to have to wave his driver's license at a bar. "Please clear the road." He wouldn't have convinced a sheep.

A car behind us honked. The officer stepped back to remove the barrier. We stepped aside.

"Hey, that's Dave," a man said. "Dave, what's going on? Are we safe?" The car drove through.

"Who's Dave?" I asked my neighbor.

"The fire marshal."

I pushed myself out of the crowd and collapsed back into the car. Dmitri had stayed put to enjoy the air-conditioning.

"Don't worry. I get you home." He turned onto Gardiner, speeding at fifty in a thirty miles-per-hour zone, then had to brake for Sunday traffic on Three Mile Harbor Road. Necks craned out of windows and convertibles, heads pointed skyward, above the tree line, to seek the telltale smoke. Drivers shouted requests for information at the homeowners who were watering their grass and trees. One man stood on his shingled roof, binoculars aimed at Fireplace Road and Accabonac Harbor beyond it. My car windows stayed up, to keep cool and calm. As Dmitri drove, I watched the leaves on the oak trees for movement. The wind stayed down.

Finally we were able to turn right onto Hog Creek Lane, which ran into the end of Fireplace

Road. Less traffic. More trees. Most of the houses in Springs are not fancy. Some vacation homes—simple wooden structures with no attention-getting architectural innovations. Few pools. The area is mostly inhabited by locals, some of them baymen, "bonackers" as they are called in the East End because originally they had made their living from the fish and shellfish in Accabonac Harbor.

A hundred feet ahead of us, Bud and Polly's daughter, Laurie, ran in the direction of The Pynes. A chocolate brown Lab tailed her.

Dmitri slowed the car behind her. I pressed the window button and yelled, "Can we give you a ride?"

Laurie stopped, turned, her expression stunned. She was breathing so hard she couldn't speak. She was wearing black cyclist shorts and an old gray T-shirt dark with sweat. The dog collapsed on the hot asphalt.

"What happened, Laurie?"

"Jim." Her chest swelled and retreated. She tried to get her feet going, but couldn't. The dog sat up, panting, ready to take off again.

I got out of the car. "What about Jim?" Jim Molton lived next door to The Pynes. He was a friend of Bud's. "What's wrong?" She tugged at me.

"Jim called. I've got to go." She tried her feet again. The dog ran ahead.

"We'll drive you."

"I'm faster." She started to cry.

"What's wrong?"

"My dad's house is burning."

FOUR

I PUSHED LAURIE into the backseat and got in behind her. The dog jumped onto the front seat as if he'd always belonged there. Dmitri hit the accelerator. With the horn blaring, we passed The Pynes and curved left on Fireplace Road. I gripped the door handle to keep from swaying. Laurie crashed against me. The car nosed toward a mailbox, than veered back onto the road. The dog stayed put, obviously used to crazy driving. Cars got out of our way. Ahead of us, black smoke billowed above the tree line. The leaves on the trees fluttered.

During the divorce proceedings, Bud had moved from the big house into one of the cottages at The Pynes. After the lawyers settled the divorce agreement, Polly had kicked Bud off the property and he'd bought what real estate agents call a post-modern. I had seen it from a distance.

Bud Warren's house was just south of the Merrill Lake Sanctuary, a three-story wooden house trimmed in white, swooped by incongruous arches, and layered by too many terraces. It didn't fit into the simple, back-to-nature spirit of Springs, but it had the merit of a view of Accabonac Creek, the harbor, and the sunrise. It was less than two miles from The Pynes.

Dmitri braked two inches from a fire truck's front bumper. Hose Humpers, stenciled in gold letters, spread across our windshield. Laurie ran out, the dog after her. "Steve!" she yelled to a firefighter coming out of a yellow truck named Bonackers. The dog jumped up on him with an ecstatic yelp. Steve gave Laurie a quick hug, then disappeared behind some trees, the dog following.

Voices called Laurie's name. I got out of the car and recognized some of the tenants of The Pynes. The officer held them back.

"Hey lady, you better get back here," he called out to me. I stopped by the fire well, luckily placed twenty feet from Bud's driveway. I couldn't see the house, only two firefighters hacking at the underbrush. There was no roar, just the crackle of wood being eaten by flames hungrier than termites. No cicadas or birds. Lots of heat. Dry. As if the fire had burned away the humidity. Or maybe it was just my throat, gagging from the acrid reek of smoke.

"Who are you?" Dave the fire marshal wanted to know. A tall man, wearing a firefighter's helmet. Soot covered his strong jaw. His khakis and navy T-shirt were dirty and soaked. His boots were muddy. His voice was cocktail-party light.

"Simona Griffo, vacationer. Laurie needed a

ride." I turned to look for Dmitri. He was still in the car, struggling to unbuckle his seat belt.

"Is Mr. Warren okay?" I asked.

"House's empty. Bud Warren's damn lucky we weren't all out at Pine Barrens. What do you know about this?"

"Nothing."

Dave walked over to Laurie, who was clutching the mailbox, as if to keep herself from running into the burning house.

I followed, stopping at a discreet distance while the fire marshal hugged her. This was a village, I reminded myself, the city dweller. He'd probably known her since she was knee-high. Steve had disappeared into the thickness of the trees. He'd ordered Tanner, the Lab, to go home. The dog was now trying to hide behind the crowd.

"Your dad's not in the house, Laurie," Dave said. "That's what counts. Most of the fire's knocked down. South side of the house is in bad shape, but we've managed to save the rest. Fire started in the kitchen, as far as we can tell."

"The kitchen?" Laurie's voice wavered. "That's Dad's workroom. Oh god, all his artwork, his papers." She stopped her mouth with her fist, her eyes fixed on Dave.

"Sorry, Laurie. I'm gonna have to wait 'til the men take up the fire before I figure it out proper. You know anything about this, see anything?"

"What?" Laurie raked her hair with a shaking hand. "What are you talking about?"

"How'd you find out about the fire?" Dave asked in his slow, calm way.

"Jim Molton called. He lives next door to us."

"You were at home?"

"No, I was at . . ." She dropped her hand and swallowed. "I was at Steve's house. I was asleep when he got the call." She turned cooked-lobster red. "Jim saw Steve driving with his helmet on, followed him over here, and called me. He couldn't find Dad."

"Where's Jim now?"

"What's up?" Dmitri's bulk trudged up to the fire marshal. He aimed his Swiss Army knife at the hem of the sky. "Black smoke." My eyes followed the blade. The smoke was dissipating, paling to pewter gray. I wondered why Dmitri was waving a knife. Then I saw the jagged hole in his T-shirt. At the hip. At least he hadn't slashed Stan's seat belt.

"What's your interest?" Dave asked Dmitri, his voice a notch less calm.

I jumped in. "We're acquaintances of Bud Warren's." I told him about seeing Laurie's father row off into the fog at 6:30 A.M. "He was headed west, toward Lion's Head Rock."

"He does that every morning," Laurie explained. "On clear, calm days he goes clear across the bay to the Gardiners Island windmill. Otherwise, he does the coast. West or east. He's usually gone about two hours."

"Well, he should be heading back here by now," Dave said. "Somebody better go warn him real gentle about losing half his house. And now, folks, you better get out of here. The fire isn't over yet." Dave glanced up at the trees. They were swaying. The wind had come up. From the southeast.

We drove Laurie back to The Pynes in silence. At the beach Dmitri helped her lift a kayak off its trestle and push it in the water. A few cottage tenants flapped around her to ask questions, to commiserate. She waved them away. The fog had lifted. Laurie slipped on a red life vest, identical to Bud's, dropped into the kayak, and paddled into Gardiners Bay to find her father.

Dmitri headed down the curling finger of land that is known as Gerard Drive, toward Accabonac Harbor where the bonackers dock their boats. He planned to borrow a floating anything that would accept his size. He wanted to be close to Laurie when she told her dad. Just in case his heart couldn't take it.

It was now ten o'clock. Bud had been gone more than three hours.

FIVE

'M STAYING," I ANNOUNCED. The cottage screen door slammed behind me. "Hey, what happened?"

Willy was sweeping up litter in the middle of the living room, his face mottled with anger. "Damn garbage bag broke!"

"Don't swear!" Stan called out.

"Come on, I'll do that." I grabbed the broom. Willy wouldn't let go.

"No, it's my fault. I gotta do it."

Dad's orders for sure. I'd learned to stay out of disciplining moments between father and son. "You're lucky it's the recyclables pile." It was cleaner.

Stan was eating breakfast in the small glassed-in porch, his back to the bay.

"I'm going to stay at least until tomorrow morning," I said. We didn't have to give the keys back until noon on Monday. "Dmitri will drive me to the Jitney." I slumped down, facing my sullen lover and the view.

Stan scooped up cornflakes. "You look beat."

"I have to stop getting up at dawn. The fire was at Bud Warren's house," I raised my voice so Willy could hear. "It's under control now."

Broom still in hand, Willy walked in and sat down next to me. He hadn't found his dad easy to take. Two days into our vacation he'd asked, "What's bugging him?" He hadn't believed me when I told him I didn't know. Now I regretted not having brought them some cinnamon donuts.

"I heard all the fire engines." Willy's knee jerked fast enough to compete with Lilco in lighting up Long Island. "It had to be real close." He would have loved to have run out to watch. Stan must have stopped him.

I smiled encouragement. "You didn't miss much."

Willy is a dead-ringer for a Norman Rockwell cover—baseball cap over blond hair, blue eyes, and freckles. Except for the haircut. Skate, I think they call it. I've dubbed it the chronic fatigue chop. The barber fell asleep halfway through.

Stan could usually play Rockwell's friendly patrolman. Brown, cropped hair, five-foot-ten, well-built without bulging muscle, a rear end that makes me want to reach out and touch it, and a kind, quietly handsome face that begs to be kissed. As for me, I don't think Rockwell did a picture of an Italian with a nose that meets jutting corners, a body that would float in gale-storm waters, an olive-skinned face that blends into a crowd, and shoulder-length brown hair that looks like roadkill if I don't wash it every day.

"Fire seems to have started in the kitchen," I said, "which I'm told is where most fires get going. I didn't go there to gawk, by the way. Laurie needed a ride and in case you haven't noticed"—the "you" was directed at Stan—"she runs The Pynes since her mother died last year. And it was her father's house that burned."

I propped up my feet against the windowsill. I let my mouth rest.

Serene light was bouncing off the bay, pushing the fog away. I sat and stared, forgetting all problems. Then Dmitri passed in a speed boat, heading toward Lion's Head Rock, following the coastline at low speed. Jim Molton was at the wheel. No sign of Laurie or Bud.

"Why are you staying?" Stan asked. He'd noticed the boat too. He didn't like Jim.

"It's seven degrees cooler here than New York and looking at the bay beats spring cleaning."

"I told you to wait. I'll help when I get back."

"We've skipped one spring, might as well wait for another? Not a bad idea. If I can get a place to sleep, I might stay a couple more days."

"Did you get all the garbage?" Stan asked his son.

"Yes, Dad. And I dumped it in the right bin too." Willy shuffled quickly back into the main room. He looked scrawny in his oversized T-shirt and Bermudas, as if he'd been left naked in the dryer too long. "I've got to pack." Something he'd already done. So had

Stan. Their two bags were zipped and ready by the
front door.

"You think you can be of help," Stan said, metic-
ulously scraping up the last three cornflakes in his
bowl, "even though you don't know these people?"

"The Good Samaritan has lost out to crass capitalism." I picked up a raisin from Willy's bowl. "I
have an eight o'clock appointment with Bud Warren
in the cool waters of the bay." His burning house had
wiped out my doubts about getting involved.

"Curiosity has nothing to do with capitalism."

"He's paying Dmitri and me to look into his
wife's death."

Stan stood up, chair scraping back. "Willy and I
better get going. I want to beat the traffic."

"Stan."

"What?" His expression frosted over.

"That's all I get? 'Willy and I better be going.'
Aren't you at least going to complain that I'm not
doing a load of wash for you?"

"I can do my own laundry."

"Complaining would be more than welcome as a
form of communication."

He lifted his chair back under the table.

I stood up, sat back down. "Stan, for the
umpteenth time, what's wrong?"

"For the umpteenth time, nothing. I can't be
Mister Happy on request, Sim, okay? It's too hot,
that's what's wrong."

The weather had nothing to do with it, of that I
was sure. At the end of May, Stan had been pro-

moted to first-grade detective, a happy event in any cop's life. A week later, his partner, Raf, and I had thrown him a party to celebrate. Stan's reaction to a chorus of "Surprise!" was as clear as a glass of water. He didn't like it.

Matters got worse when Raf proposed to his girl-friend of five years in front of everyone. Tina turned as red as the salsa and slammed Raf with a flat "no." They took their fight into the kitchen. Stan turned up the stereo to drown out their voices. The neighbors across the street got angry and called the police. The police found one first-grade homicide detective being feted by fifteen cops and their girlfriends, laughed it off, and left. The evening was not fun. Life had barely picked up since.

Stan has always been a closed person—I knew that going in—but in the past three months he'd slowly withdrawn into a corner I couldn't reach. I asked about his cases. Stan didn't elucidate. Raf, a willing source of information when I was dating Stan, had shut up since I'd moved in. It was time we communicated on our own, he said.

I asked again. And again. Stan denied his mood had anything to do with work or another lover. Then he denied his mood.

Willy was taking the bags out to the car. I lowered my voice anyway.

"If you want out, just tell me."

Stan looked at me with his overly serious expression, his eyes darker now that the humor had gone. "Do you?"

"No." I loved him. Stan was steadfast, loyal, kind, sexy. A dream man now looking for a laugh track.

I followed him into Willy's bedroom while he obsessively checked for forgotten items. A wood-paneled room. Twin beds, a narrow closet. On the wall a two-tiered shelf with a child's gleeful collection of seashells. Lots of sand everywhere plus a fat-bellied spider spinning in one corner.

Stan checked in every nook and cranny, as though it were a crime scene, then moved on to our bedroom, an exact replica of Willy's room, except for the queen-sized bed and an oil-painting of a basket full of corn. The only stuff lying around was mine.

He stepped back into the small living room. He looked under the sofa first.

"Stan! Willy cleaned up beautifully."

Then under the coffee table.

"What was in that garbage anyway? The White-water files?"

Stan raised himself up, his face flushed. "Just checking." I gave his rear end a pat. Not as a gesture of affection, exactly. I think I was trying to loosen up those muscles.

Stan stopped in front of the bathroom door. "You'll be careful?" Behind him I could see his electric toothbrush on top of the hot-water heater. Stan never forgets anything. Except to talk.

I moved to the kitchen counter. He followed. I debated telling him about the toothbrush. "Dmitri will watch over me," I said.

"That's great reassurance."

"I see a pretty rusty twinkle in your left eye." The twinkle was coming from the window's reflection. I fingered his cheek. He was about to grab my hand, then thought better of it.

"Bud Warren heard I was a homicide cop," he said. "He talked about his wife the first day we were here. That same day I called up Captain Jay Comelli of the Suffolk County police. He'd looked into the death a year ago. He's satisfied it was suicide. There was a note—"

"Which showed up three days later."

Stan shrugged. "It happens. I told Warren he should accept the facts. The victim had been treated for depression, she had no friends to speak of, she'd gone through a divorce, her daughter barely spoke to her, there's nothing to look into."

I dug my feet in. "I want to hear what Bud has to say."

At the screen door Stan stopped again. Outside Willy was leaning against the open car door, arms and legs crossed, head down. From the tape deck Darius of Hootie & the Blowfish was sha-la-la-ing at top volume about going home. Willy didn't want to see us or hear us.

"Did you dump the garbage?" Stan asked him.

"Yes, Dad." Willy's head stayed down.

"I'm sorry, Sim," Stan said. "I thought this vacation was going to be great. I should have left myself at home."

"I would have missed you."

"Thanks." He tried for a self-generated twinkle, but didn't make it. "I'll call you from one of the shelters." He pecked at my lips.

I pecked back. "Be careful." He was going off to the White Mountains of New Hampshire with Willy, sleeping in the woods, heating up canned soup over a fire—a men-meet-nature type of thing. I wouldn't have joined them even if they'd wanted me to. I'm a firm believer in flushable toilets.

I followed Stan out to the car, pleased that I hadn't told him about his toothbrush. I hugged Willy. To my surprise he hugged me back.

"Don't worry," he whispered in my ear. "I'll take care of him."

What about me?

SIX

DMITRI CLUNKED ACROSS the floorboards outside the bedroom, waking me up. The smell of frying onions convinced me to open my eyes. Frying onions, carrots, tomato puree. I blinked at my watch. It was three P.M. I'd slept more than four hours.

"What are you making?" I yelled out.

"Borscht!" Dmitri filled the doorway. He was still wearing his gym outfit. My beach towel, a replica of a dollar bill, hung from his belt. It now looked like a butcher's apron.

I sat up. "I'm happy to see you're protecting that designer getup of yours." I untwisted the Indian skirt from my legs. My shirt was wet with sweat. So was my hair. "I hate borscht."

"It put red in your cheeks."

"And on my towel. I prefer blusher, but *grazie* anyway." I followed him, barefoot, back to the main room—half living room, half kitchen. A wood-backed sofa and two white wicker armchairs faced a low bookshelf and a picture window with the bay spreading beyond its frame. The day had turned into a shiny blue postcard that made my eyes ache. The white windmill of Gardiners Island and a couple of sailboats added the usual quaint touch.

I picked up some clean clothes draped over a chair and went into the bathroom. I showered under a strong jet of hot water. Heavenly pressure. In Stan's shower, back in the city, the best we could hope for was a tinkle. Sufficiently awake, I thought of sailboats. And wind. Drying myself, I shouted, "How did Bud take the news of the fire?"

Dmitri didn't answer.

Dressed in clean navy slacks and an oversized white T-shirt, I walked back into the living room to find Dmitri stooping in front of the radio by the window.

"How did Bud take the news of the fire?" I repeated.

Dmitri straightened up, pocketing something white. "I don't know."

"What did you find?"

"I not find Bud." He twitched. "I get too seasick."

"What did you put in your pocket?" I was remembering the fuss Stan had made about a broken garbage bag. "Come on, what is it?"

"Jim put me off at his restaurant and I thump ride to town." He turned on the radio.

"You *thumbed* a ride to town." I held out my hand. "No hiding from a partner."

Dmitri dropped a paw into his pocket and handed me a worn, folded sheet of paper. Covered in Russian.

"I'm sorry." I gave it back. "I thought it was something Stan was looking for."

"Trust me."

"I do." It was Stan I was having trouble with. Dmitri and I had become buddies last October when I'd climbed into the London Town car he was driving and hired him as a temporary bodyguard. A week later he'd nearly gotten me killed, but by then I was hooked. Seven years younger than I am, he's become the brother I never had. Stan enjoyed his company almost as much. I say "almost" because Stan keeps a tight rein on his feelings.

"Did you get a whopping ticket for parking in front of a fire hydrant?" I asked.

"What I get is borscht ingredients. At Barefoot Contessa. Very fancy beets. Police too worried about fire to give tickets." Dmitri chopped cabbage with a slow stroke. "You think Bud want his check back now?"

"I'm sure he's got insurance. He won't need that thousand dollars." The radio announced that 1,200 firefighters from all parts of Long Island were battling the stubborn blaze. The fire was not going to be over by nighttime. So far no loss of human life. "What happened with the fire at Bud's house?"

"Men are gone. House stands but one side is bad. Line of trees burned out. Fire moved to creek. That was good."

More than good. The Merrill Lake Sanctuary,

143 acres worth, part of the Accabonac Harbor Preserve, was just north of Bud's house. To the south more homes, one of which was the Jackson Pollock farmhouse, which has been turned into the Pollock-Krasner Study Center, now a historic landmark. I poured cold spring water into a glass and gulped it down. My mouth felt charred too. "Wasn't the wind blowing from the southeast when we got there?"

"Yes. Before no wind. Now entire property, entire road one big dirty ashtray."

I lifted the cover of the pot. My nostrils had missed the beets and turnips.

"You're making heat, Dmitri." I turned off the radio.

"Warm inside, cool outside."

A Dory Rescue Squad boat crossed the picture window.

"After men finish with Bud's house," Dmitri said, "they go to Pine Barrens. Planes going to drop water from sky."

I glanced at the phone by Dmitri's elbow and wondered if Stan and Willy had made it back safely.

"Stan call while you sleep."

"I would have heard the phone ring." Dmitri doesn't like me to worry.

"All right, I call his car. They are both okay." Dmitri likes to take over. "On Triborough Bridge, in company of thousand cars and Blowfish."

"Thanks."

Dmitri skimmed froth from the pot. "Willy should listen to Tchaikovsky, Rimsky-Korsakov."

"The closest he's gotten to classical is *Saturday Night Fever*." Another Dory Rescue Squad boat made its way across the window. "If the wind was coming from the southeast, why did the fire work itself down to the creek, which is east?"

"Something stinking in Denmark."

"Are you thinking arson?"

"Black smoke means flammable liquid."

"Who says?"

"Trust me."

I didn't. That second boat was giving me another slow thought.

"Have Bud and Laurie come back?" I asked.

"I make borscht. I don't see them."

I slammed out of the cottage and ran down to the beach. Laurie's green kayak was still gone. So was Bud's scull. Almost nine hours had passed since he'd disappeared into the fog.

I walked back up to the grass levee, looking for people. The place was quiet. Too late, I slapped a horsefly off my neck. Even with a strong wind the heat was brutal.

During my week's stay at The Pynes, I had gotten friendly with three people: Bud; Jim Molton, the next door neighbor who liked to spend a lot of time at The Pynes when he wasn't at his restaurant; and Rebecca Barnes, a year-round resident since the first year Polly had built and rented out the cottages.

Remembering Jim's intrusive smile, I chose Rebecca.

SEVEN

REBECCA BARNES WAS AN ARTIST. Her still lifes, illu-
minated by the Vermeer-like Hamptons light that
had attracted to the area artists as famous as de
Kooning, Pollock, and Motherwell, had made her
almost as well-known as Jane Freilicher. Rebecca
had chosen to live in the second row of cottages that
lined the back of the property, where the glare from
the water was mitigated by distance and the shelter
of trees.

"I'm worried about Bud," I said, walking in. The
cottage was filled with the tools of her trade. Against
her picture window a jagged row of vases and glass
jars. On the bookshelf and coffee table a jumble of
art books. One armchair held folds of different fabric
in springtime colors. Against the back of the sofa, a
thin stack of the unsold paintings from the Guild
Hall show earlier that summer. I'd fallen in love with
a 10"-by-14" pastel of a blue bowl of white peonies

resting on the edge of the water. It looked like an offering from a grateful Poseidon. Fifteen hundred dollars I couldn't afford.

"Worrying about that man is a waste of time." Rebecca stood in front of her kitchen counter, filling up two glasses. She saw me, she added a third. "He can afford another house if he doesn't want to rebuild. Never liked that one anyway."

"You or Bud?" I took the glass she offered.

"For once we agreed. Post-modern junk is what it is. They should all burn down, they ruin our landscape."

"He chose it because it was close to The Pynes."

"You think you're clever for figuring that out."

"Very."

Rebecca gurgled, her version of a laugh. She was a broad-shouldered woman in her sixties, six-feet tall, with sharp cheekbones and jaw, an even sharper nose that hooked to the left, clear gray-blue eyes behind wire-rimmed glasses, and streams of gray hair and wrinkles running helter-skelter as if looking for the source. She wore a blue smock over black slacks and Birkenstock sandals. Most of her was covered by rainbow hues of pastel dust.

"Shouldn't Bud be back by now?" I asked.

"There's no knowing what Bud will do at any point in time." She sounded suddenly angry.

"I saw the Dory Rescue Squad boats." I drank what looked like liquid sunrise. "Delicious. What's it made of?"

"One part each of orange and cranberry and two

parts tonic water. Tiepolo colors give me a boost. Looked like you could use one too."

"I'm fine now. Thanks to your drink and a long nap."

"The Dory Rescue Squad is Steve King trying to impress Laurie. He's a volunteer firefighter, a volunteer rescuer, he'll do anything to get her to pay attention."

I recognized the old dismissive trick, one my mother loved. It kept her heart from jumping out of her throat when she was worried sick. So Rebecca cared about Bud, more than she was willing to let on.

"Laurie's kayak's not in its place either," I said. That third glass of sunrise liquid sat on the counter, waiting for whom?

"William Morris Warren is a fool." Rebecca crossed the room with four strides. "He sits so high-and-mighty on that dumb contraption I get an itch to find the ejector button and rocket him up to the moon, except the moon would spit him right back." She opened the door to the porch that she'd turned into a studio. A rectangle of fuzzy afternoon light dropped onto the linoleum floor. The space was filled by a long L-shaped worktable made of gray planks resting on trestles. Underneath the planks were boxes of pastel crayons, garbage bags full of shells and beach debris, more odd-shaped containers, and dead branches. All I could see then was a corner of the table and a dried sunflower in a brown jug.

Rebecca had let me visit her studio earlier in the week, after she'd seen me fumble with my time while

Stan and Willy went off kayaking in the harbor. I'm always afraid those things will turn over and my hips will get stuck inside. We'd chatted a long time about Italian art, with me doing most of the listening.

"We've all told Bud to junk the thing," Rebecca said. "He doesn't even listen to a nor'easter. Save his heart. What about Laurie? She's had enough troubles. She doesn't need this." Neither did Rebecca, I translated.

Rebecca banged the still-full glass on the counter. "There isn't much we can do but wait. They'll find him. Now what was Bud talking to you about this morning?"

"Why did you turn away when he waved at you?"

"I haven't spoken a civil word to Bud since the day Polly died."

"May I ask why?"

"You may not." Two sharp eyes peered at me. "That fool was talking about Polly, am I right? About her being murdered. He even cornered your friend."

"What's your opinion?"

"Of course it was suicide! Bud doesn't like to lose."

I doubt strongly voiced opinions. "Did you see the suicide note?"

"I found it." She banged the glass again. "'I'm sorry' written out forty times on good stationery. Polly used to make Laurie do that when she was a kid."

"You found the note after three days. Where was it?"

"Difficult woman, Polly was. Not likable by a long shot, but she had her good points. She had no tolerance for fools." Rebecca gave me a look that would turn a plum into a raisin.

"I'm a well-meaning fool. I also heard Polly had had bouts with depression."

Rebecca gave me another hard look. "How do you know?"

"After Bud talked to Stan, Stan checked with Captain Comelli out in Yaphank."

"Bigger idiot than that Comelli, God would have had a hard time making. He and his men walked right by the suicide note. According to them she should have left arrows pointing to it."

"Where was the note?"

"Behind Laurie's law school graduation picture. Polly Pynes committed suicide. May she rest in peace and let us get on with our lives. Come on out, Dodo. Simona's a friend. It's time to clean out your arteries."

Dodo stuck his neck out from the studio. A man way past seventy, shrunken, with a scowl on a face that had been left out to dry the day he was born and promptly forgotten.

Rebecca waved a long arm. "Simona, meet Dodo Parsons. The Parsons date back to the beginning of the white man's conquest of this particular fistful of heaven. An industrious lot. They claim they owned all of Springs once. For all I know they may have."

"I am a Parsons in name only." Dodo came forward slowly in a rumpled, dirty seersucker jacket, a frayed blue shirt with its collar buttons missing, a green knitted wool tie, and a brand-new pair of jeans bottomed off by rubber-thonged sandals. A seaman's cap covered his head. He trailed sand.

"All I own is a metal detector and my Alice," Dodo said in a punctured muffler voice. "Great man, Lewis Carroll. His words are universal."

"Dodo prefers to play the local eccentric," Rebecca explained. "Every village has one. Around here I'm considered his female counterpart."

"You don't drink." Dodo neared the counter, extended his arm. We shook hands. He smelled of whiskey and sea salt.

"I've seen you on Atlantic Avenue Beach," I said. A couple of times during my morning walk I'd watched him shuffle along, stooped low, with his headset on, waving the metal detector across the sand, a child's yellow shovel and pail hanging from his arm. I never saw him find anything.

"I'm afraid I can't say the same about you," he said. "Hot days make me feel very sleepy and stupid."

"This will wake you up." Rebecca rammed the other glass in his hand.

He drank from it reluctantly. "How did you get me to look sober?" His thumb pointed to the studio.

"Drew you while you were fast asleep. For the rest I used my imagination. Artists have some, you know."

"'Curiouser and curiouser!'"

"Bud's gone missing again."

Dodo shrugged. "'The race is over, but who has won?' Not Bud."

"Why not Bud?" Rebecca asked, frowning.

"'When I used to read fairy tales,'" Dodo said, "'I fancied that kind of thing never happened.'"

I had no idea what he was talking about.

"What do you know, Dodo?" Rebecca took him seriously.

"Only what I see, Becky. Drunks have no imagination." Dodo walked back to the porch. We followed. The room extended beyond the cottage, giving an expanded view of The Pynes. It was almost five o'clock and the sky was beginning to leak orange. Shadows lengthened, swallowing up light. Dodo pointed his thumb again. East, this time. Gulls flew in couples away from the dropping sun. The cicadas were going strong. A crow cawed. The wind rustled. The tide was coming in. The only sound of civilization was Laurie's sprinkler system.

Jim Molton and Steve King walked silently on grass toward the main house. Steve's brown Lab, Tanner, and a florid, elegant woman trailed at a respectful distance. From the twist of the men's bodies, we could tell they were holding something between them. As they turned past the woodshed, that something became Laurie. She was walking. Barely. Her legs going through the motions, without being able to bear her weight. Her head was bent low. She was still wearing the black cyclist shorts and gray T-shirt. She was drenched. Shoeless. She hadn't taken off her life vest.

Rebecca sprinted out of the porch and across the grass. "Laurie!"

Laurie turned. In both hands she held another life vest. As red as hers. Twice the size.

Bud's vest.

EIGHT

HOW'S LAURIE TAKING IT NOW?" Jim Molton asked. Dmitri and I were sitting at the bar of his restaurant, Jim's Pit. Inside, the air conditioners hummed at full speed. Outside, a sea breeze brought relief to the wide wooden deck. Diners, inside and out, feasted on seafood specialties and watched the sun drop into Three Mile Harbor. The sky was raspberry sorbet topped by blueberry cream.

Below the restaurant, the small marina was crammed with boats that sold in the high six figures. Jim's speedboat was moored there along with Kennelly's seventy-foot Hinkley sailboat. If I craned my neck I could see past the narrow inlet to the right, where the commercial fishermen docked off a wide strip of asphalt. Only five boats. One of them was *No Wife*, Steve King's trawler.

"We don't know anything," I said. "Laurie's locked in her house with Rebecca. You were gone before I could reach you." I'd wasted precious minutes just standing and staring in disbelief. "Steve left about twenty minutes later and refused to talk. What happened?"

"First clue was the life vest," Jim Molton said. "Jake Bennett's kids, Ronnie and Joe, were out fishing on the Gardiners Island side of the bay. They were setting their nets around a school of bluefish when there it was bobbing in the water. You can't miss that red. Ronnie and Joe didn't make anything of it. They were too busy with their runaround net."

"So?" Dmitri nudged.

"Sorry." Jim raised an arm to someone behind us. He nodded to a couple walking by, showing off an automatic smile that was nothing like his intrusive special: startling white teeth against buttery skin the color of toasted almonds and dark brown laughing eyes.

"When they hauled the net in, Ronnie kept the vest thinking he could make a couple of bucks," Jim said. His face had turned serious again. "Then the kids saw Steve and the rest of the rescue squad. Ronnie hailed them down. Laurie was in the boat with Steve. She took one look at the vest and broke down. Steve brought her over here. We took her home. That's when you saw us." Jim refilled my wine glass with Pinot Grigio.

Dmitri asked for more vodka. Warm this time. "Russian way."

Jim stopped a busboy and gave out orders. "Thanks," he added before the kid rushed off.

"What about Bud and the scull?" I asked.

"Clue number two, the damn scull with the rowing machine, riskier than Ginnie Maes. Once the vest was found, the Coast Guard got called in. Half an hour ago, Steve phoned. They found the scull out in Cherry Harbor, overturned. The rowing machine part got stuck on a lobster trap."

"Excuse me, Jim." A young anchovy of a girl dressed in her grandmother's black girdle whispered in Jim's ear. Dmitri gave a cursory look at her hair and her bust. One was nonexistent, the other too short.

The name Melanie came out loud and clear.

Jim shot up. "Be right back." His hand brushed my bare arm as he passed.

"Melanie who?" Dmitri asked.

"Griffith."

"Ah, she's good."

I could see her in the bar's mirror, wearing jeans and a spanking white T-shirt that matched her teeth. Jim was kissing both her cheeks. He was in crisp khakis and a blue-and-white-striped shirt, cuffs rolled up, no tie. His brown hair, darker and longer than Stan's, curled nicely down his neck. A very pleasant-looking man. But so was Stan, I reminded myself.

"You get a movie star in your restaurant," I said, "everybody else will come in hoping to get a sighting." I'd taken a half-hour long shower and decked myself out in a beige linen pantsuit I'd bought expecting to hit at least one of the in restaurants during my week's stay in the Hamptons: Nick & Toni's,

Della Femina, the Laundry. And Jim's Pit, this year's hot spot. With Stan, the linen had stayed unwrinkled.

Dmitri had outdone himself with a black silk shirt, a wide silvery Countess Mara tie he'd gotten at a used-clothing store on lower Broadway, black wool pants gone shiny at the knees, and tan Desert Storm boots. The two of us were doing a good job of lifting the tone of the place.

"Barbra come here," Dmitri said with a nostalgic sniff. "Baldwin brothers, Kim Basinger, Ron." He'd lived the "in" life as Perelman's bodyguard.

"Hey, I'm a star, aren't I?"

Dmitri took a gulp of his warm vodka and looked doubtful. "Maybe with Keanu Reeves who has speedboat for bus." He was staring down the bar mirror.

"Jim?" There was similarity. They shared a sullen, sexy look. "Jim's smile is better."

"Will bank stop check now Bud is dead?"

"Dmitri!" I wrinkled my brows at him. "Have a heart."

"My heart is size of America, my pocket is size of kopek."

"The check's dated before his death, there shouldn't be a problem."

"We go ahead?"

"Bud wanted an answer, and, dead or not, Bud is going to get his answer. That's the least we can do for an advertising legend." The plan had the added advantage of keeping me distracted from my personal life.

Dmitri glowed. "Now he never find out we are not professionals."

"You stay here and try to find us two rooms. I know it's next to impossible, but try. Go to Danceteria later tonight. Maybe you'll get another tip while doing the Electric Slide." That's how he'd clued me in on The Pynes.

"Slide is not chic. What about Laurie's cabin, with air-conditioning?"

"I think we should stay independent. Plus I don't quite see myself going up to Laurie and saying, 'May we stay here so we can prove your mother was murdered?'"

"There is my office."

"The police frown upon people sleeping in cars. Maybe we'll crash some yacht. Listen, tomorrow here's what we do. I'll take the six-fifty Jitney—" Jim's hand seared my neck this time, stopping speech.

"Sorry. How about dinner on me? With me?" He flashed the real smile this time. "I got a free table."

Dmitri rose. "I have Siberian hunger."

"Great." Jim linked his arm in mine and led us off to a table in a glassed-in corner. He sat down with us.

"Finish up about Bud," I said. A college-age girl dressed in khaki Bermudas and a blue shirt gave us menus. Dmitri gave her a big grin. She had lots of hair.

"I'll order for you if you like," Jim said, "but personally I think it's patronizing."

I agreed. "Grilled swordfish for me and a salad. Thanks."

"But you shouldn't miss the clam pie. It's a local specialty."

"Clam pie it is," I said. The man was hard to resist.

Dmitri ordered clam pie, and four other items. He does that even when he's paying. Jim didn't need to order. Another bottle of Pinot Grigio appeared at my elbow. Dmitri got more warm vodka.

"Where was I?" Jim asked.

"Scull found in Cherry Harbor," supplied Dmitri.

"That's all I got."

"Bud must have had another heart attack," I said.

"Maybe, but clue number three is missing— Bud." They hadn't found him. The Coast Guard called off the search when it got dark. They would resume in the morning. "Helicopters are going to join in now that the brush fire in Pine Barrens is under control."

"One thousand, two hundred acres of state forest preserve scorched," Dmitri said.

Jim dug into a rare steak. "With the rumors flying around, I feel like I'm back on Wall Street." He offered me french fries.

I took one, just to be friendly. The clam pie was good, but I would have eliminated the dough. "What was the vest doing without a body?"

"Survey says: suicide."

"No," I said. Dmitri shot me a warning glance. He finds me too trusting.

"Why not?" Jim asked. He twisted his head to beam me with worried eyes.

Because Bud wouldn't have hired us to find out about his wife. Because he wouldn't have made an appointment with me for that night. "Bud didn't seem like that kind of man."

"Bud was crazy about Polly," Jim said. "He fought that divorce with everything he had. But he lost, and Bud, my friend Bud, was a sore loser. Her committing suicide blew him away."

"So he commit suicide also," Dmitri said. "Passion is ruler of world." He'd finished his fried calamari and was now facing a heap of shrimp pasta. "Read *Anna Karenina*." Dmitri talks big Russian authors, but he prefers paperback romances. The happy endings give him hope.

"Anna Karenina"—he smacked his lips—"she define passion!" Half his vodka bottle was gone.

I gave up my wine. Someone had to drive home. "Bud thought Polly was murdered."

Jim shook his head. "That rumor got going because the suicide note wasn't found right away. And there were enough people who would have loved to hold Polly underwater for about a year or two. Me included. Bud started believing the rumor. It was easier than facing up to Polly's taking her own life. Don't believe murder."

"I can't believe Bud committed suicide."

"I don't like it either," Jim said. "I considered myself a friend. I want to believe I'd spot something as bad as that. In the bond business I could tell which way the wind was turning even before the wind."

"People are not bonds." Vodka leads Dmitri to profound statements.

"Maybe he's not dead," I said. I wasn't so clear-headed myself.

"That's another rumor," Jim dropped his elbows on the table, "that he's done a disappearing act."

"Why would he bother?"

"I don't know. The fire at his house? Steve said the fire marshal's pretty sure it was arson. Laurie doesn't know yet. A slow-burning candle in a plastic vat of gasoline."

Dmitri wagged a finger. "Work of amateur. Gasoline very dangerous. Fumes strong. Can explode in face of arsonist."

"He must have known what he was doing," Jim said. "They found bits of melted plastic next to the open oven door. If the candle blew out for some reason, the vapors from the gasoline would have gotten to the pilot light and there'd still be a fire. Only reason it didn't all go up in flames is that someone spotted it early. Some locals are thinking that Bud set fire to his house and then took off."

"Why would he?" I asked.

"There doesn't have to be a reason, I guess. The locals judge our brainpower by inverse proportion to the amount of money we make." Jim smiled.

Something must have happened to my face. On the drive back to The Pynes, Dmitri started lecturing.

"Old Russian proverb says, 'Third person is light in the bedroom.' Even if third person only in head."

"What are you reading now? *Passion Heat* or *Sweltering Love?*"

"Chekhov. *Uncle Vanya.* In English." He sniffed. I didn't bite. "Everyone unhappy about sex."

"I have not brought Jim into my bedroom in any form whatsoever!"

"Maybe time you do. There is also good Italian proverb." Dmitri had spent a year in Ostia, a beach town just south of Rome, where emigrating Russians congregated, waiting for visas to Canada, the United States, and Israel. The Italian link had tightened our friendship.

"I know the proverb you mean: 'Check the water for salt before quenching your thirst.'"

"'Love is like the moon, if it not grow, it wane.'"

NINE

THE NEXT MORNING, MONDAY, the traffic on the Long Island Expressway came to a halt. Sudden flare-ups in Pine Barrens had brought the firefighters back in full force. The driver of the Jitney turned up the volume of his radio. We heard about the federal government promising to send in C–130 tanker planes that could carry five thousand gallons of water each. I clutched the bagel that the Jitney provided along with the *Times* and watched helicopters and crop dusters zooming through the smoke. They looked like toys trailing water buckets that belonged next to sand castles. The radio announced a local food drive to feed the firefighters.

I let go of the bagel and studied the newspaper. There was no mention of Bud Warren's disappearance.

At noon I was finally in New York and at home. In the oven-hot basement I stuffed dirty clothes, including Dmitri's, in one of two communal washing machines. I was a quarter short of the required $1.50, had to run back upstairs, borrow from Willy's glass jar, clamber back down, push the button, only to realize I'd forgotten the detergent. Back upstairs I discovered Stan had used the last of it. He'd even left me a carefully printed Post-it where I was most likely to see it: in the refrigerator, on top of the jar of sun-dried tomatoes.

I gave up on laundry, called Bud's agency, WSK, and got put through to Kennelly's secretary. I introduced myself, mentioning my agency for added clout, and asked for an urgent appointment with her boss.

"This is in regards to?" she asked cautiously.

"Death," I said.

"Death what?" a male voice squawked. Lester Kennelly had picked up the phone. Death always works.

"Possibly Bud Warren's." I was counting on him not knowing. Jim Molton had not been able to reach him or his wife.

"What are you talking about? Bud's supposed to be here in forty-five minutes."

"Forty-five minutes? I'll be there." I hung up. Advertising people react to windows of opportunity with speed, not kindness. I showered and slipped into my meeting suit, a gray cotton DKNY outfit that screamed advertising exec on the rise. I toned down the Hampton tan with some powder, lined my eyes, decided against lipstick for a somber effect, and rushed to the door. The phone rang.

Dmitri. He'd spent the morning combing the beach for the man who'd found Polly's body—Dodo. No luck. And no news on Bud. "Your cottage we can have for week if we promise not to light cigarette." The original renters had been scared off by the new flare-ups. The Pynes, like all of Springs, was densely wooded. There was no sign of rain.

"Five hundred dollars to sublease for week," Dmitri said. That was half of what Stan and I had paid and half of Bud's check. Dmitri was all for sleeping on the beach.

"We're taking it. We're not in this thing for the money."

"So why?"

"We're fulfilling a last wish."

"If he alive, we get more money. I need cash. I wish to go back to Moscow."

"You were there in May." He flew over once a year to pick up hair to resell to wig makers over here. Russian hair, mostly light colored, fetched a good price.

"Pavel took his wife to Red Sea," Dmitri said, munching, probably into another Dreesen donut. "I not see her." Pavel's wife was Dmitri's great love. She reciprocated. It was always platonic, he assured me. Pavel was his brother. He would never betray his brother. "I think Pavel suspect."

"Just pray Bud's alive. We're taking the cabin. I've got to go. I'll call you later." I was about to hang up.

"Willy call."

That stopped me. "Everything okay?"

"Collect from bottom of Mount Jefferson. I accept."

"Yeah, okay. What did he say?" Willy had called me maybe five times in the two years I'd known him.

"He want you to know Stan talk about you lots."

"Great. How? She's a nag? She's the love of my life?" My finger snaked across the dust on the windowsill. "She's the worst housecleaner I've ever lived with?"

"Lots of talk about you cooking good."

"That's me, the pasta lady. They're eating out of cans."

Dmitri breathed loudly. He loves drama. "Willy worried about you guys."

I was moved by Willy's concern. Maybe he could get his father to open up. "Did he leave a number?"

"They are going up Mount Adams."

"Thanks. I'll call you when I know what time I'm coming back."

"Rebecca love love borscht!" Dmitri yelled just as I dropped the receiver back in the cradle. God bless him, he'd used an article!

WSK was located on Hudson Street in the top half of a six-story, yellow brick ex-manufacturing building from the 1920s. Its wide double windows overlooked Hudson to one side and St. Luke's walled-in garden on the other. Three blocks to the south Saatchi & Saatchi Advertising had once ruled. When Saatchi fell to infighting and bad management, the joke on Madison Avenue was that Kennelly bragged he'd sold God on a campaign to change the path of the sun in order to put S&S under WSK's shadow. WSK was an important agency, but not quite as big as Kennelly's ego.

I didn't know about his ego, but the man had the girth and hustle of a linebacker. He was at least ten years younger than Bud, with a large, craggy face that was surprisingly friendly. His hair was trimmed short, gray-blond. Bud was the creative brain, Kennelly the business one. I wondered how they'd gotten along. At my agency, HH&H, the bottom line and creativity were in the ring daily.

"I called Laurie." Lester Kennelly sat down in a Donghia armchair at one end of the vast room. I'd dropped down on the softer-looking sofa. The Power of Color was the office theme. A blue area rug, a lemon yellow desk the shape of an Elsa Peretti bean. The six-seater sofa I was sitting on was celery green. Lester Kennelly sat in fuchsia pink. Black ultra-modern floor lamps. A pale wood streamlined unit held the TV and VCR. The only art on the wall was a bright blue David Hockney pool.

"She wouldn't come to the phone," he said. "What's going on?" Kennelly knew by then. One doesn't stay at the top of a nationally renowned ad agency without having information at one's fingertips. He also had a house in East Hampton, on prestigious Lily Pond Lane, where telephone and electrical lines are buried as deep as the owners' pockets. Once I'd alerted him, he had people to call on.

He was sizing me up, trying to figure out where I fit.

I mentioned I was a friend of Bud's, stretching the truth a bit, and related what Jim had told me, including the arson fire at Bud's house.

Kennelly pressed a button on the phone at his elbow. "Charlene, Bud's Sport campaign has probably gone up in smoke. Warn Creative." He turned to me with a pleasant smile.

"Is that for Sport4Life?" They were WSK's biggest clients.

"New product campaign. The sample came in on Friday. The client was expecting our final proposal tomorrow. Bud had gotten a new idea he wanted to work on over the weekend." Kennelly drummed his fingers on expensive tan trousers. Under the matching jacket he wore a blue oxford shirt and a Nicole Miller sailboat tie. "Arson's hard to believe." His eyes focused on the David Hockney pool hanging behind his desk. "His heart finally got him?"

"The more persistent rumor is that he committed suicide." I hugged my arms. The temperature in the office was cold enough to make you long for the street, where the temperature had reached ninety-nine degrees. "Because of the life vest."

"Maybe he took off the vest to go swimming."

"Not very probable. The scull would have drifted away. I'm sorry a complete stranger is bringing you the news. Jim Molton tried to reach you and your wife last night. In East Hampton and here in the city. I don't know why he didn't call this morning." Actually I did. Jim liked to sleep late. He'd claimed that was one of the reasons that he'd gotten out of the trading business.

"I screen my calls. Jim Molton didn't mention an emergency."

"I had hoped to meet you at the barbecue Saturday night." Which wasn't true. One CEO in my life is enough and that's my boss. But I'd seen Kennelly at the Amagansett Market Saturday morning, lining up for breakfast among the roses and the giant hibiscus with the rest of the summer crowd. I was curious why he hadn't shown up at the barbecue. Rebecca had called it a revered annual event in the Warren-Pynes family. The party had also been given on the eve of the anniversary of Polly Pynes's death. A friend would have shown up.

"My wife went, although she didn't stay long. Amanda spends the entire summer out there and only likes parties that raise money for worthwhile causes. Bud hated them. The rich rubbing rear ends with the richer, was his take on it. I see nothing wrong with it. A lot of money gets collected." Kennelly stood up, walked behind his desk. "Saturday night I needed to go over marketing strategies for Sport4Life. Then around ten o'clock, when I heard about the Pine Barrens fire over the radio, I packed it in and went to bed. I got out early Sunday morning. I couldn't afford to get stuck in the Hamptons." He fished in a drawer. "Now, of course, I wish I'd gone to the barbecue."

Kennelly tossed a photo toward me. His aim was

perfect. The picture hit my lap. Three men—Bud and Lester Kennelly in younger days with a third balding man who was holding up a Clio, an award given to the best TV commercials. They were on a sailboat.

"Our first award, for Grin toothpaste. 'Grin your cavities away, your blues will disappear.'" Kennelly dropped back in his pink chair, emotion a light way back in a dusty corridor of his eyes. "Bud was the best. I was a lucky bastard to snare him. He'd gotten a lot of recognition at Doyle Dane Bernbach, but its heyday was over. This was back in 1976. Bob Shepard and I were both account supervisors at Ogilvy & Mather, going nowhere. One day Bob and I were having lunch in our usual coffee shop on Forty-sixth Street, writing up plans on a napkin about going out on our own. In walked Bud, a man who could have gone to the Four Seasons every day. Money never did mean much to him, which can be infuriating when you're trying to run a business." He ran his hand over a closely shaved cleft chin.

"We'd been eating in the same coffee shop on and off for a year. But that day, he acknowledged us. For the first time. He sat at the counter, asked for coffee, then turned around and asked us if we'd join him."

The red thermos. I wondered if somebody had found it. Thermoses float. So do bodies. Eventually.

"A week later I bumped into him in East Hampton." The intercom buzzed. Kennelly pressed the botton. "Yes, Charlene?"

"Mrs. Kennelly's on line one."

"I'll call her back."

"She just heard. She's very upset."

"I'll call her back." His finger came off the intercom. "Where was I?" His voice hadn't changed.

Nice marriage. Maybe I had nothing to complain about with Stan. "You bumped into Bud in East Hampton."

"That's right." His face softened, the memory obviously a pleasant one. "We're both at Iacono's buying chicken for our wives. You should try their chickens. Free range. The best. Two henpecked husbands. This is back awhile when it was still okay to expect women to do the shopping. Anyway we started laughing. That's when my lightbulb lit up," Kennelly said. "The three of us—Warren, Shepard, and Kennelly. It took me six months to convince Bud. He liked the idea, but he didn't want to turn his back on Bill Bernbach." For a busy man Lester Kennelly was doing a lot of reminiscing.

"We put in sixty thousand each. By the end of the first year we were drawing salaries of thirty thousand. Nothing even then, but we called the shots. We even got a great chicken account. And now look at us." His eyes locked onto the Hockney pool again, a painting that must have cost well over a million. "We made a great team."

"Is there any reason Bud would want to disappear?"

"The agency is about to sign the biggest deal yet."

"You just said Bud didn't care about money."

A crinkle of a frown. "He cared about the agency."

"A merger with Chass\Dayton?"

He glanced at his watch, one of those underwater Tag-Heuer numbers with so many knobs it could launch a spaceship. "That's a bad rumor, like Bud's suicide. If you're a friend of Bud's, how come I don't know you?"

"I'm new. Saturday night at the barbecue, Bud Warren paid my partner a retainer of a thousand dollars. Sunday morning over coffee he asked me to look into his wife's death." I unfolded the check I was going to deposit once I left WSK. *Ti prego, Dio*, don't let this man ask me for my PI license. "This piece of paper doesn't make a very convincing suicide note."

"So you think he faked his own death?"

I let my breath out. "It's been done before."

"He had no reason to. Plenty of money. His health was on the mend. He was the only creative head in Manhattan, maybe the world, who worked full-time long distance."

"With faxes and computers, that's not so difficult."

"You can't communicate leadership by E-mail." Kennelly pushed his thick neck out of a too-tight collar. "Bud had no reason to quit his life in any way whatsoever."

"He thought his wife was murdered."

Kennelly didn't seem surprised.

"Is that what you think too?"

He gave his watch another look. "I plead the fifth. Bud is my partner." He stood up, a clear indication our conversation was over.

"He hired three detectives to look into her death," I followed him to the door, "but his records probably burned up. Do you have their names?"

"Sure do. The agency paid for them. Charlene will get them for you." He opened the door and gave his assistant instructions. A bony, broad-shouldered woman with hair the red of clowns' wigs and fists for cheekbones put down a sheaf of papers with an audible sigh and stood up on four-inch heels.

"Thanks."

Kennelly smiled. We shook hands. His was warm. I waited until Charlene had left her desk, then said, "Bud wasn't pleased with the detectives' results."

"Neither was I."

"Why?"

"It seems that the only person who could have murdered Polly was Bud."

TEN

CROSSED THE FLOOR, looking for Charlene. I passed windowless cubicles occupied by harried ad execs in their shirtsleeves, with telephone receivers dangling from their ears and suit jackets draped over backs of chairs. They ate the Korean deli specials served up in clear plastic containers—eyes on the latest market research—while talking on the phone, wooing the fickle client.

Framed tear sheets of successful print ads hung like trophies along the corridor wall. Sly Stallone dangling in midair from a red rope: *Sport4Life Saves Your Life*. A beautiful blond couple sleeping on a mattress while world-famous art streaks above them: *Sleeping Is a Fine Art on Magic Mattress*. Grin toothpaste, Fingerfast computers. And on and on.

I found Charlene at the other end of the floor, in a windowless room next to the women's bathroom. She was surrounded by stacks of metal files. In one corner a printed sign above the copier asked: PLEASE

DO NOT COPY BODY PARTS. I tried not to think about what that meant and let my eyes rest on the new set of colors. Mercifully gray on gray. Except for Charlene with her clown red hair and purple-and-green suit, all of which fit the Power of Color theme of Kennelly's office. I guessed she was in her mid-forties.

"Bud dead?" Charlene asked. She sounded Long Island or New Jersey. As an Italian I can never tell which accent is which.

"There's a good chance he is," I said.

Charlene unlocked the P file drawer. "He was a nice guy." The interest indicator stayed low.

"Did you know his wife?"

"Nice guys are dumb."

"You didn't like her?"

"I stuck her in the P file. For Polly Pynes, part-ners, and pains in the neck." Charlene's fingers walked along the stuffed file drawer. Her nails were dried blood red. Her lipstick matched.

"How was Mrs. Pynes unpleasant?"

"She used to butt in on creative. If an ad she didn't like hit the magazines, she'd tell everyone how awful it was." She leaned a well-padded hip against the drawer. "Now, Mrs. Kennelly, she's a doll. I used to work for Bud and when his wife called, it was, 'I want my husband,' like he was something I was gonna serve with pickles and cole slaw. When Mrs. Kennelly calls, it's 'Hello, Charlene, how was your weekend? Happy Birthday, Charlene, my husband's bringing in a little present for you. If you don't like it, please exchange it.' And her being a busy lawyer too." Charlene turned a cheekbone to the ceiling to show off the Elsa Peretti silver bean on her ear. "Christmas present. Why're you asking about Polly?"

"Bud hired me to look into his wife's death."

"No kidding?" Charlene leaned into the file drawer again and eyed me with interest. "You don't look tough enough to be a detective."

"There's no truth in packaging."

She smacked her forehead. "I'm in advertising. I should know that."

"Some people think that Bud killed her."

Charlene went back to searching for Polly's file. "I'd've hired a hit man, but Bud was a softie. He took his wife's death real bad." She pursed her lips. "Where the hell is that file? Ah, here it is, out of place." She extracted a thin file and scraped her heels over to the copying machine.

"Who else has keys to the file drawers?" I asked as Charlene pocketed them.

"What's that got to do with Polly Pynes?"

"Her folder was out of place and you look like the type who files in the right place."

She frowned. "Yeah, I'm real good at it. Except it's been kinda busy around here and I'm burning out." She rested her elbow on the copier and gave another sigh. "This women's lib stuff is real overrated."

"So is marriage. Who else has keys besides you?"

"The partners, Lester and Bud."

"What happened to Bob Shepard, the third partner?"

"He sold his shares back last year. Now he lives in the Caribbean." She gave me a don't-you-wish look.

"It's even hotter down there," I assured her. "Plus they get hurricanes."

"One's passing through this office right now."

"Bud's disappearance?"

"That too."

"The Chass\Dayton merger is on again?"

"Never heard of 'em." She winked.

I was right! I couldn't wait to tell Gregory at my office. That piece of gossip was going to earn me at least two slices of pepperoni pizza and start everyone working on their résumés. A merger meant a lot of people would be looking for new jobs. Perhaps mine.

"Do you keep files on all the partners' spouses?" I asked.

"It's not stuff that's gonna interest anybody. I must have misfiled it. I'm human, you know." I peeked at the open file drawer. Lester and Bud's files were as fat as one of Dmitri's romance paperbacks. So was Mrs. Kennelly's.

"What kind of stuff?"

"You know. Their birthdays. What flowers they like, that kinda stuff."

And a track of the perks disguised as promotional necessities: the decorator for the apartment, the trip to London for a client lunch that gets extended to ten days in Scotland, the clothes to keep up appearances, etc., etc. Business as usual. From the thinness of Polly's file she hadn't gotten—or wanted— many perks.

Charlene pulled out three invoices from the file, folded them so that only the names and addresses showed, punched in a number in the copier control box, and pressed the button. Some hapless client was going to get billed seventy-five cents for those copies. It adds up by the end of the year.

"One of these guys is dead," she said, handing me the copies. "Like a month after he came to collect his money, I read about it in the paper. He was trailing some rich woman and her lover with a camera. She popped him right between the eyes. You'd better watch it."

"Which one is dead?"

"Dan Hartman."

That left Richard Knight and James McCreedy.

ELEVEN

WITH HUNDREDS OF HUNGRY Long Island fire-fighters in mind, I walked to Balducci's on the corner of Sixth Avenue and Ninth Street. It's like a crowded corner of Italy—jam-packed with all the food my country has to offer. I tore off a number at the deli department and waited. Four years of my New York life had been spent half a block away. I'd been miserable, happy, lonely, and sometimes ecstatic to be on my own. Last October I'd moved to Seventy-seventh Street to live with Stan. The Upper West Side has its share of great food shops—Zabar's, Fairway, and Citarella concentrated in one convenient block, on the same side of the street yet—but I'd sprouted my American legs in Greenwich Village, with daily excursions to Balducci's.

I bought ten softball-sized balls of mozzarella, three pounds of prosciutto, half a pound of arugula, and eight rounds of freshly sliced semolina bread. A

good-sized chunk of my share of Bud's check—which
I had yet to cash—was gone.

I let four cabs pass before I found an air-
conditioned one, the WSK freeze having worn off.
On the Upper West Side I had the cab wait with my
Balducci stash while I bought detergent and cellophane wrap at D'Agostino and then deposited Bud's
check across the street. At home, I dropped my bags
in the vestibule and headed for the basement with
detergent. In the apartment I turned on the kitchen
air conditoner, peeled off my limp DKNY suit, lowered the blinds, and headed for the refrigerator to
fish out sun-dried tomatoes from the oil-filled jar.
Licking my fingers, I dialed Dmitri. Bud still hadn't
been found. The Pine Barrens fire was spreading. I
let paper towels soak up most of the oil while I listened. He'd found Dodo sleeping in a duck-blind
boat.

"I leave him to you. He speaks funny. What does
'imperial fiddlesticks' mean?"

"Abandon Chekhov and try Carroll." I bit into a
dark, wrinkled tomato, instantly feeling at one with
happiness. "Find out if the thermos Bud took with
him yesterday has showed up. It's red, with a chip in
the cup."

"Important?"

"I don't know. The vest was found. The boat was
found. Where's the thermos?"

"Where is Bud?"

"I'm afraid he's going to turn up much too soon."
I dropped another sun-dried tomato in my mouth

and told Dmitri about my meeting with Kennelly. "Friendly. Reminisced a lot. Are we okay on the cottage?"

"I hit bargain. Three hundred dollars for week. You save two hundred."

"I save?" Dmitri is a master at creative accounting. As an Italian it's something I'm used to. "We're partners. We pay and save fifty-fifty."

"I sleep on beach. Raf call, looking for Stan. And Jim call also."

"What did Jim have to say?"

"He want to take you out to dinner tonight. Nick & Toni's, I tell him."

"Dmitri! He owns his own restaurant."

"I know. Jim's Pit. But Jim want to take you everywhere. Hamptons extravaganza! He not invite me so I tell him I'm busy."

"I can't go."

"Chekhov say it is immoral to suppress youth and vital feelings."

"What about you and Pavel's wife? You see her twice a year, you don't touch her, you're thirty-two years old, and you won't even date anyone else. I live with Stan. I can't go out with another man."

"Pavel's wife is great love of my life. Is Stan great love of your life?"

I chewed on an arugula leaf. "What are you getting at?" It left a bitter taste in my mouth.

"Make finding out part of investigation." Dmitri hung up.

After I'd made six or seven sandwiches, Raf

called. He'd just come back from visiting his mother in San Juan.

"I've gotta get hold of Stan."

"Did you try his car phone?"

"No answer. He's already up some mountain." He was breathing hard. "Stan gonna call you?"

"From one of the shelters. What's wrong, Raf?"

"Nothing. Just tell him to call, okay?"

"Come on, Raf. What's going on?"

A long breath. "Stan say anything?"

"About what?"

"Work, what else? Old case of ours is breaking. He's gonna be very happy when he hears it."

"Which case?"

"Simonita! Work and home are milk and lemon. Put 'em together, they curdle." His voice was wound up so tight I thought it would jump at me any minute.

"You okay, Raf? Are things with Tina any better?"

"Sure. Tell Stan to call pronto. It's important." He hung up.

He wasn't telling it right. I thought of calling Tina, but that would have taken up the rest of the afternoon. Instead I dialed Jim McCreedy. He had a Manhattan address. I got a recording.

"This number has been disconnected."

The phone book gave me the same number. I made more sandwiches for the firefighters and tried Gregory, my one true friend at work. I wanted to tell him about Bud Warren, about the possible Chass\

Dayton merger with WSK. I wanted above all his cool advice about Jim. Gregory's voice mail said he'd be out of the office for the next three days. At home his answering machine told me he'd be back on Thursday. August. Vacation time.

Sandwiches piled up on the counter. When my back started to ache, I sat on a stool and tried Richard Knight, who lived two subway lines and forty-five minutes away. Somewhere in the crowded heart of Queens. Knight answered on the first ring.

I introduced myself and explained about Bud.

"You a PI?" His voice would have made a good Brillo substitute. I pictured a half-empty bottle of Old Forester at his elbow, a Luger in his shoulder holster.

"A friend." PIs have low tolerance for unlicensed detectives stepping on their turf. "A good one."

"My Hamptons connections tell me he's belly up somewhere in the bay."

"They haven't found him yet."

"I say he took a powder."

"Took a powder?" The first thought that came to mind was Bud going to the ladies' room. Sometimes I get my American idioms mixed up. "Do you know any reason Mr. Warren might want to disappear?"

"What's in it for me?"

"A late lunch. Early dinner." I was still hungry and didn't want to eat the sandwiches. "In Manhattan." I also wanted to get back to the Hamptons at a decent hour. Not for dinner. Maybe

just a drink and a chat. Jim knew all the players.
"That's my offer, Mr. Knight."

"Plus a C."

"Vitamins?"

"A century."

"I can give you an hour at the most."

The Brillo pad scratched hard. "I want a hundred bucks! And it's Dick."

"That's a lot of money, Dick."

"I should charge more. You're the third person in
a month who wants that file."

I nearly sliced my finger off on that one. "Who
are the other two?"

"We have a deal?"

"No food. And I'll come to Queens."

"Look, I got clients beating down my door right
now. Wives out in the dunes with the lifeguards,
husbands bonking their secretaries on the conference-
room table. Vacation time is hot for me. This afternoon
I gotta go to Southampton to look into a kidnapped
cat. A lotta bucks are involved. So I'm gonna have
to fit you in later."

I convinced him to let me ride along to
Southampton. Dmitri would pick me up from there.
"We can talk on the way."

"Okay, meet me at Willets Point, that's the Shea
Stadium stop on the seven train. It's an elevated station. I'll meet you at street level, at the bottom of the
stairs. At four o'clock, pronto."

"How will I recognize you?"

"Dick Knight's got a lot of armor."

Knight, armor. A joker. To make sure we wouldn't miss each other, I told him what I was going to wear. Navy slacks and a white short-sleeved shirt. He liked the idea of slacks, but told me to bring a jacket. Maybe he did fashion consulting on the side. Or he had a convertible. I made a mental note to remember ice packs for the sandwiches. And a scarf. The convertible was probably red. He sounded like the type who was into penis enhancers.

I updated the message on the answering machine. I finished making sandwiches. I touched my toes to relieve my back. A view of the dirty floor reminded me of the laundry. I ran down two flights. Some kind tenant had dumped the wet clothes on the table. I threw them in the dryer. This time I'd brought along enough money. I sat on the basement steps, leaned my back against the hot wall, and sweated.

Over a glass of Pinot Grigio, I'd get Jim to give me a quick bio of Polly, Laurie, and Bud. I'd follow up with intelligent, pertinent questions such as "Who's your dentist? Stan could use a smile like that." Or "Is your usual good mood spontaneous or medicinally induced? Stan could use some Prozac." "Do you have a shrink? Does he do cops?" Then of course, the biggest question of them all: "Why would you want to hold Polly Pynes underwater for a year or two?"

What was I going to do about Stan? Keep worrying? Keep trying to figure him out? Call Raf back and wring out drops of information?

My mother's voice came in loud and clear. "*Chi

rompe le uova, fa la frittata." Who breaks the eggs, makes the omelette. Let Stan get out of his own bad mood.

Nick & Toni's. Mamma, what was I going to wear?

TWELVE

DICK KNIGHT'S ARMOR was black leather. From neck to toe. On his head, a black helmet. Plastic. Another helmet, this one white, sat on the backseat. Between his legs, a roaring motorcycle, shiny black and sparkling chrome, long and sleek, with barely enough room for Knight's wide posterior. Tied to each sideview mirror, a limp red cowboy kerchief.

Dick snapped the visor up and looked down at my feet. He had squinty eyes. "You said nothing about movin' out with the furniture." In a very loud voice, he was referring to my duffel bag stuffed with a week's worth of clean clothes and the two Macy's shopping bags filled with plastic-wrapped, ice-packed sandwiches.

"You said nothing about making the move on a death machine," I yelled back. I'd lugged the stuff down and up too many stairs to give up.

"It's my steed. A Harley-Davidson Bad Boy, the best of the cruisers." He snapped the visor back down, turned his animal off, and pulled out a bungee cord from inside his jacket. Five minutes later we were off for the Long Island Expressway, sandwiches squashed in his saddlebags, duffel bag tied to my back, a white helmet on my head, and my heart in my throat. I kept my mouth shut. Partly because the noise of the motorcycle didn't make conversation easy. Mostly because I didn't want bugs on my teeth.

After an hour and a half of dancing from one jammed lane to another at seventy miles an hour, we hit Exit 70 and got onto Route 111. I saw Grace's on the other side of the road. I tapped Dick's shoulder and pointed.

"I'm buying," I yelled.

As soon as the words were out, he swung the motorcycle across the road, doing a U-turn ten feet in front of a green Bentley.

"Fuck you!" the Bentley screamed.

"Manners and money don't mix no more," Dick declared after he came to an abrupt halt in front of a picnic table. He turned off his motor. The sudden silence was deafening. I wobbled off the seat and leaned me and my duffel bag against the picnic table for a moment.

"You're a rookie rider, aren't you?"

That didn't merit an answer. Besides, I was too busy trying to remove my helmet. My head had swollen. When I finally got it off, air tingled pleasantly across my wet scalp.

"I bet I got a welt across my stomach from your

arm," Dick said. He removed his helmet in one easy swoop. A man who looked in his late forties—maybe younger if he was into drugs or alcohol—he had chin-length gray hair plastered down with sweat and the weight of the helmet, a round, lined face with paunchy cheeks, a squashed nose, meaty lips, small eyes the color of dust, and a chin weak enough to need a beard.

I unhooked the bag from my back and shrugged out of my jacket. The heat was unbearable.

"Aren't you dying in that leather?" I asked.

"It's like my second skin." He slid off his bike, kicked out the bike's stand, and undid a few zippers. Knight was shorter than I by an inch, which put him at five-foot-three. "We're gonna eat out here 'cause of the bike and I wanna smoke." He straddled over the bench, taking possession of the table from a family of four who were about to sit down. "Two dogs with chili, sauerkraut and onions on the side, french fries, caffeine-free Coke." He held up his hands. They shook. "Too much coffee."

"It's self-serve around here, macho man."

Knight shrugged. "I got to watch Bad Boy. Unless you wanna. If anyone touches the bike, shriek." He stood up and held out his shaking hand. If he could trust me with his baby, I could hand over my wallet.

"One hot dog, plain," I said, "and a Diet Coke. Thanks."

"Park the body. I'll be back."

I watched his boots scuffing across the gravel.

He walked splay-footed, and you could have driven a beer truck in the space between his legs.

I parked. Bees hummed around the plastic ketchup bottle. I wiped the table with someone's leftover napkin. Grace's isn't much to look at, but it serves the best hot dogs on Long Island. Once a roadside stand, success had expanded it into a one-story glassed-in building with indoor and outdoor tables. Local people share tables with the Hamptons-bound, Grace's dogs their only point in common. Dmitri and I cherish hot dogs. They're representative of America.

I ran after Dick, ducking my head inside the glass door. "Make it two dogs. One to go with all the trimmings!"

"So why do you think Bud Warren murdered his wife?" I asked after we finished dressing our hot dogs with ketchup and mustard. I slipped the hundred dollar bill under my Coke can, where we could both keep an eye on it.

"He had means, opportunity, and motive."

"As for means, anyone could have held her head down. She was a small woman." In Rebecca's studio, I'd seen an old picture of Polly standing between Bud and Laurie on the beach. Laurie towered over her.

"I'll grant you that, Simone. A size four and she was full of muscle relaxants. They found no marks of struggle on her body."

"It's Simona, with an 'a.' If they found no marks, why are you so sure she was murdered?"

"Take my word for it." He chomped into his hot dog. Chili oozed onto his hand. He sucked it off. I noticed with satisfaction that the bees favored his side. At the table behind me, the family of four began to squabble about who got to squirt mustard where. I would have moved to Dick's side, but I prefer mustard to bees.

"I'm supposed to pay a century for your word?"

"Look, opportunity narrows it down," Dick said. "Bud was the last person to see her. They had a big public fight the night before, right on the beach at The Pynes. She said she was goin' to put a restraining order on him if he didn't leave her alone, this over-heard by most of the residents, plus his partner Kennelly and his wife who were sitting in their Jaguar waiting to take him out to dinner. Bud let her know she'd ruined his life and his daughter's." Dick took another, more careful, bite. The chili ended up in his mouth the first time around. "The next mornin' he comes over to apologize, that's his line to the police. She's out kayakin', he grabs his kayak, which she was lettin' him keep at The Pynes, don't ask me why if she don't want him around—"

"She had ambivalent feelings." I understood that only too well.

"That's shrinkspeak. I say she was nuts. She's not there, he goes after her. Bud Warren admits all this, you understand? He has to. That Dodo bird sees him. You meet him yet? He fell into a rabbit hole years ago and can't find the exit sign."

"Therefore a terrible witness."

A black limousine with darkened windows swung into the parking lot. The chauffeur got out and went inside. The engine stayed on. Air-conditioning.

"The old lady, Rebecca Barnes, she sees Bud Warren too. In fact she's with Dodo bird takin' her morning walk on Gerard Drive, draggin' him along to sober him up." He started on his second hot dog. Mine disappeared after three bites. Bees are a good incentive to eat fast.

"Dodo backs up Rebecca's story." Knight's voice scratched through the chili. "This is not a guy who normally talks to cops, you understand." Knight threw back his head. It didn't go far. His neck was too short. "One time he spent the night in the clinker for destroyin' that dummy they keep out in a police car." His laugh needed a Robitussin rubdown.

"You mean Manny the mannequin?"

"Manny, that's the guy."

The limousine chauffeur came out carrying six hot dogs wedged between his fingers. Paper napkins bulged out of the side pocket of his uniform.

"So now we have two witnesses." Knight slammed the butt of his Coke can on a bee. "These mother—"

"Witnesses to what?"

"Bud and Polly meetin' out in Accabonac Harbor. He was buggin' her again and she threw her paddle at him."

"What time did this happen?"

"Eight o'clock in the mornin'. By one o'clock Dodo bird finds Polly lyin' sweetly in the rushes behind the old Pollock farmhouse. Drowned dead."

"Backtrack a minute."

"I got me a catnapping to take care of."

"One more minute. Dodo and Rebecca. What else did they see?"

"Nothin'."

"Did someone see Bud paddle away by himself? Are there no witnesses after that? That's a pretty popular stretch for walkers. Any residents see anything?"

"Zip. Nada. Kayakers are a dime a dozen. I even got to ask Pierre Franey, the food guy. He's got a house on Gerard. He was making bread when I came by. Offered me some too. Never thought a frog could be friendly. Great bread.

"The police, then me afterward. We canvassed everyone nearby. Even the people facin' the harbor from Fireplace Road. Who's gonna remember somethin' you see every day?"

"How did Bud account for his time after he left Polly?"

"He kayaked into the bay and met up with Steve King, who was in a dory, checkin' lobster traps. King corroborates. He hauled Bud onboard, and they were together for about two hours. Now those two didn't get along, everybody I talked to confirmed that. So what did they talk about for two hours, huh?" He lit a Camel and took a deep drag. "Steve King's been after Bud's daughter for most of his life. Whose side is he gonna be on? Besides, by then Polly Pynes was maybe good and dead. Time of death was put down between eight in the morning and noon. They can't pinpoint it any better than that."

The wind must have shifted because the bees

changed sides. Dick was eyeing the one crawling across my left eyebrow, his hand in midair.

"Please don't try to kill it." I could see myself showing up at Nick & Toni's looking like a one-eyed bandit. "What about motive?"

"Plenty. First of all everyone says Bud was still crazy about Polly."

Dmitri's favorite reason for anything—passion.

"Me, I say ego worked into it. He's a real proud man and she dumped him."

I sat perfectly still, waiting for the bee to move on. "I don't buy that as a motive for murder."

"There's the money. She's dead, he don't have to pay seventy-two grand in alimony each year."

"It seems Bud doesn't care about money."

"She got half of his stake in WSK as a divorce settlement."

"Are you sure?" Every partnership agreement I'd ever heard of made sure shares didn't get dispersed in the event of death or divorce.

"Plus there's the land. I'm tellin' you, that woman was greedy. And nuts. She divorces the guy, but when she croaks a year later, he gets The Pynes. That's worth a cool mil."

I sat up at the risk of getting stung. "What about Laurie?" The bee flew away. One of the kids behind me started screaming.

"She got the main house and the rest of her mother's assets, which was about two hundred thou." He reached for the hundred dollar bill.

I snatched it before he did. "That's your evidence?

Didn't you look into anyone else who might have had a motive?"

"Sure. Her daughter, the fisherman boyfriend, the restaurant guy next door, plus half a dozen other people who would have been glad to see her dead for one reason or another, but Bud's the one who got spotted with her shortly before she died." He stood up, dropping his cigarette in the Coke can. "Listen, I gotta go."

I clutched the bill. "The police had the same information you have, yet they didn't arrest Bud."

"No hard evidence. Man's won a lot of respect in the community. He's always givin' money away. Plus the suicide note."

"You're not holding out on me?"

Knight straddled his bike. "I swear on Bad Boy, Silver, Trigger, and Rocinante. Now give me that C and let's cut out of here." He zipped up, put on his helmet, and throttled the engine.

"Who else asked for the file?" I tied the duffel bag on my back.

"One's confidential." He threw the other helmet at me. "I got paid."

"The other's the police?"

"How'd you figure that?"

"Who else could force you to give something away free?"

"You're right on both counts. Last Thursday my file became police evidence." He cracked a knuckle and did a slow shoulder roll to underline his newfound importance. "Why do you think Buddy boy lammed outta Springs? The cops are finally closin' in on the man."

THIRTEEN

WOODS LANE ENDED. Dmitri swung the pink Caddie onto Main Street. He'd picked me up at the fire station in Southampton where Dick Knight had dropped me off. Where I had left fifty soggy sandwiches, which was not much considering 1,200 firefighters were out there. The fire in Pine Barrens was still going. The C–130 tanker planes the government had promised hadn't arrived. The wind was strong.

Dmitri had spent time at the East Hampton Library looking into accounts of Polly's death in the *New York Times* and the *East Hampton Star*. The only thing that he'd discovered was a new romance author.

Bud had not been found.

As we drove by Town Pond I asked Dmitri to park the car. "I always forget to savor." I willed myself to relax against the car's seat. Dmitri crinkled paper. A humid waft of mustard and onions reached my nose.

"Hot dog cold, but good."

"I'm not talking about your hot dog. Look out the window." To enter East Hampton Village is to experience a time warp, to step back into a well-groomed American Colonial town, an idyllic painting by Constable, a papier-mâché re-creation of Once Upon a Time.

"Block the traffic out of your mind for a minute. Rest your eyes on the pond, the elms, the burying ground." I could almost see the cows grazing between gravestones, the geese honking as they made their way to the water in an orderly line. "Inhale the sheer loveliness of the place. The history."

"I memorize guidebook." Dmitri pointed northeast. "Mulford House built in 1650s." His mouth was full. "President Tyler live in studio for summer of 1845. In 1660 Maidstone Arms Inn was Osborne tannery. Clinton Academy—" He stopped. I wasn't listening.

We were close to the ocean. It was four or five degrees cooler here than in the city, but still uncomfortably hot. The Caddie had no air-conditioning. The smell of hot dog and its fixings mixed with the pine scent from a newly installed cardboard tree dangling from the rearview mirror. No bees. I leaned my head back and watched the play of late afternoon light on the pond. I suddenly felt sad.

"What is three centuries to you, Simona? Rome has sewer twenty-six centuries old." He licked his lips, his fingers. "I bet a dollar I know what you're thinking."

"You'll lose."

"Thinking dinner with Jim. It make you romantic."

I shook my head. "The houses are made of wood, not marble. That's the difference between East Hampton and Rome. Here the beauty is fragile. It's been lovingly preserved with a lot of concentrated effort. And most of us just rush in with the beach toys—the Mercedes, the cellular phone, the Calvin Klein outfits—with a frenetic need to find the best party, the hottest restaurant, the 'in' beach, someone to sleep with. We don't stop to taste the beauty."

"You are thinking history with Stan is at end. That make you sad."

Dmitri can be infuriating. "I am thinking fire. After twenty-five days without rain, one tossed cigarette and it's *addio* East Hampton."

"The Barrens are far away."

"Bud's house is not."

"That was arson."

"It's the result I'm worried about, not the cause." A police officer was strolling our way. "Get this pink hearse moving, you big lummox, or you'll get a ticket for illegal parking. Your luck can't hold out forever. In fact, you owe me a dollar."

"Ha!"

"And buckle your seat belt."

Dmitri eased the Cadillac back into traffic. "I wear new shirt."

This one was purple, with long sleeves he kept buttoned. The rest of him was wrapped in black sweatpants, turquoise socks, and Teva sandals. Dmitri hooked the seat belt over his shoulder without buckling it and waved at the police officer as we passed.

I was about to nag Dmitri about safety, but then decided that Mamma's rule about breaking eggs applied here too. I relayed the information obtained from Dick Knight instead. "He's holding out on us. He's sure that Bud killed Polly, which means he has some hard evidence against Bud that the police didn't get in their own investigation."

We crossed Newtown Lane, teeming with dinner traffic. It was five minutes after eight. Jim wasn't going to pick me up until 9:45. Our reservation at Nick & Toni's was for ten o'clock. Grace's hot dogs would keep me operating until then.

"Why police interest suddenly?" Dmitri asked.

"Knight wouldn't or couldn't tell me. He might be worried about getting his license revoked. All I got out of him was that they asked for his file last Thursday, four days ago." This had happened two days after Stan had talked with Captain Comelli, who had assured him the police were satisfied Polly Pynes's death was a suicide. Either Comelli had lied to Stan or he'd received new evidence since that talk.

I let out a soul-clearing sigh. "Yesterday morning seems ages ago." We passed Pantigo Road, which leads to Amagansett, hugging the left for North Main Street. "Did Bud's thermos show up?"

"Coast Guard can't find body, they look for thermos?"

"I felt pretty awful after drinking Bud's coffee."

"You look it too."

I started picking at the torn upholstery. He hates that. "I thought it was the heat, but now I wonder." The last time I'd felt compelled to take a four-hour nap was after I'd decided to leave my husband. I'd swallowed ten milligrams of Valium to get me through the next week. "I bet that coffee was spiked."

Dmitri chuckled. "See what I do for you after I leave library." He slapped the glove compartment open, used a chamois cloth to fish out a small orange plastic bottle, and dropped it on my lap. It smelled of smoke.

"Don't touch it!" Dmitri warned.

I raised my hands in surrender. The bottle came from a New York City pharmacy. The label had Polly Pynes's name on it. "Take one tablet at bedtime," I read. "May cause drowsiness. Valium. Five Mg." No refills. The date was July of last year. One month before Polly died. "Where'd you find this?"

"Bottle is empty."

"I can see that. What did you do, break into Polly's house?"

"I find in Bud's bathroom sink in burned house."

"That's a crime scene!"

"No police. No kitchen door. I step over yellow tape and walk upstairs. It is not B&E."

"If not breaking and entering, how about trespassing, obstructing justice, and aiding and abetting an arsonist."

"Bottle has nothing to do with arson."

"First rule of being a detective—don't touch the evidence. You're not an American citizen, you probably don't even have a resident alien card. They'll ship you back to Russia for good!"

"Trust me. I come back with new name."

I gave up. "You were lucky the stairs didn't collapse."

"I tiptoe."

"How clever. Anyone see you?"

"Two ducks, one egret, and too many seagulls. I swim there from Gerard Drive. I swim back. Very long, very cool."

"Valium isn't exactly hard to come by. An overdose can get you pretty sick, but it won't kill you, and any doctor will prescribe Valium. So why did Bud keep his wife's pills all this time? And please don't tell me for sentimental value."

Dmitri scratched his mustache. "Because one day he knows he follow in footsteps of beloved wife. He take pills in coffee. Out in ocean he take off vest, he plunge into ice water, and lets darkness overtake him." Dmitri's voice shuddered. He would have been great in a Boris Karloff movie.

"Dick Knight would say he fed them to Polly, hid the bottle, then left it in his bathroom, empty, to make the police think he committed suicide." I fanned myself with the chamois cloth, a waste of energy. "If that was the case, he'd make sure the thermos was found. He'd leave a note. If he planned to commit suicide, fake or otherwise, why give you a one thousand dollar check to investigate his wife's death? Why make an appointment with me?"

We passed Cedar Street on our left. I looked back. Only one engine was parked inside the fire station. Using the chamois cloth, I carefully put the pill bottle back in the glove compartment. Mission accomplished, I dropped down on the seat.

"You are popped, Simona."

"Pooped."

"Popped. Like pin in balloon."

"Both." We veered right for Fireplace Road and I climbed over to the backseat, pushing Dmitri's romance books in a corner with my feet. I stretched out. "Remind me to show you the picture of a hairless cat named Uma. If we find her, she's worth eighty thousand dollars to Dick Knight. I think he might be more forthcoming for that kind of money."

"What you say?" Dmitri asked. Apparently I'd been mumbling.

"I said wake me up when we're home."

FOURTEEN

A JOLT AND THE SOUND of shattering glass woke me up. Dmitri shouted something in Russian. Another jolt propelled me against the back of the front seat. I heard a loud thud. The car veered sharply, bumping over something. I was on the floor of the backseat by then, trying to find something to hold on to that was a little firmer than *Love Forever*. The car stopped with a crunch and the shudder of a dying beast. The car horn bleated.

"Dmitri, help!" I flailed arms and legs. My hips were stuck.

Dmitri didn't answer and the horn kept up its racket. I wriggled, pushed, sucked in my stomach, and finally popped one hip free. I scrambled back up and leaned over the front seat. The steering wheel had disappeared inside Dmitri's chest. His head lolled at a twisted angle. I swallowed hard several times to keep from panicking and reached over to touch below his ear. Gently, for fear of moving him.

He was alive. Tears poured down my face as I punched 911 on the cellular phone.

"Where are you?" the operator asked.

"Somewhere on Fireplace Road," I shouted over the horn, looking out of the windshield for a mailbox, some specific reference point. The front of the car had met up with one of those wide, sturdy, centuries-old trees the Hamptons are famous for. Out of the side window a shadowy row of variously shaped stone slabs told me I was where I wasn't ready to be.

"We're in a cemetery!"

"There are no cemeteries on Fireplace Road."

"I don't know where I am."

"We'll find you." The operator hung up. I was grateful for his optimism. I didn't budge, afraid the opening of a car door might cause Dmitri to move and hurt himself even more. When I had fallen asleep, we'd been fifteen minutes away from The Pynes. How we'd ended up against a tree in a cemetery was beyond me. Behind me was a paved road and a thick forest of the usual cedars. No houses that I could see. No traffic. Help was coming soon, I prayed. The light was dim. Above a thick tapestry of trees, a patch of mauve sky; below, a sobering green clearing with scattered tombstones, flowers, and lots of dead.

I let my eyes rest on Dmitri's broad back, the twist of his neck. I couldn't help but think of the whales they sometimes find on the beaches of Long Island. Legendary creatures that make a wrong turn somewhere. Who usually die.

I bit my lips out of anger. I wanted to kick Dmitri for being so stubborn, to tear that stupid new purple shirt to shreds. "Why didn't you buckle your damn seat belt!" I wanted to scream.

I told him a joke. Dmitri didn't look like he could hear it, but maybe then he could. "Do you know what a lie for the good is?" I shouted. The car horn was still going strong. "A man comes home early from work. In the bedroom he sees a naked man in his wife's closet. 'What are you doing here?' he asks—"

A pickup truck stopped behind us. Tanner, the Labrador, jumped out from the back. Steve King got out of the driver's seat. They came toward us at the same fast pace.

"I've called nine-one-one," I yelled. "He shouldn't be moved."

"What about you? Are you okay?"

"I was telling him a joke. Dmitri loves jokes." My cheeks were getting wet again. It was the dog's doing. He'd gone over to Dmitri's side, his snout raised high, working overtime. He was smelling blood. I hadn't seen any blood, but then Dmitri was hunched over. I couldn't see much. "This man finds a naked . . ."

Steve King reached in the open back window and put his hand on my head, the way he might with his dog. "I'm sure it's a very funny joke, ma'am, but we don't want your buddy shakin' up laughin', do we? You might want to think about takin' one big long breath. Then doin' a couple more."

I followed orders, immediately feeling better. Steve dropped down on his haunches to face me more or less at eye level, his hand resting on the open window. It was leathery and tanned, covered with cuts. It smelled of the day's catch he had just taken to Stuart's Market Place in Amagansett. That's why he'd been on this road, he said, on his way home. I kept my fingers on Dmitri's neck to feel his life ticking.

Steve explained that we were in the Green River Cemetery off Accabonac Highway and Old Stone Highway. "Some pretty famous folks are buried out here." His voice was loud and steady. The car horn wouldn't let up. "Frank O'Hara, he was a poet. The painter Jackson Pollock and his wife, Lee Krasner. 'Everyone's dying to get into Green River Cemetery' is the local sayin', but I never did see anyone wantin' it as bad as you two." He chuckled. I thought my joke was better. If I could ever finish telling it to Dmitri.

"I don't know what happened," I said. "I was sleeping."

"Your back bumper is smashed, your taillights are gone. Some drunk roared into you, and your buddy lost control of the car."

Dmitri groaned and lifted himself off the car horn. The sudden silence lasted only a few seconds. I yelled, "Don't move!" The dog barked and the ambulance's siren wailed down the road.

Dmitri looked down at his precious new shirt. It was covered in blood from a cut on his chin.

"How do you feel?" I asked.

"Like Russian revenge."

The police arrived as the paramedics eased Dmitri out of the Cadillac. I gave them our names, our East Hampton and New York addresses. I'd been asleep. No, I hadn't seen what hit us. Dmitri hadn't either. That's all the information I had, I told them. Mentioning our interest in a year-old death that might or might not be a murder seemed unnecessary. The hip I'd popped free burned, my left shoulder ached, and I could feel one cheek swelling where it had smashed against the door handle.

Steve King supplied his drunken driver theory. As he talked—he knew the cops by their first names—I took a peek at the front of his truck. It was in pristine condition. I gave Tanner an extra scratch behind his ears to cover my guilt. The man had only been kind to me.

He even offered to accompany me to Southampton Hospital, but Dmitri wouldn't go in the ambulance without me. On the way over we held hands. His chin had hit the top of the steering wheel. His temple had rammed against the windshield pillar. The paramedics thought that was what had knocked him out.

Lying on the gurney, bandaged up, Dmitri looked ashamed. What had happened was at odds with the way he saw himself. Fearsome, courageous, bigger-than-life. And always more clever than the next guy.

"Someone is after us," he announced.

I laughed. "It's hard to believe we're a threat to anyone at this point. I subscribe to Steve's drunk-on-the-loose theory." Dmitri could have been right, but the two paramedics had their ears bent in our direction. It wasn't the place or the time.

"No drunk," Dmitri said. "Three times he hit me. I'm sorry, Simona, it is my fault." He explained that he'd taken advantage of my napping in the backseat to turn onto Old Stone Highway and head for Amagansett. Fifteen minutes later he'd walked into FizzEd, where Kelly Klein was keeping herself trim with step aerobics. She'd been contemplating a haircut. Dmitri had tried one more nudge of his charm to seal the deal. "Klein hair! Big bucks!"

She'd changed her mind. She was contemplating a divorce instead.

"After I go for home." He closed his eyes.

"Ten dollars you'll come home with me tonight," I bet him.

"No contest."

"Okay, I'll bet the opposite and I'll raise it another ten."

Dmitri accepted with a thumbs up. I stroked his mustache with my free hand. His hand tightened over mine. He was in a great deal of pain.

"So what is end of joke, please?"

FIFTEEN

WHAT'S THE DEFINITION of a lie for the good?" I repeated to a young doctor with peppermint on his breath. I was in the ER of Southampton Hospital. Dmitri had just been whisked off for X rays.

"You tell me." The doctor shined a light in my eyes.

"A man comes home early from work. He finds his wife in bed and a naked man in her bedroom closet. 'What are you doing here?' the husband asks. The naked man shrugs. 'Waiting for the bus.'"

The doctor held up a hand instead of laughing. "How many fingers?"

"Four." Next I told him who the U.S. President was: "Billy Crystal."

This time he laughed. I didn't.

"Hey, cheer up," the doctor said. "Your friend's going to be fine."

"You promise?"

He got distracted. A soot-covered firefighter lumbered in on his own two feet, his arm in a makeshift sling. Two nurses rushed to his aid. A teen with a bad cut on his shin sat on a bench, next to his rollerblades, fiddling with a Walkman. A mother was hushing a crying little girl, reassuring her that not all ticks carried Lyme disease.

I asked Peppermint Breath about the Barrens fire. It had jumped Sunrise Highway and was threatening Westhampton, about twenty miles farther east. The C–130 tankers hadn't shown up yet.

"No casualties so far." He raised crossed fingers, dropped two ibuprofen pills in my palm, and told me I'd survive.

"Thanks." Tomorrow I'd make more sandwiches. I walked out into the hall, called information, and got Jim's telephone number. His machine answered. The big clock on the wall told me it was 10:17 P.M. I tried Nick & Toni's. Jim was at the bar. While my stomach groaned at the thought of the food I was missing, I explained about the accident, going into details to make sure he believed me. My stomach has always led a separate life.

Jim worried about me for a couple of minutes. Over the phone his voice came across high-pitched, a little manic. I could picture him standing at a trading desk, shouting sell and buy orders into the phone at lightning speed. I thought of Stan with his calm, furry voice. Would he have been this worried?

"I'm fine, Jim. Really."

"You're not just joshing me?"

"No. The doctor assured me I'll see another sunrise."

"Good. Get a taxi. Join me now. Our table isn't ready yet anyway. The usual twenty-minute wait to remind your patrons how hot you are. Drives me nuts. Come on, I've got your Pinot Grigio waiting for you."

"I'm sorry. I have to stay with Dmitri. Besides I look like hell. Thanks, though."

He said he understood.

"Maybe you'll take a raincheck?"

In two weeks when the cheek flattens out and the bruises go and I've hashed things over with Stan. "Sure thing."

I checked with a nurse about Dmitri. "As soon as we know anything ..." She glided off on sparkling vinyl tiles. I swallowed my pills and settled down to wait in the hallway with a Diet Coke and peanut butter–cheddar cheese crackers from a vending machine.

Forty-five minutes later Jim walked into the ER, carrying a large wicker basket. In crisp blue slacks, a collarless off-white linen shirt, and loafers *with* socks, he was a welcome sight. An orderly pointed him my way. I waved. Jim opened up his smile. "Picnic time!"

I slipped a leftover cracker into my pocket. "You're crazy."

"I know how to offer a deal." He dropped down next to me, close enough for me to pick up the scent of sandalwood. "You have to be starving." He leaned over to remove the lid of the basket. Steam rolled out along with the delicious smell of food. He brought out cloth napkins, silverware, and two foil-covered plates. "Wild striped sea bass in saffron broth with New Zealand cockles and sautéed pea shoots, Nick & Toni's best. I put the Pinot Grigio in Snapple lemonade bottles. Hospitals aren't into alcohol. Dessert is peach tart."

We ate right there, in the hallway outside the ER. We got a few disapproving and envious glances. I stuck to Coke because of the pills, but I was high enough on attention not to need any stimulants. I even forgot that my cheek looked like a baseball mitt and that Dmitri's blood was on my shirt. Jim didn't seem to notice either. The wild sea bass had a crispy skin and moist, white flesh that filled my mouth with a melting luxurious taste. It was the best fish I had ever eaten. I saved my half of the peach tart for Dmitri.

"I want to know more about this accident," Jim said after stacking the dirty plates in the basket. He'd finished both Snapple bottles of wine and his cheeks shone red through the tan. It was cute. "You think someone's after you?"

"What are you talking about?" I hadn't told him Bud had hired us.

"Lester Kennelly called me this afternoon. He had you checked. You don't have a PI license."

"Never said I did. Who needs a title or a piece of paper to get things done."

Jim laughed. His eyes sparkled. "Not me."

"If you think someone might be after me, then you do think Polly was murdered."

"Let's say her death was convenient."

"To whom?"

"I brought you something else that's interesting." From the breast pocket of his linen shirt he slipped out a folded piece of paper. "About a month ago, Bud came over to my restaurant. He likes to eat there every night and sometimes he stays until closing time, nursing a brandy." I liked the way Jim referred to Bud in the present tense.

"I try to find time to sit down and chat." Jim tapped the paper on his other hand. "He talks to me about work, his latest ad campaign, sometimes he'll worry out loud about Laurie. She's got a law degree but she's shoveling dirt out at Bayberry Gardens."

"From the little I know about him, I got the feeling he wasn't a great communicator."

"Prefers his computer to people. At least that's what he says. I see him as a lonely man." Jim laughed. "He says we're two of a kind."

"Lonely?"

"I don't know." The red of his cheeks spread across his face. "Whatever. Anyway, a month ago he came to the restaurant with a notepad and all through dinner he took notes. When I sat down with him for our usual chat, he showed me this list. He wanted my input." Jim offered me the folded piece of paper. I opened it up. The WSK logo was on the top left. Underneath it, Bud's name was printed, com-

plete with title: Chief Creative Officer. Underneath
the title, a list of names.

STEVE KING
REBECCA BARNES
DODO PARSONS
JIM MOLTON
LESTER KENNELLY
LAURIE

"What does this list represent?"

"A list of suspects."

"In his wife's death?"

Jim nodded.

"Your name's on it! He gave you a list with your
name on it?"

"Bud liked things on the up-and-up. I think he
was testing my reaction. Wouldn't surprise me if he
presented this list to all his suspects."

"Well, you did say you wanted to hold Polly's
head underwater for a while."

"The front bumpers of both my cars are in mint
condition." Jim stood up, pulled at his belt, paced to
the vending machine, pulled all the knobs. "God, I
hate hospitals. The smell is enough to—how much
longer is your friend going to be?"

"You don't have to stay. I loved the food and the
company. Thank you."

"Oh Jesus, I might as well tell you." He sat down
again. "I bought my house from Polly. That was four
years ago. I'd just left the Street, with some heavy

financial losses and an eight-year relationship down the tubes. Wall Street runs from a river to a graveyard. I was ready to jump into one end or the other. I thought I'd go back to nature and find inner peace and all that. Springs seemed right. Low-key, but close enough to East Hampton in case I started to miss the action. Plus I had that great view. No one would think of me as a loser. God this sounds dumb."

"Human."

His face relaxed with relief. "Thanks. You saw my place, it's got a great bay view. But Polly liked to keep control of things and wouldn't sell me the land the driveway's on. The only way you can access my house is to drive through Polly's property, which really cuts into the worth of the place. At the time I didn't think it was a problem. It was still a good deal and I was still cocky. I'd soon get enough money together and she'd sell. Last year the restaurant took off and I had some money. There was a great Richard Meier house for sale on Georgica Road that I wanted. I even found a buyer for my place who was willing to go way over market price *if* he could also buy the land the driveway was on. Polly strung me along, asking for more and more money, then gave me a flat-out 'no.' That's not enough to kill, but almost."

I looked down at the list again. "Bud included his own daughter on this."

"As I said, he was trying to provoke reactions."

"What reasons would she have for wanting her own mother dead?"

Jim smiled apologetically. "Laurie's a friend. You'll have to ask her."

"What about Steve King? He's at the top of the list."

"Steve thinks The Pynes belongs to him. His father, a bonacker like Steve, owned it. Back in the late forties, after a bad winter, Polly offered less than half its value. Steve's father had a wife and a son to feed, so he accepted. Steve's made a big deal of this."

"Well, I checked his front bumper. Not a wrinkle on it. What about the others on the list? Rebecca, Dodo, Bud's partner."

"I asked Bud about that. He said if I didn't know, it didn't matter. Lester has been trying to divorce his wife for more than a year. She's holding on tight. When that news first hit, village rumor had it that Lester and Polly were an item. In my opinion, that's a crock."

"Why Rebecca Barnes? She's wonderful."

"I don't know, but liking the boss of the company doesn't make her stock worth beans. All I can tell you about Dodo is that he drinks too much and that Polly used him as an errand boy. As for Kennelly, he and Bud had a few work-related arguments that I know of. Lester didn't want him to quit New York. Most of their disagreements boiled down to money versus art."

"Did Bud talk to you about a merger with Chass\Dayton?"

"I know it fell through last year."

"Did Bud tell you why? Or mention Chass\ Dayton in the past month?"

"No on both counts. Are you saying Chass\ Dayton is connected to Bud's death?"

"I'm just trying to find out as much as I can. What are the chances that Bud staged his own death?"

Jim looked suddenly weary. "None. Bud was a straight shooter, hated dishonesty."

"Hard to believe for an advertising legend."

"He gave the public the truth about a product. He just presented it with an interesting twist. That's what made him great." Emotion clenched his face. "I don't want him to be dead."

I reached for his hand. "What's so special about the Richard Meier house?"

"He's a great architect. All right, he's hot, he's doing the Getty Center in LA, he costs a lot of money. It would have been a trophy house. I'm not proud of myself for wanting one, but I like the idea that I can afford something big again. Come on, what do you expect?" His voice rose. "I was a commodities trader for eleven years! You can't shake it off just like that. There's nothing wrong in wanting the good things in life."

I let go of his hand. "Jim, I haven't said a word."

"You sent disapproving vibes."

He'd gotten the signals mixed up. I'd been thinking that despite his need for a trophy house, he was very attractive. And likable. My fingers were itching to slide across his lips.

This time I stood up. I excused myself from Jim and hobbled back into the ER room to talk to the nurse. This time she made a phone call. "The doctor will be right down."

Fifteen minutes later, with my cheek out to pumpkin proportions and my joints stiffening to concrete, Dr. Peppermint Breath told us Dmitri had five stitches on his chin; a contusion on his left temple, which was the probable cause of his loss of consciousness; and three cracked ribs that had not perforated his lungs. Only rest would heal him.

"He's bellowing to go home."

I've never been happier to lose twenty dollars.

SIXTEEN

THE PHONE WOKE ME UP. I rolled out of bed to answer. Dmitri had spent the night on the sofa that Jim and I had lowered him onto. He'd refused the bed, afraid he wouldn't get up again until his ribs healed. We couldn't afford to rent the cottage for that long.

It was the East Hampton Town Police. The Kirkwood Garage had the Cadillac. The officer gave me the telephone number. They'd found the car that had rammed into us. "A '94 blue Honda Accord reported stolen yesterday afternoon at 5:05 P.M. from an Ed Starner residing on Napeague Lane. Know him?"

"No."

"His story checks out. We found the car on Neck Path. They must have abandoned the Honda right after hittin' you. Probably got scared outta their wits. Drunk kids. We found a dozen beer cans and a couple of smudged prints we're checking into. If we come up with anything we'll get back to you."

The phone rang again. This time it was Stan.

They were about to try a new mountain, taking the Ammonoosuc Ravine Trail up Mount Washington. They planned to hike up to the summit and then back down to the tree line to spend the night at the Lake of the Clouds hut.

"What a lovely name," I said.

"If you're thinking romantic, it isn't." Stan had on his sleepy voice. I could feel it low down. "You get bunk beds, twelve to a room. Last year a guy snored so loudly that the whole crowd ended up laughing. It didn't wake him up."

"You're having fun?"

"The weather's good."

Great answer. "What about Willy?"

"He wants to talk to you. Hon?"

"Yes?"

"I love you."

"I guess I know that." Telling me wasn't good enough. "Anyway, your toothbrush has been watching over me. I bet you forgot it on purpose."

"I didn't, but an electric toothbrush isn't much use when you're camping."

"Uh huh." Lighten up, *bello mio*.

Willy got on the phone. Weather was big for him too. Or so it seemed. I got to hear about how there could suddenly be a snow storm, how the highest winds ever recorded in North America came from the weather station on Mount Washington. He was about to go into the flora and the fauna of the place when Stan must have finally walked away from earshot.

"I know what's wrong with Dad," he whispered.

"What?" I whispered back.

"We camped out on Mount Adams last night. In the middle of the night Dad had this vomotose nightmare."

"Who wouldn't? Sleeping bags were meant for mummies."

"Wait a minute." His voice moved away. "Hey Dad, could you get me a soda, please? I'm real thirsty." He came back to the phone. "He mumbled a lot. I listened real hard. He kept talking about cherries and blue maggots."

"You're sure that's what he said?"

"Oh yeah, and I know what it means too. He's worried about Granny."

"How do you get Granny from cherries and maggots?"

"She used to make the best cherry pies. Now she says she's too tired. Maggots are what eat you up when you're dead. Do you think Granny's dying?"

"No." The boy had a galloping imagination. "I'll bet you guys had steak last night."

"How'd you know?" His voice sounded awed. I'd just scored big.

"Because red meat makes him toss and turn and burp and I don't know what else." Gives him gas for one. "Get your dad to stick to chicken or fish, and he won't have any more nightmares, okay?" Willy promised. I babbled on about missing both of them for a few minutes. Stan came back on the phone. I asked him if he wanted me to call his mother for him, check up on how she was.

"I talked to her last week. She's fine. In fact, she left for a ten-day Caribbean cruise yesterday. Not even the heat stops her."

So much for dying. "Tell Willy," I said. "He'll get a kick out of it." We exchanged goodbyes. He didn't ask about my case. I didn't tell him. I forgot all about Raf's message.

I stumbled into the living room on stiff joints and went straight for the iron skillet. *Tocca ferro*, touch iron, a must for superstitious Italians. I placed my forefinger and little finger on the skillet in centuries-old, ward-off-the-evil-eye fashion and hoped that maggots and cherries had nothing to do with Stan's mother or me.

The ritual over, I went looking for Dmitri. He was outside in a pair of cut-off gray sweats I'd washed yesterday, feet and chest bare to the sun. After spearing myself into an oversized T-shirt, I joined him and told him about the cars. "They think it was drunken kids."

Dmitri shook his head slowly and cracked open a hard-boiled egg against the picnic table. In front of him, a platter of boiled potatoes, three eggs, and four hot dogs nestled around a jar of hot mustard.

"How did this food get here?"

"I make while you snore."

"Don't let anything happen to you," I said. "I'd miss you too much."

"You'd miss my food."

"That too."

I dipped a hot dog in mustard and munched. The

bay was slick with sunlight. The only mark in the sky was a scratch left from a jet. The Gardiners Island seventeenth-century windmill across the bay was sparkling white, the blades in a perfect X. It was still too hot, but a breeze gathered up humidity in slow brushstrokes and sent it to some other corner of the island. The place ought to have been heaven.

"Jim showed me a list of possible suspects that he claims Bud gave him," I said. I propped it up on the refrigerator in front of the compostable/noncompostable list. "Steve King, Rebecca, Dodo, Laurie. It was on WSK stationery, maybe in Bud's handwriting. I'll have to check."

"You don't trust Jim because you like him too much."

"I'm trying to do my job. Jim's name was also on that list."

"But he give it to you."

"Diversionary tactics." Charming ones at that. I lowered myself gingerly on an Adirondack chair and wondered if I could somehow get the recipe for Nick & Toni's wild striped sea bass. My feet ended up on a bench. I leaned my head back. Work could wait.

Dmitri lifted the food platter and extracted a photo from underneath. "Why you have picture of this cat?"

"That's Uma. Not a pretty sight, is she?" Uma was a Blue Cream Sphynx cat with short, fine down that made her look hairless. Huge ears, a white muzzle, pink chest, and a purple-gray coat that ended in a rat's tail. "The breed has health problems. She has to be bathed and towel-dried frequently or else she leaves a stain wherever she lies because she has no fur to absorb the grease. She was born on David Letterman's fiasco of an Oscar night."

"Uma, Oprah. Oprah, Uma." Dmitri dipped a potato in the mustard jar and dropped it in his mouth.

"That's the one. She's being hotly contested in a divorce. The husband hired Dick Knight to find her. The husband also thinks the wife took her. Mr. and Mrs. Reed Lawrence III. The cat disappeared a week ago from the Lawrences' Southampton house on Dune Road. That's all I know. It would be great if we could help Knight on this one, but Uma is probably on her way to Australia. Mr. Lawrence is offering eighty thousand dollars for her safe return."

Dmitri's mustache twitched. "Name is not new to my ear. Maybe Lawrence is friend of Ron. I put Mike and Phil on to this." Dmitri's friends still worked for Perelman. I like to refer to the Russian gang as the three musketeers. Dmitri opts for the "Karamazov brodders."

"Good idea." I reluctantly stood up and did a slow stretch. It was past ten o'clock. "I'm going to start with Rebecca." The least likely suspect.

"Check if she have borscht left over." He ate another potato.

"Indian giver."

"You know what Russian revenge is?"

"Siberia."

"Napoleon, he invade us and what do we do? We

burn fields. We kill cattle. Thousand of French troops die of hunger. We die too, but they die more. Same with Hitler and Mussolini. Russian revenge is hunger. So I eat."

"Makes perfect sense." I grabbed the last potato and walked back to the porch to get dressed.

"The Coast Guard!" Dmitri called out.

I turned around. Three boats were crossing the bay, heading straight for the windmill. I ran inside and yanked the binoculars off the porch wall. "One's a police boat. They're docking on Gardiners Island."

"Someone moves blades of windmill in cross position."

"That's why the windmill has always been painted white," Rebecca said, walking toward us. Her blue smock flapped with her long, purposeful stride. Wisps of long gray hair floated around her face, stern and beaky with bad news. "When the pirate ships came, the Gardiners would warn the people on this coast by changing the position of the blades to a cross. That was at least two hundred years ago."

"Why would they do that now?" Dmitri took the binoculars from me and aimed them at the windmill.

"The caretaker called the police. He found Bud by the Great Pond. Quite dead. You can only get to the pond by kayak, and then only at high tide." She pointed to the island and moved her finger northeast, underlining the fading coastline of the 3,350-acre privately owned estate that stretched toward Montauk. "There's a ridge of sandbars out there. The

Gardiners used to put lights on them to wreck ships and haul off all the goods. The Great Pond is at the very tip." Rebecca swallowed slowly, her only other sign of emotion besides the harsh light in her eyes and the disjointed speech. "The gulls gave him away. Great swoops of birds, the caretaker said. They piqued his interest. At first he thought it might be a deer carcass. The island is infested with ticks."

"I'm sorry, Rebecca," I said.

"Thanks. I'm a hardy old bird, but I would like some company. I drove Dodo out early this morning to Asparagus Beach to hunt for treasure. He can't afford to miss a day. It helps keep his balance." She gestured toward the chair. "We all need that. May I?"

"Of course. Laurie?"

Rebecca dropped down in the chair in a fast, graceless gesture. "She's with them on the boat. She refused my company."

"Should we wake Jim?" I sat on the bench beside her. Dmitri went inside our cottage.

"Jim's not family. I've left word for Steve King. He's out in his trawler. His Dory Squad buddies will let him know by radio. All we can do is wait and see what Laurie needs."

After asking about our accident, Rebecca said, "You should put some seaweed on that cheek."

Dmitri came back out, his chest covered with a clean, wrinkled blue shirt. His hands held three glasses and a pitcher of orange juice and vodka.

We drank. We toasted Bud. We waited.

"The Indians called the island Manchonake,"

Rebecca said. "The place where many have died." She gave a thin-lipped smile, her eyes hooked at the foot of the windmill, at a harbor too far away to see. Dmitri refilled her glass.

"Bud once told me I painted only still lifes because I had no love for living things." Rebecca caught a stray hair and twisted it on her long, bony finger. "Cézanne painted still lifes because he was too scared of the female figure. Bud couldn't admit that a person can be strong and assertive and still have a pocket of fear dictating his choices. Her choices." She clasped the splintery arm of the Adirondack chair. "Still lifes. *Natura morta*, the Italians call it. The French, *nature morte*. Dead nature. I always thought it was such a bleak way of looking at the loveliness of a still moment. Until now."

Rebecca stood up. "I have to pick up Dodo."

"Give me car keys, I go," Dmitri offered.

"We'll all go," I said.

"No." Her voice was firm. "A Gardiner once called the island a sandbar of sorrow. I think the tide's been bringing The Pynes a hefty share of that sorrow."

SEVENTEEN

DMITRI AND I WAITED in silence, sharing the binoculars. The temperature rose. Sailboats moved across the bay. Seagulls swooped. Water lapped. I went inside the cottage and called Lester Kennelly at WSK. I got his assistant.

"Lester's in East Hampton. He went out late last night," Charlene said. "We were working late. His wife called. She was worried about Laurie."

I told her about Bud's body being found.

"Lester called an hour ago. We're all numb over here. And going crazy."

"I can guess. 'Sport4Life Saves Your Life' was Bud's famous tag line for all Sport4Life products. Now he goes and kills himself just when the agency is pitching a campaign for a new product. Doesn't look good for WSK."

"You got it," Charlene said. "We're doing damage control. Me, I'd love to quit."

"You'd get bored."

"Yeah, I know. Hey, I remembered something. That Polly Pynes folder that was misfiled? It wasn't me. I didn't touch it for months."

"Maybe your boss took it out."

"King Kennelly? He wouldn't know where the file room is. No, it was Bud. I remember seeing him in there about three weeks ago. He was using the copier and he had a file under his arm."

"Was there anything missing in the file when you showed it to me?"

"No. It didn't hold much to begin with. Just those detectives' names and the lists of expenses Polly had filed when she was still entertaining for Bud in the city. Old stuff. Anybody come after you with a gun yet?"

"No." Not with a gun.

"You be careful now."

I thanked her and hung up. I summed up my conversation for Dmitri, leaving out the gun part. If Italians are good at taking imaginative leaps, Russians are masters.

Dmitri and I for once agreed. Neither of us could see a reason for Bud wanting to look in his wife's file. It didn't seem likely that he couldn't remember the names of the detectives he'd hired.

Dmitri took over the phone. The garage asked for ten days and $1,200 to fix his car. He groaned and went back to his perch on the sofa to sleep off the news. The clay color of his face announced that his pocket wasn't the only thing hurting.

❂   ❂   ❂

By lunchtime, the news that Bud's body had been found had spread through The Pynes. A cluster of residents gathered on the narrow strip of beach. In hopes of something useful, I hitched up my skirt and waded in the water nearby.

They commiserated, picked news from one another, and gossiped: Bud hadn't been the same since Polly's death. He worked too hard. Polly had been the death of him. His daughter didn't help. No, Laurie was nice, but she was young, a little confused. With that mother! Why wasn't the girl practicing law, after all that money he spent? It was the fisherman's fault. Steve King, he'd sucked the brains right out of that sweet girl's head. Polly still loved Bud. What? No way! Then why'd she leave him The Pynes?

The West Side psychiatrist with a permanently curdled face dropped the word "murder" in conjunction with Polly's name.

"Shame on you," Laurie's defender said, a sunworn woman with a parrot on her shoulder. "You tell him, Captain Dan. Shame on you." The bird fluffed its feathers, cocked its head, and refused to comply. "Suicide. Both of them," she said.

"Suicide," the bird repeated.

The chubby economics professor from Queens College dissented. "Statistically, a heart attack makes the most sense."

"What about the floating life preserver?" the psychiatrist asked. "What, statistically speaking, did he do with his scull? Tie it to his ankle?"

The economics professor did a belly flop in the water at that point, leaving me sopping wet. It cooled me off, which was the only good thing so far.

"What do *you* think happened to Bud?" I asked the psychiatrist.

He took a deep breath. His chest stayed puny. "It's difficult to give a considered opinion. He was not my patient, but I did see a Suffolk County police car in Polly's driveway yesterday afternoon. Captain Comelli was in it. The very man who worked on Polly's—"

"Hey, Doc!" the professor yelled from the water, waving binoculars. "They're leaving the island."

Doc gulped air to restore his dignity. The rest of us watched in silence as the Coast Guard and police boats slowly crossed the bay, trailing a swarm of gulls.

Our silence was broken by the sound of a truck pushing up the driveway. We turned in unison. Captain Dan squawked.

Steve King parked his pickup by the woodshed next to the big house. He had his baseball cap and his sunglasses on. The dog waited beside him.

"That man reminds me of a vulture," the doc said.

"You're full of it," the professor said.

The parrot woman sighed. "He's desperately in love."

"In love," Captain Dan repeated.

I left them to squabble and romanticize, and went over to thank Steve for helping us the night before. I added that I felt for Laurie. Her father had seemed to me a very nice gentleman. He simply nodded. Tanner wagged his tail once. Asking Steve about his two-hour talk with Bud on the morning of Polly's death would have to wait another day or two.

So would my talk with Laurie. I said goodbye, turned around, and headed for Rebecca's cottage to borrow her old Buick. There were easier, more practical issues to take care of that afternoon.

Rebecca pointed with her charcoal stick at the keys on the kitchen counter, then resumed drawing an osprey in the act of landing on its nest high above the shallow water of Accabonac Harbor. The wings stretched across the page. The charcoal strokes filled them with majestic motion.

"That's beautiful," I said, picking up the keys.

"It's not a still life."

I drove the seven miles to East Hampton, first stopping at the garage to leave a deposit for Dmitri's car. At the A&P I luxuriated in the icy air-conditioning until my body started to creak. A sign from the Ladies Village Improvement Society asked for more sandwiches for the firefighters. At the checkout counter kids were cheering the arrival of two C–130 tanker planes.

"Did you watch 'em on CNN?" the bagger asked, pimples bright against his tan. "Five thousand gallons! Splat! Totally cosmic!"

"It's a crying shame it took them so long," the

man behind me said. "Go trust the government!"

I hauled my gallons of spring water into the car—plus enough whole wheat, ham, and cheese for another fifty sandwiches—and headed over to Claws on Wheels near the railroad station for East End specialties: Shinnecock littleneck clams, just-picked corn, and ripe tomatoes.

The clams had sold out. I did a quick menu change. The firefighters were getting pure Americana this time, but Dmitri was going to get sweet Italian revenge. Cool Pasta by the bay.

Next I drove down Pantigo Road to Buzz Chew and rented a car, picking a dark blue Chevy that wouldn't attract attention in case we needed to follow anyone. Or in case someone was waiting to ram us into the cemetery again. Buzz Chew promised to deliver within the hour.

When I turned into the driveway of The Pynes, Laurie was waiting for me.

EIGHTEEN

LAURIE FLUNG OPEN THE CAR DOOR, her face livid with anger. "Where's that Russian man?"

"Dmitri? Sleeping in the cottage, I think. Laurie, I'm so sorry about your father. Is there—"

"He's not in the cottage. He's not anywhere around here. Where the hell is he? If you don't find him, I'm going to call the police!"

"Laurie, calm down. Come on, sit down, we don't have to make this public." I patted the passenger's seat. Laurie hesitated, looked back at the cottages. Curtains were fluttering. She sat down, slammed the car door shut, and curled against it. She was thirty-one going on an enraged twelve. But then she'd just lost her father.

"Why do you want to call the police, Laurie?"

"That man tossed my dad's place!"

"No, Dmitri wouldn't do—"

"Don't tell me what he'd do. I saw him!"

Please Dmitri, no.

"He was swimming away down the creek and he had a plastic bag hanging from his mouth! Upstairs at Dad's place was a mess."

"Let me explain, Laurie."

"Just find him." She sat up, suddenly subdued. I followed her gaze. Rebecca was coming toward us with her usual determined stride, blue smock flapping. Laurie fingered the door handle. "Please. I need help." She opened the car door and slipped out, running to Rebecca like a lost child who'd found her mother.

I couldn't figure her out. Nor did I know where Dmitri could be. There was no note in the cottage, but the bicycle that had been propped behind the daybed on the porch was gone. I called Ron Perelman's house and asked for Mike or Phil, Dmitri's buddies. I was informed they were both out on a mini cruise with their boss. I put the food away. Dmitri had ploughed through the bread, the tuna fish, and two frozen bagels that Stan had left behind. Russian revenge.

I climbed into Rebecca's car again and drove to the visible heart of Springs—Ashawagh Hall, at the corner of Fireplace Road and Old Stone Highway. Just beyond the old school, now a community center, was the General Store that had been around since the 1840s and where Jackson Pollock had—sometime in the late 1940s, early 1950s—traded one of his canvases for sixty dollars' worth of groceries. Dan Miller had hung the small "drip" painting in the store where the locals had laughed at it and called

Dan a fool. Years later the "fool" sold the canvas for $17,000 and bought himself a plane.

Dmitri cherished the General Store's blueberry scones, but no one had seen him since Sunday. Same thing at Dreesen's and at the ice cream store in Amagansett. FizzEd was next.

I walked into the middle of a step aerobics class and shouted over U2 if anyone had seen Dmitri.

I got my answer from a woman with an all-bones body a butcher might sell for broth. "If he shows his ass around here, he's an obit." Her haircut was bad.

Other women joined in: "Crow meat!" "Road kill!" "Fish bait." They all had delirium tremens haircuts. I got out of there and headed home.

By now a knot had formed in my throat. Two hundred and fifty pounds with three cracked ribs riding on a rusty bicycle. If any of these women had beer-guzzling boyfriends, my partner was an easy target.

Suddenly Dmitri was in front of my bumper on Fireplace Road. He'd come out of the parking lot of the liquor store. I hit the brakes, then I honked. After that I screamed: "Do you want to get yourself killed? Do you want to kill me? Why the hell didn't you leave a note?" Dmitri pedaled, wavering between the two lanes. Under his weight, the matchstick bicycle. Or so it seemed. He had two bottles of wine strapped to the rack. He also had a rope tied to his wrist. Tied to the other end, a trotting furry mutt. Two feet high and about seven feet wide.

A moving van zoomed toward us, honking.

"You're going to kill that dog! Move to the side!" The van got closer, honked again. Dmitri finally veered to the right. The mutt did not resist. I drove up next to them. "What are you doing?"

"I look for Uma."

"What's at the end of that rope doesn't meow."

"I was in animal shelter. They find her tied to a tree in Merrill Lake Sanctuary. Sunday after fire at Bud's house."

"What's her name?"

"Sabrina. She is Audrey Hepburn in her eyes."

"Not in her hips."

"Very pregnant."

"Wonderful. By the way, no dogs are allowed at The Pynes."

"We sneak her in."

"Did you toss Bud's house?"

"Toss like football?"

"Toss like making a mess of the place while you were looking around."

He turned around only long enough to show me his insulted expression. "Dmitri always very careful." He narrowly missed a tree.

"Laurie doesn't think so."

Behind us cars honked. We were hogging the lane, going too slowly. I pulled over at the first intersection, forcing Dmitri to swing with me. I then tried to make him relinquish the dog. She was a black-and-white longhaired mix, with a lot of spaniel in her. Floppy ears, big liquid eyes, a tongue that was practically washing the asphalt. Looks designed to fill your heart with instant love. The second that I unwound the rope from Dmitri's wrist, she started howling.

He grinned. "Sabrina adore me already."

"So do your victims at FizzEd. The hairdresser you made a deal with is probably going to end up as lobster bait. You're lucky if you get away with only three cracked ribs."

"Plus five stitches and bad contusion on temple."

"And water on the brain."

"You think they ram me into cemetery?"

"Yes, I think they ram you. Unless it was Laurie. She was angry enough. I'll have to ask her if she likes beer." I'd been scratching the dog's ears all this while to persuade her to try the backseat. I didn't convince her. The howling persisted.

Dmitri got off his bike to pick her up. She yelped with happiness. "If she loses babies, it is your fault!"

"Mamma! I've had it. Here, you drive her home." I handed him the keys. "Get a blanket from the cottage to wrap her in. If we're lucky, the neighbors will think you bought a sack of Long Island potatoes. I hope she likes spaghetti."

Dmitri took off with Sabrina in the front seat, licking his face. I hoped Rebecca didn't mind a few dog hairs. I got on the bike. I hadn't ridden one since I was twelve. The tires looked paper-thin and the seat reminded me of a gynecological tool, but I was full of optimism. Everyone always says once you've learned, you never forget.

They're wrong.

NINETEEN

WE TOOK LAURIE A PLATE of Cool Pasta and a bottle of wine as a peace offering. I limped. To complement my aching shoulder and bruised cheek, I now had a skinned knee and a twisted ankle. The mutt, satiated by spaghetti and ketchup, was gratefully asleep on the sofa, her snout buried in Dmitri's dirty shirt.

"Thanks," Laurie said, stepping back into her kitchen. "I haven't eaten all day." On the kitchen table was an untouched casserole, two chocolate cakes, and a meat loaf, each with a note attached. The neighbors bringing sustenance to the grieving. We both murmured our condolences. I was dying to find out the details, but had the good manners to wait.

"I'm sorry about today," Laurie said, leaving the wine bottle on the table with the rest. She held on to the pasta. "I had some anger to vent." She had the bloated, startled face of someone who'd just awakened from a nightmare. Except that she was still in it. Her curly brown hair was wet, her round face dark with tan. Dark lashes ringed swollen brown eyes. Her jaw was wide, her lips thin. She smelled of soap. When she smiled, Laurie radiated joy. In a week at The Pynes I'd seen her smile once. At the barbecue Saturday night, when Jim had whispered something in her ear. She'd taken off right after that.

"I do not toss," Dmitri declared.

"I know that now." Laurie glanced at Dmitri's bandaged chin. "And I'm sorry about the accident."

"It wasn't you who bumped into us?" I asked, just to make sure.

"I might have if I'd found you last night."

"Many angry women look for me." He kissed her cheeks three times in proper Russian fashion.

She almost dropped the pasta plate, but she looked pleased. I suspected she came from a family where a handshake was considered a declaration of love.

"Why no dogs allowed in Pynes?" Dmitri asked, revealing his priorities.

At the same time I asked, "Why is Dmitri off the hook?" Laurie dealt with Dmitri while she led us out to the porch. "That's the only one of Mother's rules I'm keeping. We accept drop-ins for short, supervised visits." Her face flushed with sudden color. She was probably thinking of Steve and his Lab. "No overnights. The tenants want the place to stay clean."

Dmitri and I sat on wicker chairs the color of wet

sand, facing the water. The walls were painted the color of dry sand, the floor shallow water blue. The pillows were pale gray. The lamp at Laurie's elbow was covered with white shells and dropped golden light on the glass table. The lamp repeated itself in the windowpane, looking like a distorted moon. Outside it was dark, except for a thin stubborn glow on the western edge of the bay. The porch door was open to let the weak breeze in. The cicadas, crickets, and katydids were deep in conversation.

"What made you change your mind about Dmitri?" I asked again.

"Give me a minute." Laurie ate the pasta quickly, to get it over with, while we sipped the sunrise drink Rebecca had left.

"Yesterday afternoon," Laurie finally said, "I got inside Dad's house for the first time since the fire." She lowered the empty plate on the floor and crossed her legs. She was wearing tan shorts and a light blue Bayberry Gardens T-shirt. "The fire marshal had taped the place off. No one's supposed to go in there, but I had to see the damage for myself, see if I could spot any telltale signs about the arsonist, something only I could recognize. The whole kitchen section was gone. Computer, all of Dad's files, his work.

"The fire didn't get upstairs to the bedroom side. There's just smoke and water damage, but every-thing—furniture, knick-knacks, Dad's clothes—" Her eyes filled with tears. She grabbed a glass and tried to drink. It was empty. I poured more juice into it.

She took a long drink. "The upstairs wasn't vandalized. No ripped mattress, slashed upholstery, or stuff like that. It was just messy, and Dad, I told you, was neat. Someone had gone through the place in a hurry. Open drawers, clothes on the floor. I called Dave, the fire marshal. The place looked like that on Sunday too. That's how I know it wasn't Dmitri."

"You mean someone had gone through the house before the fire?"

Laurie nodded. "The arsonist even took down the curtain rods. They're hollow."

"Whatever he was looking for couldn't have been too big then. Jewelry?"

"No one in the family wore any. Nothing was missing that I could tell. If Dad left money lying around, it would have been in the kitchen where it burned with everything else." She sat with her back to the water, her eyes aimed at Dmitri. "You talked to Dad at the barbecue a long time."

Dmitri looked at me.

I nodded.

"He hire us to find your mother's killer."

"Mother committed suicide!" Laurie blushed with anger. "Dad refused to get that into his head!"

"You want us to give money back?" Dmitri stood up and started pacing. His ribs were hurting again.

"Captain Comelli came to visit you yesterday," I said. Laurie turned to face me, anger in her eyes. "Yeah, he swayed in here, full of himself, insinuating that he had new evidence on Mother's death."

"Did he tell you what evidence?" I asked.

"He kept waving a copy of Mother's suicide note

and saying that maybe Dad had taken off, implying that he'd killed Mother. If you knew Dad, that's like saying Mother Teresa stole from the kitty. I don't mean he was a saint. He wasn't even a good father, but he was honest to a fault. If he'd killed Mother, he would have turned himself in five minutes later."

She had a skewed definition of honesty, but then she'd gone to law school.

"I told Captain Comelli he was a smug little prick," Laurie said. "It's the new me. Assertive. I also told him Dad was killed."

TWENTY

"COMELLI DECLARED IT was a crazy idea, of course," Laurie said. She folded her legs up on the armchair and hugged them tight. "He suggested I take a stiff shot of whiskey."

From where I sat it didn't sound like bad advice. She was having a bad case of the shivers. I leaned over and clasped her wrist. "What was the medical examiner's verdict?"

"Death by drowning, which doesn't take too much imagination."

Dmitri raised an arm, finger pointed skyward. "It is how he drowned that is question."

"Dad's been taken to Hauppauge. To the Suffolk County Medical Examiner's office. It's going to take them twenty-four to forty-eight hours for a preliminary report. I'll have to wait two weeks for Toxicology." She smirked. "His death is not considered suspicious enough to warrant faster treatment."

"Why do you say that he was killed?"

"Someone tossed his house and then burned it. Then Dad drowns. All in the same morning."

"Many odd facts in situation." Dmitri nudged me, finger still pointed. "Tell her."

I started with the empty Valium bottle Dmitri had found in the upstairs bathroom.

"I am sorry, Laurie," Dmitri said with a hangdog expression. "You are right to be angry." His apology did not move her. Her eyes stayed on me, eager for more information. I explained how I'd shared coffee with Bud from his thermos Sunday morning.

She propped her chin on her knee. "Did Dad say anything about fearing for his own life?"

"No, but after drinking that coffee I felt very wobbly. We think it might have been spiked. If Bud had spiked it, there was no reason for him to offer me some and get me all drugged up. Maybe whoever spiked the coffee used Valium and left the bottle in Bud's bathroom."

"Yes!" Laurie lifted her head. "To make us think Dad killed himself."

"And killer," Dmitri added, "he sets fire to Bud's kitchen so we think suicide note is burned up!" He sniffed for approval.

"That makes perfect sense!" Laurie declared.

"Let's go slow here," I said. "If that's the case, whoever it is isn't very clever. He risked burning up the Valium bottle too."

"Lousy idea," Dmitri admitted.

"The fire marshal says you can almost always tell

when it's arson," Laurie said. "It's finding out who that's the problem."

"How many people knew Bud always took a thermos of coffee with him?"

"He's gone off in that scull with his red thermos every morning since March. The whole East End knows about it."

What the whole East End didn't know was that for three foggy mornings in a row, Bud had shared his thermos with me.

"Dad was a methodical man," Laurie went on. "He wanted order in chaos. Advertising was chaos. That's one of the reasons that he came to live out here. He thought nature was methodical. Like he was." She stopped to swallow.

"He'd set up the coffee machine the night before," Laurie went on. "It was on a timer and at five A.M. sharp it would brew his coffee. He'd have a cup at the house and pour the rest in his thermos and drive over here. He liked to watch the dawn come up from home. The Pynes was home to him. I offered him the big house when Mother had died and left it to me, but he wouldn't even stay in one of the cottages. He said that would be taking advantage. 'A visit's okay. Your mother wouldn't have minded that.'" Tears came. Dmitri produced a handkerchief the size of a place mat, fringe and all.

"Who had access to the house?"

"Dad refused to lock up. It was his way of holding the clock back."

"Okay," I said, "we've just come up with a whole

scenario that sounds plausible, but it's not enough to convince anyone that Bud was murdered. You must know something else, Laurie."

Dmitri agreed with a nod. "Like motive, maybe."

Laurie chewed on the inside of her mouth for about half a minute. "Dad was furious about something," she finally said. "Last Thursday morning, around ten, I walked into his house and heard the tail end of a phone conversation. In all my life I've heard him raise his voice twice. The day Mother died and last Thursday."

"What he say?" Dmitri asked.

Laurie shut her eyes. Her fists clenched. "'You've got until Sunday!' Then after a long pause he said, 'I trusted you.' He sounded so hurt."

"A friend!" Dmitri whispered, eyes wide. Betrayal fascinates him. He is incapable of it.

"Sounds like it," I said. Bud had thought the same about Polly's murderer. Someone she had trusted.

"Dad hung up after that. When I walked in, he was shaking and trying to light a cigarette. He hadn't smoked in ten years."

"Did you ask him why he was upset?" I asked.

"I was afraid he'd have a heart attack."

I didn't believe that, but I didn't pursue it. "You can ask NYNEX for a listing of his local calls for the month, assuming he generated the call."

Laurie's face turned red. "I did. The next day." She ran a hand through her hair. "His heart. I was worried."

"I would have done the same thing," I said. If I feared Bud was talking to someone I cared for. "Have you gotten the list yet?"

Laurie looked relieved. "They said a week."

"Let's try to make sense of what you've told us already," I said. "Last Thursday your father yelled at someone and was unusually upset. It sounds as though he was demanding something from someone. A friend presumably, and since Bud made a point of being honest, we can assume it wasn't extortion. Maybe someone stole something from him and Bud gave him a deadline to return it. That would explain the 'I trusted you.' Then Sunday morning, right after your father left to come here, while it was still dark, someone, presumably the same person who had been on the phone with him, searched your father's house, then torched it. If your father was asking for something back, why search the house?"

"It's the other way around," Laurie said, her anger gone. "Dad's got something this other person wants."

"But then the phone conversation doesn't make sense."

"They are not related," Dmitri suggested, walking to the open porch door to catch the breeze.

Laurie's eyes followed him. "Last night someone went through this place."

Dmitri slapped his thigh. "They not find what they look for in Bud's house!"

"This happened while you were sleeping?" Creepy.

"I don't think so," Laurie said. "Amanda invited me over for dinner in East Hampton. Amanda, she's Lester's wife, Dad's partner?"

I nodded.

"Amanda likes to play mother hen. She stuffed me with meatloaf and TLC. After dinner I was so exhausted from kayaking all over the bay, worrying about Dad, and all that food, that I fell asleep on her sofa and didn't wake up until after two o'clock."

"Was Lester there?"

"After I woke up. He followed me home to make sure I was okay. I gave the prowler plenty of time to go through the place undisturbed."

"You don't lock either?" Dmitri asked.

"I'd left the bathroom window open. It gets moldy in there."

I shifted in my seat. I was getting stiff. "When did you notice someone had been here?"

"This morning. Little things, like the paintings in the dining room were straight when they've always listed to the left. The cereal I'd spilled on the kitchen counter had been cleaned up."

"Was anything missing?"

"No. I don't know what it could be or why he thought it was here. No one's lived in this house for a year."

"Which makes it a perfect hiding place," I said.

"But why murder, Laurie?" Dmitri asked. "We need strong motive. You know, maybe?" He flashed his best avuncular smile.

Laurie sighed. "Before hanging up, Dad said,

'Monday is too late. I've already made the appointment.'"

"You suspect someone?" I asked.

"No!"

I said, "Lester Kennelly was expecting Bud at WSK on Monday."

"It's a different appointment. Dad and Lester set that up at the beach Saturday morning. I was there." She didn't sound pleased by that. "Dad believed in a strict value system and he could get pretty self-righteous. Maybe he was going to get this person fired from his job or report him to the police. The guy killed him instead."

"You don't think his death is related to your mother's?"

Laurie shook her head vehemently.

Dmitri and I let silence fall while Laurie chewed one side of her mouth again. I listened to the summer night sounds outside the porch. I couldn't distinguish what creatures were making what noise, but I was pretty·sure that Bud's daughter wasn't telling me the whole truth. Or at least she was leaving out her fears.

"I only came back to The Pynes last summer," Laurie said slowly. "I stayed away for more than eight years trying to forget this place and some of the people. Now I feel like I'm dragged along the bottom of the harbor by a haul-sein, but there's no one there to pull me out." She lifted her face. "I have to solve this thing." Her gaze was strong, intent. "Can you understand that?"

"Yes." After a blow like that, she needed to regain control. "You need to convince the police your father was murdered."

"About the only way that will happen is if the medical examiner finds a gunshot wound in the back of Dad's head. Either Dad had a heart attack that drowned him or Captain Comelli's going to stick to his Dad-the-Wife-killer-Kills Himself-to-Avoid-the-Law theory. It does good things to his ego."

"The big scary cop routine."

"Right on."

"On his side, Comelli's got the fact that your father took off his life vest."

"I know, he rammed that one down my throat."

Dmitri said, "Maybe empty Valium bottle convince him. Simona will testify Bud's coffee make her sick." He glanced at me.

I answered with a sheepish grin. "Sorry, I forgot the bottle in the Caddie. We'll get it from the garage tomorrow and take it to Suffolk County Homicide in Yaphank. It would help if they found the thermos."

"Thanks." Laurie let go of her legs. "I need your help on this. The police aren't going to move until they have the toxicology report and then it might be too late. If Dad trusted you, I do too. I'll pay you what he'd agreed."

Dmitri sat back down. Slowly. A dirigible landing. "Two hundred a day each plus expenses. Five thousand bonus if killer get arrested."

"*One* hundred dollars a day each." I gave Dmitri

my dirtiest expression. "*Two* thousand if killer is arrested."

He stroked his bruised temple. "Big regret. I forget."

"Are we on?" Laurie stood up.

I looked over at my partner. Dollar signs were falling in place on his eyeballs. He had to pay his cousin's wife for the Caddie, pay the garage for repairs; he wanted to visit his great love in Moscow. I needed a reason to stay out of Manhattan and avoid cleaning. And soon maybe I'd need the extra money. To look for an apartment, for example.

"Yes!" we said in unison.

"Great!" Laurie glanced at her watch. "I know you'll want to ask a lot more questions, but I'm bushed now. In the morning Amanda and Lester are driving me into the city early to see WSK's lawyer about Dad's will. Dad kept his papers in the kitchen. Now they're burned." Laurie led us back to her kitchen. I carried the plate I'd brought over, now empty.

"Did Lester ask you about Bud's campaign for Sport4Life?"

"Yes." She bit her lower lip. "He's not heartless, you know. He really cared about Dad."

"Could Lester have gone through your dad's things?"

"No, what Lester's looking for is a big drawing. Dad worked on heavy paper. God forbid if anyone tried to fold it."

"What about suspects?" I asked. "Any ideas?"

She reached over to the refrigerator and removed a sheet from a fish magnet. "Dad wrote this up." She handed it to me.

Bud's suspect list. Same WSK paper, same handwriting, same names. The order was different. First Jim, followed by Rebecca, Dodo, Lester, Laurie. And a long blue stain. If I hadn't seen Jim's list I wouldn't have known Steve King's name was under that ink.

"Bud made up this list after Polly's death," I said.

"It applies to both." Laurie opened the screen door. Moths flickered under the porch light. The night creature chatter was deafening. "My parents didn't connect with a lot of people. Dad loved only his work. Mother thought she was above most people and most people stayed clear of her."

"How are these suspects linked to your parents?"

"Well, they all live around here. Lester is Dad's partner, as you know. He only comes in the summer. He had a low tolerence level for Mother. She enjoyed interfering in Dad's work."

"What about Rebecca?"

"She's been around since the beginning of The Pynes. Dad liked her, but Mother turned hot and cold toward her."

"Rebecca stopped talking to Bud after your mother died."

"She won't tell me why. Jim's great. Both Mother and Dad liked him, but Mother wouldn't sell him the land to his driveway. I guess Dodo Parsons is on there because he was Mother's errand boy."

"Dodo Parsons," Dmitri repeated.

"She called him her Sad Hatter. He's drunk half the time, but harmless. Rebecca's trying to help him out." An apologetic smile flickered across her face. She said nothing of Steve King.

I decided to skip him for that night. She wouldn't have told me the truth anyway. "Why did your father put you on the list, Laurie?" I asked instead.

"I told you, he was honest to a fault."

Dmitri looked horrified. "Polly was your mother!"

"That doesn't change the fact that she made my life miserable. And I really wanted the land she'd always promised me. Two good reasons for murder. Except I didn't kill her. Dad got the land, but you probably already know that. It's good gossip." Her resentment was as deep as the night beyond the screen door.

"Good night," I said. "We'll talk tomorrow."

The visitor she'd been expecting came just as Dmitri and I reached our cabin. Steve in his pickup.

"You know something funny?" I said to Dmitri.

"I know funny. Stalin go to Siberia and meets soldier. 'How goes it?' Stalin asks. Soldier shrugs. 'Can't complain.' 'Damn right you can't.'"

"All right, you know something odd?" I could hear him grin in the dark. "Laurie saw you take something from Bud's house, but she didn't ask what it was."

"You tell her."

"Yes, but much later. If I thought my father had been killed I'd have asked the minute you walked into my house."

"Maybe she is not curious as you."

"Or maybe she already knew."

"You know something good?" Dmitri said.

"What?"

"Jim not lie to you about list."

I found myself smiling.

Ten minutes later, while Sabrina the mutt was peeing in the darkness of the bushes, the pickup careered out of The Pynes with a roar. By the sound of it, the visit hadn't been fun.

TWENTY-ONE

WE NEED STRONG MOTIVE," Dmitri said, rising from his sofa like a geological mass. The dressing on his chin had fallen off, revealing five Frankenstein-like stitches. His left temple looked like an ink-splotched blotter. Sabrina ran off his lap to whimper by the screen door.

It was eight o'clock the next morning, Wednesday. The radio was announcing that the Pine Barrens fire was still eating up acres. More than three thousand so far. The heat was expected to break in the next day or two. I'd already talked to the fire station and made an appointment to see Captain Comelli at two o'clock. Dmitri had interrupted my contemplation of Stan's lonely electric toothbrush.

"How about this for strong motive?" I said. "Polly's killer knew Bud was on to him." Why did that darn toothbrush make me feel guilty? For what? "That would explain the phone call Laurie overheard." Bud was giving the killer until Sunday to give himself up. On Monday he was going to the police.

"But why hire the DimSim Agency?"

I wrapped a paper napkin around the offending object and stuffed it into my duffel bag in the bedroom. "Probably Bud had a few loose ends he'd hoped we'd tie up for him."

"Good, Simona. I buy."

"That floating life vest bothers me."

"Bud cannot drown with vest on."

"But how did the killer get it off of him without Bud catching on to what was happening and putting up a struggle?"

"Which would leave marks on his body."

"*Esattamente.* What is the killer looking for, and why arson?"

"Evidence that says he is Polly's killer. He not find it. We know this because Monday night he go to Laurie's house to look."

"He didn't find it at Bud's so he burned up the place out of anger?"

Dmitri moved his big head in a papal nod. "We look for person with bad temper."

The phone rang before I could tell him how crazy that was. It was Billie from Stan's squad room. A reedy black woman with three black belts in judo, she is in charge of the computer system but on the side plays amateur psychiatrist for the staff. She hadn't helped me much with Stan, but then he's staff, I'm not. The blue glue.

"How can I reach Stan?" she asked. "He's not answering his car phone."

"He's communing with mountain lions and having bad dreams. I don't expect him to call for another couple of days. Is this an emergency?"

"I just need to talk to him. How are you, honey? Life treatin' you good?"

That didn't sound like Billie. Much too sweet. "Raf's been looking for him too." I'd forgotten to tell Stan.

"Raf's just worried about the blue magnet. That's nothing compared to the Mayor's office calling every couple of hours."

"Mayor's office? Is Stan in some kind of trouble?"

Billie laughed. "No way. Just politics. If he calls, tell him to give me a call. And Raf too while he's at it."

"I will. What's a blue magnet?" Stan had been dreaming of blue maggots.

"Hon," Billie said with unusual patience, "we like to speak in code around here, keeps us together. Blue magnet's just the code name for a case we've been working on. Nothing more than that."

"Is cherry another code name?"

"Naw, cherry's just something good to eat. And don't go thinking I'm being vulgar." She hung up.

I slammed the phone down. "I hate it when I don't know anything."

"You know a lot about food."

"What's that supposed to mean?"

"Maybe restaurant business more interesting than cop business."

"Very funny."

Sabrina banged her snout against the screen door, big wet eyes in the beseeching mode. I gingerly reached for the blanket. My shoulder muscles were in full second-day rigor, my hip was still sore, my knee looked like it had fallen on a Parmesan grater, and I hadn't bothered checking my face in a mirror.

"We have a problem here." Meaning Sabrina. It was much easier to focus on the dog. "If we keep coming in and out with a bundle in our arms, someone's going to think we're trafficking babies."

"Sabrina!" Dmitri scowled. Sabrina dropped her head between her paws. "I take you out an hour ago!"

"It's not her fault. She's pregnant." I threw him the blanket. "Her bladder's acting up."

"Women like this too?"

"From what I hear."

"How much longer?"

"Not more than two weeks by the look of her."

Dmitri wrapped her up while she licked his ear. "I find solution."

A doubt tickled the back of my throat. "You're not going to give her away, are you?"

His eyebrows shot up to the roof. "Are you crazy!" He covered Sabrina's face and stormed out of there, screen door banging in my face.

I stumbled after him. We'd tossed for the bike and car. He'd won. "Don't forget to get that bottle from the Caddie."

Dmitri dropped his bundle in the front seat of the rented Chevy. "You are chicken pecking!"

"Hen!" I yelled at the retreating car. As Dmitri reached the road, Rebecca's Buick swung behind him. "Damn!" I yelled even louder. Now I was going to have to chase after her in that dratted bike.

The sky and the ocean were two different shades of gray. The sand seemed endless. Sandpipers scurried ahead of us, jabbing the sand nervously with nail-thin beaks. Gulls squatted on the edge of the wet sand with their usual dumb scowl. The air was redolent of the salty, sweet smell of a new beach day. It also felt about five degrees cooler.

"According to the dispatcher you're the one who reported the fire at Bud's house," I said. Dmitri had taken pity on me and circled back to The Pynes. We'd followed Rebecca to Atlantic Avenue Beach, where he'd dropped me off. "You didn't leave a name, but she recognized your voice."

"I don't waste many words on people," Rebecca said. She walked ahead of me on her longer legs, with her sweats-covered body bent forward. The wind was strong.

"She heard you give a lecture at the Pollock-Krasner Study Center."

"I have no trouble talking about art and history." Rebecca pointed back to the Atlantic Avenue Beach entrance, to the house that sells snacks and beverages. The human tide was rising. "That used to be a Coast Guard station over there. The beach was called Coast Guard Beach then. During World War II four Germans swam here from their submarine, almost fooled a Guardsman with their fluent English, but gave themselves away when they offered him a bribe. He sounded the alarm while they walked to the train station and bought tickets out of here, calm as could be."

"Were they ever found?" The wet sand felt cool on my feet.

"Fifteen days later. Got executed for their visit."

"How did you know Bud's house was burning?" I asked.

She lengthened her stride. "You've got me pegged for the arsonist?"

I skipped to catch up and told her about Laurie's murder theory, how she'd asked Dmitri and me to help. The direct approach was the best, we'd decided. Whether we shocked them, annoyed them, or only piqued their interest, we would get reactions, and those reactions, we hoped, would tell us something. Besides, Bud had led the way with his suspect list.

"Now we call it Asparagus Beach," Rebecca said, "because people stand and look like stalks while they check out the scene, hoping to be seen. And picked I guess. And here you are picking me. As thief, arsonist, and maybe even murderer."

"Bud wrote up a suspect list after Polly died."

"He waved it under my nose too. I gave him the last good laugh I've had in a long time. How did I know about the fire? I was taking a walk in the Merrill Sanctuary Sunday morning. That's right by Bud's house. I saw smoke. I called the fire department. It's that simple."

"Did you see the dog?"

She stopped. "What dog? Steve's?"

"A pregnant black-and-white mutt someone tied to a tree in the sanctuary and abandoned."

"Bastard! There's a huge fine for doing that. Find the dog's owner. That's something worthwhile to pursue." She started walking again.

I followed. "You didn't go to see how the fire turned out?"

"You find that odd?"

"Frankly, yes. Laurie said you were friends."

She forged ahead against the wind, sharp nose first. "I've been renting that cottage long enough."

"Come on, Rebecca. Stop! I'm not trying to pin Bud's death on you. Or Polly's. You're on Bud's list. I want to know why so I can move on to the others. Did you stop speaking to Bud because he put you on the list?"

She dropped down on the sand next to a seagull. The bird left with an indignant waddle. "I stopped speaking to Bud for my own reasons."

"Why did he think you'd kill his wife? Because you were in love with him?"

"Clever Simona, she has it all figured out."

"Help me then." I lowered myself down beside her.

"I will not."

Stubborn woman. "Did you have an appointment with Bud on Monday?"

"Whatever for?" Her gray-blue eyes were curious.

"Know of any appointment he might have had?"

She shook her head. "Why is it important?"

I shook my head. "I wish I knew. Tell me about Dodo."

"He's a sweet man. Even Polly liked him, and she didn't like too many people. He called her the Red Queen. 'Off with her head!' Polly loved being thought of as a nasty monarch."

"Why is Dodo on Bud's list?"

"Why is anyone? His daughter's on there, for heaven's sake! That's crazy."

"She had a strong motive."

"'Imperial fiddlesticks.'"

"What about Laurie's relationship with Steve King?"

"Love and hate. Laurie's loved him since she's been thirteen years old, she's hated him because he didn't finish high school, because he wants to fish for a living, because he doesn't fit into the comfortable middle-class life her parents have prepared her for. He's loved her since he set eyes on her. He was twenty-nine to her thirteen."

"That age difference is enough to get a parent upset."

"If Laurie is to be believed, he didn't touch her until she was twenty-one. He also hated her for being heir to what he considers his land."

"Jim told me the story."

"The Pynes will always stand between them."

"She should have just walked away from home and land."

Rebecca eyed me with clear eyes. "Life is that clear-cut for you?"

I thought of Stan and my attraction to Jim. "I'd like it to be. Is Steve the reason Laurie stayed away from The Pynes?"

"Him and a few other people. Laurie's mother sucked the marrow from her spine, forced her into law school, and forbade Steve. Her father buried his nose into his work and demonstrated his great love for her by putting Laurie on a murder-suspect list. For years Steve's been telling Laurie to cut loose and follow her heart, poverty be damned! Poor Laurie doesn't know which way to turn. Could he have killed Bud and Polly? A very definite yes. Would he? I hope not. It would destroy Laurie."

"With Bud's death, she's finally inherited all the property."

"She's going to have to make some tough choices now. After Polly defrauded Steve's father by underpaying for the land, his friends chipped in with loans to help him buy it back at the price she'd paid. It had been in the King family since the first settlers practically. Polly apparently laughed in their faces and said she might sell it for double the money. The next winter the old man and Steve's brother drowned at sea. Steve was a three-month fetus at the time. The feeling the bonackers have is that the two King men wouldn't have risked a bad sea if they weren't trying to earn enough to get that land back. Awful woman, I must finally admit."

"Laurie insists Polly committed suicide."

"But you'd rather believe Bud?"

"A few people aren't telling the entire truth." I cocked my head at Rebecca.

"Go easy on Laurie."

"I intend to. For one thing she's my client."

"I'm glad to hear it. Now what is so important about a Monday appointment?"

"What was Bud Warren to you?"

We hit an impasse.

TWENTY-TWO

I TOLD DMITRI I'D MEET him at the Honest Diner on Main Street in Amagansett. The village, a few miles east of East Hampton and just south of Springs, still has a few relics from the past, such as the nineteenth-century double-towered Presbyterian church and Miss Amelia's 1725 wood-shingled cottage, now turned into a museum. Mainly Amagansett flows with restaurants and bars. In fact, its Indian name means "place of good water."

The walk from the beach to the diner was almost two miles. In the sun. I was ready for lots of water, good or bad. Dmitri hadn't gotten there yet. After an unusually short wait—summer life in the Hamptons is somewhat saner in the middle of the week—I got a table and ordered coffee and four slices of freshly baked farmer's bread. I started leafing through *Dan's Paper*, a freebie that's the social bible of the Hamptons.

"You should really go all-American," a pleasant

voice said, "and try the Red Eye Gravy with Grits. If we hang around here long enough, we can have the Roadside Meatloaf for lunch."

We?

Jim slipped in the chair opposite me. He was assuming a lot. Why didn't I mind? "What are you doing in someone else's restaurant?"

"Checking out the competition. Any good-looking men around? Sorry, that's dumb."

"Just a little." I hadn't been paid that kind of silly attention in what felt like a long time. The waitress came with our food and Jim ordered black coffee and a double rasher of bacon. He was wearing wrinkled blue Bermudas, a black T-shirt with the words, "Not Tonight, I'm Reading," and he looked as though he'd been up most of the night.

"I'm sorry about Bud," I said. "You'll miss him, won't you?"

Jim rubbed his eyes. "I dedicated a bottle of vodka to him last night. The least I could do. And I just talked to my chef. We're adding a Bud Warren special to the menu."

"Which is?" I stupidly looked in the mirror by Jim's right shoulder. My cheek looked like a mix of corn and blueberry muffins—yellow, blue, and mushy.

"Bud liked grilled tuna and grilled shrimp, and he always wore bow ties so it's—"

I pushed a hefty chunk of hair over half my face. "Bow-tie pasta with tuna and shrimp, a little garlic sautéed in olive oil, a few red pepper flakes—"

"And cilantro!" He leaned over. "You like to cook?"

Jim had such incredibly white teeth. "Love it." I broke my bread in half and offered him some.

"How about dinner at my place tonight? We'll cook together."

The toothbrush loomed large. "No, thanks."

Jim leaned back into his chair. "The cop."

"The cop."

"He looks like all his moves are getting foiled."

"Stan's having a tough time." And Jim was far too appealing. I'm not good at sharing my affections and I've always been bad at casual sex. Even before AIDS.

"If I had you around," Jim said, "I'd be shouting for joy so long I'd give you a headache."

That felt good. "Thanks."

He brushed my good cheek with his knuckles. "In any market there's a fool."

"Double order of bacon?" the waitress asked, waiting to slip the plate on the table. She was beautiful, young, and blond.

Jim dropped his arm out of the way, but he kept his eyes on me. The air-conditioning went on the blitz. The waitress assured me no such thing had happened. I am too young for hot flashes.

"I saw Laurie last night," I said, to keep distracted.

"I know."

I raised my eyebrows. My mouth was full of bread and raspberry jam.

"I was on my porch, sloshing vodka. I saw you and the Ural Mountains bearing gifts and walking toward the big house. I'd paid my respects to Laurie earlier."

"You have a good view of The Pynes."

"I can't see the back cottages. But I did see you and Bud getting in the habit of sharing breakfast every morning."

More than likely that meant that Jim hadn't been the one who'd spiked Bud's coffee. The killer would not have knowingly drugged me too. "I thought you liked to sleep late?" I was grinning.

"That hasn't been easy with you next door."

"Jim, please."

"I'm sorry. I'll lay off." He bit into three pieces of bacon all at once.

I glanced at the door. Where the hell was Dmitri? "I saw you whisper something in Laurie's ear the night of the barbecue. Her face beamed like a lighthouse. What did you tell her?"

"Is that the problem?" Jim squeezed my hand. "You think Laurie and I are an item?"

The thought hadn't occurred to me. "Are you?"

"No, I just told her Steve loved her, that he was waiting for her. Their relationship has had more ups and downs than the Dow Jones." He spoke matter-of-factly. "After Polly's death, those two wouldn't speak to each other. I brokered their reconciliation."

"They fought about The Pynes."

"Yeah, Steve's pride, Laurie's insecurities—they

get in the way. Sometimes I've wanted to knock their heads together. After Polly died, things between them got really bad."

"Did she blame him for her mother's death?"

"She wouldn't tell me. Steve was with Bud in a dory checking lobster pots when Polly was found. That's another thing I never found out. What they talked about for two hours."

"They alibi each other out."

"In theory, either of them still could have held Polly under. The time of death wasn't pinpointed to the minute. Bud was right there and Steve keeps his dory over at Louse Point. That's only a ten-minute row from where Polly was found."

"Steve's motive is stronger than Bud's if he believed Laurie was going to inherit his land."

"Maybe. Anyway, I finally convinced them they should get together and talk it out. I made them examine their options. Sixteen acres worth a million, which you can blow in a day, or a relationship, which if you work at it, can last you a lifetime."

I thought of Steve's pickup careering out of The Pynes last night. "A trader who is also romantic?"

"I'm a sucker for a good love story." The Sabrina-like yearning in his eyes lit up. Briefly, thank God. I didn't want Jim to remind me of my ex-husband, one of Rome's smoothest rakes. I looked at the door again, then at my watch.

"Dmitri isn't coming," Jim said. His mouth was full of my leftover bread. "I was trying to hog your time. I met him over at the East Hampton Library. He charged me with driving you over there."

"Did he go over to Kirkwood Garage?"

"Don't know, but he looked like he was ready to bite the ass off a bear. He told me you're working for Laurie now. How come?"

In the car I explained that Laurie suspected her father had been murdered. Jim let out a low whistle. "I can understand someone killing Polly, but Bud? He didn't get in anybody's way. Has she got proof? What do the police say?"

I mentioned all the reasons that murder was likely: the arson, the probability that the coffee had been spiked, the tossing of Bud's house, Laurie's house being searched.

"What's Rebecca's connection to Polly and Bud?" I asked.

"Renter. A friend of Polly's, I think. I'd see Rebecca go over to the big house occasionally. Polly's bought a lot of Rebecca's art."

I hadn't noticed any during my visit with Laurie, but then I hadn't seen the bedrooms.

"Dodo?"

"Ask Rebecca."

"I have. If she knows anything, she's not telling."

"Rebecca keeps a tight lip. Jesus, this is worse than Black Monday." Jim was referring to the day in October back in 1987 when the stock market plunged.

"I'm sorry, Jim." He looked like he had just lost five hundred points. I wanted to touch him, but didn't.

In silence we drove up to the library on Main Street.

"Did Bud make an appointment with you for this past Monday?" I asked.

"I expect he planned to show up at the restaurant for dinner, as usual."

I started to get out of the car.

Jim's hand rested on my arm. "Wait a minute." His fingers were icy from the air-conditioning. It still felt good. "What's this about an appointment? Is it important?"

Curious how that date caught people's attention. "It was just a Post-it Laurie found in Bud's bedroom." One thing Laurie had asked us not to mention to anyone was the overheard conversation. Not even to Captain Comelli. At least not until we saw the phone company's breakdown. "It read 'Monday appointment,' underlined three times."

"Try his dentist." His eyes filled with concern. "Are you going to be okay? If there's a murderer out there, he's not—"

"I'll be fine. I've got the Ural Mountains on my side." I laughed and waved goodbye. God, I could get used to Jim.

TWENTY-THREE

THE LIBRARY WAS HOUSED in a one-story brick building built in the early part of the century. As the
library grew, several rooms had been added through
the years. In the entrance hall the newest books were
displayed on a window seat. An origami-like paper
model of a proposed addition sat on a table. I found
Dmitri stuffed in a five-by-five-foot room with a narrow window high on the wall. He was staring at a
microfilm machine.

"This place must have been a toilet once," I said.
"Did you get the bottle?"

"Not yet. I remember something first, thanks to
Laurie. Look at this." He pointed to the screen that
showed a page of the *East Hampton Star*, his finger
underneath a boxed-in photo.

"Seventeen August of last year," Dmitri whispered. Above the picture was the headline "Recovering
the Past: A Star Contest." The picture featured a
scraggly team of football players no older than ten.

"If you can name team, you win *Star* T-shirt."

"From a year ago? If you want it that badly, you can buy one." I tugged. "Come on, let's go."

"No, look at small picture." On the right lower corner, two inches square. I squinted hard. A woman and a man stood behind a cement mixer. A corner of a shingled house was visible, an expanse of dark gray low in the background. Gray that could have been water. The caption read "Last week's couple remain unidentified."

"Who are they?"

Dmitri straightened his back and, with a look of triumph, shook a photocopy under my nose. I backed off to see better. Reading glasses were in my near future. So was my fortieth birthday.

"Twenty-four August. One day before Polly die."

This time the "Recovering the Past" picture was of four people standing in front of a small propeller plane. The small picture showed the couple behind the cement mixer again.

"I remember reading this Monday," Dmitri said. "Looking for Polly's obit I get distracted with pictures. I remember when Laurie say name last night."

My eyes focused above his finger. Slowly I read, "Lester Kennelly was the only caller to recognize Polly Pynes and Dodo Parsons. They had just finished laying the foundations of the first Pynes Cottages in 1951."

"Dodo and Polly a couple?"

"Now we know why Dodo is suspect."

"Good for you! Now let's get that empty Valium bottle. I've got a homicide captain to meet."

"The bottle's gone?" I'd left Dmitri at the garage while I walked Sabrina. Now I was sweating and in no mood for jokes. "What do you mean, the bottle's gone?"

Dmitri shook his cellular phone in my face. "I find this which you forget."

"Who cares about the phone. Where's the bottle?"

"No bottle. I look everywhere."

"That can't be!" I strode over to the Caddie, which was parked next to a thick stand of trees behind the garage in an open space of packed earth choking with weeds that anyone could walk into. Nothing in the glove compartment. Even though I was pretty sure the compartment had stayed closed after the accident, I lifted the carpet, furrowed underneath the seats, dug in between the seats. Came up with dusty fingernails, three quarters, a "Hair Solutions for Men" brochure, and the bent paperback cover of My Heart Is Yours.

I marched full of piss and purpose to the only man in the garage. "Something is missing from our car. Who had access to it?"

The man wiped his greasy hands on an even greasier rag. He was big with a potbelly that would only fit under a truck, which was what he'd been working on when we drove up. He oozed the smell of gas and car oil. "I'm the owner and I'm not responsible for stolen property. Says so right there." Kirkwood twitched his left shoulder, behind which hung a sign too dirty to read. Whoever in the police department had picked this garage had to be intimately related to the owner. The place, on some back road of Amagansett, looked like the set for Quentin Tarantino's next film. "If you're thinkin' it was me," Kirkwood said, "you're dead wrong."

I shaded my eyes from the sun. Kirkwood, with a shiny black streak running across his forehead, looked familiar. "I'm not saying you're responsible. I just want to know if you saw anyone near the car who shouldn't have been near the car."

"When I'm under the chassis, I can't be worryin' about who's doing what. The cars are locked. Most of 'em aren't worth stealing. Some aren't even worth fixin'." Kirkwood walked over to a soda machine, the only clean sight in the lot. "So what's missin'?"

"A pill bottle."

"Drugs?" He fed coins into the slot.

"No! Besides, it was empty."

He offered me a Coke, which I took. He wasn't so bad after all. "So what's the sweat?" he asked.

"It's a bottle the police are interested in."

"Something to do with your accident?"

I made a noncommittal sound.

"Look, I got friends in the department." That much I knew. "Maybe I can help."

"No thanks." It didn't make sense getting involved with the local police. In a couple of hours I was going to talk to the man in charge—Captain

Comelli of the Suffolk County police. "You didn't see anyone loitering around?"

"Nope. But as I said, I don't see much except the underbelly of cars. And at night, well, the place is open. Can't fit all the cars inside the garage. Sorry about that."

"Where do I know you from?"

"Sunday's fire at Bud Warren's house. You're the lady with the bulky friend. You walked right by me. Bill Kirkwood." He lifted his palms to show me more grease. "I won't shake hands."

"Simona Griffo."

"Well, Simone, tell your Russki he should take better care of his car. It would be a beaut after a complete overhaul."

Who wouldn't? "We can't afford it."

"Story of my life. If it was a bottle of pills, are you sure the ambulance guys didn't take 'em?"

I called from Dmitri's phone. The two paramedics weren't on duty and neither was the driver, but I got their names. I went back to Kirkwood and was handed a phone directory for the entire South Fork, which back in the city would have barely contained SoHo. I found my men, the driver was even at home. No, he hadn't taken anything, or seen anything, but, come to think of it, just as he was closing the ambulance doors, he had noticed the tall guy with the baseball cap getting into the passenger's seat of the Caddie. When he turned the ambulance around, he'd looked again. The

Caddie's passenger door was open. So was the glove compartment.

I looked up Steve King in the phone book. He lived on Driftwood, off Hog Creek Lane, where we had picked up Laurie Sunday morning.

"I'm out fishing," Steve's answering machine said. "That's work, not play. It's up to you if you want to wait for the beep. I wait for no one." Except for Laurie.

"What now?" Dmitri asked. Sabrina nuzzled his ear.

I glanced at my watch. It was past noon. "We'll catch him tonight. First a quick drive to Green River Cemetery just to check the ground. The bottle could have fallen out."

The cemetery yielded nothing except tombstones. Jackson Pollock's was the best. A massive boulder bearing a bronze plaque with his signature. Lee Krasner, his wife, had chosen the boulder. She was an artist also. And a loyal nursemaid who had left on a trip to France when Pollock started bringing his mistress into their home. On an August night, in a drunken stupor, Pollock, accompanied by his mistress and her beautician friend, drove his Oldsmobile convertible into a tree on Fireplace Road. Pollock died instantly. So did the beautician. His mistress survived. Krasner went back to her art, producing her best work. But when she died, her friends chose to bury her behind Pollock, underneath a boulder one fourth the size of his, belittling her for posterity. It made me want to scream.

"Come on, Dmitri. Let's go find Dodo."

❂   ❂   ❂

Dodo wasn't in Rebecca's cabin. Neither was Rebecca. We drove down Gerard Drive, the car crunching on the shells that seagulls had dropped to crack open. On each side of the road grew wisps of spartina grass and a straggle of wild rosebushes, their hips as red and full as August cherry tomatoes. Two young men jogged, their chests gleaming. A kid rollerbladed with his Irish setter panting behind him. Above him, barn swallows crowded the telephone cable like fetishes on a necklace. On one side the harbor, the bay on the other, both bodies of water almost white with noon light. At the end was a small beach and a canal that joined the harbor to the bay. A sign proudly announced that four plover chicks had been born.

Across the canal, a sun-drenched Louse Point. Looking west, we could see Bud's half-burned house. The parrot lady, tanned to well done, waved at me from the beach. Captain Dan squawked from his perch on a barbecue grill. No Dodo.

Dmitri let Sabrina out of the car for another pit stop. "Louse Point. You know why name?"

"I'm not betting."

"Information free. Louse singular of lice. First Connecticut people come here to fish and almost starve to death. Not enough food to feed one louse. Like Russian revenge."

"Which reminds me I'm hungry."

Dmitri frowned, eyes on his new love who was belly-high in the water. "She will drown."

"Sabrina's cooling off. If we were smart that's what we'd be doing. What do you know about a place called Little Low Drink?" Dmitri whistled. Sabrina waded farther.

"Two Holes of Water?"

He whistled again. She barked back. Dmitri tossed his flip-flops, rolled up his wool trousers, and went after her. She made him carry her back.

I enjoyed watching her drip all over him. "Next, she'll make you bring her breakfast in bed. You know what my favorite is? Bellyache Swamp."

The three of us got back in the Chevy to resume our search.

The duck-blind boat at the end of Shipyard Lane was filled with dust and empty beer cans. The owner of the liquor store suggested the Jackson Pollock farmhouse. It had once been owned by Dodo's grandfather. The painting shed was open, where Pollock had created the drip paintings that back in 1949 made *Life* magazine ask, "Is he the greatest living painter in the U.S.?" I peeked inside. The floor looked like the aftermath of a Mardi Gras party, covered with bright-colored confetti of paint. The walls were lined with photographs of an artistic life. His painting boots rested in a corner, a spattered memento along with the shed, of a genius who killed himself with liquor.

Our last stop was Asparagus Beach in Amagansett, where we tromped through the sand for ten minutes each way with Sabrina padding after waves. She got sopping wet again. Dmitri's nose turned pink. My hair coiled. All the while we wondered out loud why Steve, or anyone else, would steal an empty bottle of pills.

Our original thought had been that the empty Valium bottle had been left on Bud's bathroom sink by his killer, to make it look as though Bud were committing suicide in the same way as his wife. If so, was it Bud's killer who stole the bottle from the Caddie? Why? Could Steve be our killer? With Bud dead, Laurie stood to inherit The Pynes, land that Steve claimed belonged to him. With Bud dead, Laurie was free to marry anyone she wanted. And Steve had come courting last night. Except he hadn't stayed long.

We didn't find Dodo.

"Town Hall," I decreed. It was on Pantigo Road, in Amagansett, in a small spread of low, modern red-brick buildings set back from the road and which included the East Hampton Town police department. I headed for the buildings department.

"Why are we here?" Dmitri grumbled as a friendly woman named Amy hunted through old files for me. It was past one o'clock by then. Dmitri needed to refill his body. So did I.

"The cement mixer!"

"I am stricken by ignorance!" Dmitri's way of saying "So what?"

"We're looking for connections."

We found them once Amy brought me the building permit for The Pynes.

February 7, 1950. The Town of East Hampton

granted permission for the construction of eight identical cottages to be built according to the affixed plan on sixteen acres of land to be known as The Pynes. Owner: Polly Pynes. Architect: Charles Parsons.

Dmitri gaped. "Dodo?"

"One and the same."

After thanking Amy, we drove back to East Hampton village and joined the scene on Newtown Lane. I wanted Babette's for its great Middle Eastern hummus and tabbouleh salad with warm pita. Dmitri pushed me on. "Lentil walnut tempeh burger I will never eat!"

We stopped at the less health-conscious Grand Café and got seated outside, the place to be, to see and be seen—when the weather wasn't sweltering. I protested. For air-conditioning, there was a thirty-minute wait. Dmitri sat. I drooped. Next to us three sweatless women in black T-shirts and shorts waved white-enameled nails while they debated about Paris in the fall or the spring. I ordered a grilled-chicken salad. Dmitri asked for two hamburgers and a triple order of french fries with French dressing on the side. All that Paris talk was getting to him.

"So now we know Dodo was Polly's architect. Big deal."

"It's a start." Information Dmitri doesn't obtain, doesn't count. "Aren't you curious how a man who has a degree in architecture ends up drunk and scrounging for scrap metal on the beach?"

"You mean Polly involved?"

"Given her record for nastiness, it's a definite maybe. I think we should go talk to some old-timers."

"Rebecca."

"She's tight-lipped. While I'm with Comelli, you could try talking to some of the men who fish off the dock by Jim's restaurant."

At the mention of Jim, a gossipy glint lit up Dmitri's eyes. "You have dinner with Jim tonight?"

"No."

"Why not? Jim is nice gentleman."

"Are you trying to be a matchmaker? Is that why you sent him over to the Honest Diner?"

"You need fun guy."

I couldn't believe this. Sweet, loyal Dmitri. "Aren't your romance books all about loyalty and honor and staying true to the one you love?"

"Maybe love with Stan is over." He sounded far too sad.

The waitress came with our order. I chewed on a radish. "Dmitri, are you trying to tell me something?"

"Go out with Jim." He cut up Sabrina's hamburger while she wiggled in anticipation underneath our table. "Taste someone else. You might like." He fed her bite by bite.

I slammed my fork down. "Okay. You know something. What is it?"

"I know for a week you do not smile. Sunday night at Jim's Pit, sitting with Jim, all of sudden you smile."

"I had too much wine."

"You had nice man courting you." He poured French dressing on his mound of fries.

"I don't like this conversation."

"Look, Stan is great guy, but now you live with him. Maybe the passion gets hiccups. My books, they teach me that in love, complications are good. Pavel's wife maybe I love so greatly because she is my brother's wife and I cannot have her. It is a complication that makes for great passion."

"But you see her only twice a year and you've never even kissed her!"

"Ah, but my dreams of her"—two fingers ruffled his mustache—"they are Hollywood great."

"I need more than dreams."

"*Esattamente*. You go for Jim a little. Stan come back. Get jealous. He fight to win you back. Love is good again. Dream come true."

I laughed. "That's not exactly playing fair with Jim."

"Jim has his Pit. He can eat." To demonstrate Dmitri filled his openmouthed grin with a pound of dripping fries.

I thought about it for the split-second it took Dmitri to down those potatoes, then shook my head. "Sorry, not my style."

"Why he call restaurant Pit? I think of trap lion fall into. Not good image."

"The pit's the floor of the stock exchange."

"Where much money is made. Now I understand. You make big mistake not to go for Jim."

"Wanna bet?"

"No."

I didn't like Dmitri refusing my bet. He normally bet against any odds. Even on the Pope going for abortion.

"Okay, let's pretend Steve took the pills," I said.

"Why he take?"

"I don't know." I remembered the hand Steve had placed on my head to calm me down. Can a murderer ever be kind? "What did that empty pill bottle reveal?"

"It reveal that Polly's doctor give her prescription for Valium." A young couple behind Dmitri stood up and left their table. They couldn't keep their hands off each other.

"The first time Laurie saw the upstairs of her dad's house after the fire was on Monday." My eyes stayed hooked on the lovers. I wasn't thinking of Stan. Or Jim. "*After* you'd taken the pill bottle from the bathroom. So she couldn't have known it was there. But Steve helped put out the fire. Excuse me a minute." I took Dmitri's phone and walked to a bench down the street. This was a conversation I didn't want the Francophile ladies to overhear. I punched in the Kirkwood Garage number. Bill answered.

"Simona Griffo here. I'm helping Laurie Warren make sense of her dad's death and the arson fire. Bear with me. Do you know which firefighters checked the upstairs of Bud's house right after the fire?"

"The kitchen was keeping us pretty busy. Steve

King and I had the hoses. I didn't get upstairs until later with Dave, the fire marshal. I walked him through every room."

"Steve wasn't with you?"

"No, he was checkin' over the grounds for the umpteenth time. He gets shy when Laurie's around."

"Laurie was in the house on Sunday?"

"Fire marshal didn't like it, but she made a big fuss. We checked every room of the house together, bathrooms included."

TWENTY-FOUR

DMITRI INSISTED ON DRIVING me to Sag Harbor. His ribs were fine. He knew the back roads. He was wearing his precious purple shirt. He winced when I buckled him in. By avoiding Route 114 and taking roads dense with trees instead of traffic, we got there in twenty minutes. I was to meet Captain Comelli at the end of Long Wharf. I was grateful we didn't have to drive west, all the way to Yaphank, where Comelli had his office.

"Why Laurie lie?" Sabrina was having noisy dreams in the backseat.

"So we wouldn't suspect that she knew about the pill bottle. Laurie spotted the bottle on Sunday, but she couldn't take it in front of Bill Kirkwood and the fire marshal. She went back on Monday, but you got there before her. That's the reason she got hysterical with me and accused you of robbing her. That bottle must point to the killer. Why? I don't know." We passed Sag Harbor's most renowned building, an odd, clunky-looking church built in the nineteenth century to resemble an Egyptian temple.

"Laurie murders her father, perhaps also mother?" His tone was disbelieving. "We are not in California."

"Maybe she's protecting someone else—Steve King would be a good guess—and pretends to hire us to find out what we've done with the pill bottle. After I tell her, she goes over to the garage and steals it."

We swung onto Main Street. "What about Steve with glove compartment open? I think he is one who bump into us."

"Can't accept that all those lovely ladies have turned against you, can you? We'll ask him tonight."

Dmitri braked in front of the American Hotel, another landmark. A redhead with hair down to her bare thighs was sipping a drink on the porch.

"I have gun," Dmitri said, turning off the engine to let me know his chauffering was over. Sabrina let out an expectant yelp.

"Keep the safety on," I said. Dmitri's bullets flow like the Don. In curves. I opened the car door. Heat poured in like melted butter. "Meet me in an hour in front of the Corner Bar."

Dmitri held Sabrina back. "Two hours. I talk to fishermen. I go find Dodo."

"Sure." I looked at his new shirt. At the seat belt securely fastened. He'd never get out of the car by himself. "I bet you ten dollars the redhead keeps the hair."

"Twenty dollars."

"*Affare fatto. Ciao.*"

After a few steps, compassion got the better of me. I went back and unbuckled his seat belt. Sabrina had to pee.

At the wharf a woman tried to entice me to sign up for a romantic sunset cruise for twenty-five dollars a couple. A couple, did I look like I was a couple? Was I only half of something? I glowered at her and yelled, "No way!"

I walked on, now stuck with thoughts of Stan, who had become as romantic as that damn electric toothbrush he'd forgotten. I passed a catamaran that claimed to be the world's largest. A fellow tourist bumped into me and smiled an apology. Jim's smile took over. Was it anger or Jim? Or was my love for Stan simply shriveling up in the heat? I didn't know and this case was confusing me. I had two deaths, which were maybe both murders, maybe not. Maybe one was, and the other wasn't. Laurie had lied. Rebecca was keeping secrets. A thief was looking for something he might or might not have found. An arsonist had half-burned Bud's house. Because he couldn't find what he wanted? Out of revenge? To destroy evidence? I felt like my brain was hanging from a hundred question marks. What the hell would I do with a romantic cruise?

Captain Comelli stood at the end of Long Wharf. Medium height, stocky, he kept his sturdy legs wide apart as though he needed to keep his balance on the high seas. A white sea captain's hat shaded the top of his face. The rest of him was covered in a white shirt that showed laundry creases, khakis with blade-sharp pleats, and black, spit-shined boots that added height. He was watching me. Over the phone I'd told him I'd be wearing a Planned Parenthood T-shirt. I stopped halfway down the wharf, to see if he'd make a move toward me. He stayed put, playing it cool. To hell with him! I pushed myself down the wharf between ice cream–eating families decked in various degrees of sunburn.

Closer up, Captain Comelli turned out to be a taut-looking man around fifty with eyes bulging blue with arrogance.

I introduced myself. He nodded acknowledgment, then turned to look northeast to the entrance of the harbor and the lighthouse. "Cedar Point," he said. His voice was DJ smooth. "What do you know about Sag Harbor?"

"It's an old whaling village."

He cocked his head, as if surprised I knew that much.

"Back in the late 1830s, used to be the third-largest whaling port in the world." He leaned his elbows on the wooden railing. "Ten years later the whole industry went to the dogs. Whales got too hard to find and the California Gold Rush sounded a whole lot more appealing than ending up like Captain Ahab. Then petroleum came in and whale fat was out."

"Didn't Melville have Queequeg come to America in a Sag Harbor whaler?"

"How's an Italian know something like that?" He didn't bother to look at me.

"What's Comelli? Irish?"

"Comelli's a mistake my mother made." So much for being a *compare*. He lifted a warning finger. "Don't sass me."

"Captain Comelli, I don't care what you think of Italians or your father. I came here to talk to you about Bud Warren's death. His daughter thinks he was murdered and she may have a point. I had coffee with Bud Sunday morning and—"

"Murder isn't what the preliminary autopsy report says. No pre-death lesions or bruises." He turned to face the village, wiping his elbows where they had leaned on the railing. A fastidious man. "My mother's family used to have a house right on Main Street with the rest of the rich whaling families. No industry seemed to stick after whaling. That's why the village looks the way it does. No progress. It's like it's been preserved in formaldehyde." He turned to look at me. "Like body parts."

I didn't blink. "Captain Comelli, Bud Warren is dead—"

"There's no hurry then, is there?"

"You didn't have an appointment with him on Monday by any chance?"

"No. What would this appointment be about?"

"You're the investigating officer, you tell me."

His face tightened. "Whatever Bud Warren told you was probably a lie."

"He told me his wife was murdered."

"And he knew we knew it."

"How?"

He thought for a long moment. I was beginning to wonder if his head had wandered off on a whaling boat when he asked, "How's Detective Greenhouse?" So he knew the connection.

"High up where the air is cool."

"Lucky man. Say hello for me."

"Stan will be really grateful that you took the time to talk to me."

Comelli delivered a smug smile. He had decided to work on an IOU from the NYPD. He didn't know about Stan's allergy to my playing detective. "I called Warren on Friday, told him I wanted to have a chat. I made it sound casual. Gets 'em sweating. Fear starts eating up their guts. Works better than maggots."

There was that word again. "A year ago you decided Polly's death was a suicide."

"A year ago I didn't have the evidence I have now."

"How did you find out Dick Knight had this evidence?"

"Nothing confidential about that. Mr. Knight handed his file over in person just last week." Sweat was seeping through his shirt, stiff with starch. "He was being a dutiful citizen."

"Knight told me you came looking for it."

"He's a PI. Prevaricating instigator." He chuckled.

"Did you get that from a crossword puzzle?"

The chuckle landed in the harbor. "You seem to know a lot."

"I was going to help Bud, now I'm helping Laurie."

"A shoulder to cry on and all that."

"'All that' covers it." I told Comelli about my drinking what I was sure was spiked coffee. I told him about finding the empty Valium bottle in Bud's bathroom. I told him about Bud making an appointment with me for that night, about his $1,000 check. I told him about Laurie and Bud's houses being searched. Illegal alien Dmitri stayed out of the picture.

"What got stolen?"

"Nothing, as far as Laurie knows."

He gave a dismissive shrug. "Kids lookin' for easy money. No harm done. Bud's death—suicide." A man full of certainties.

"That's exactly what the killer wants you to think," I said. "Can't you even entertain the idea that there might be a different way of looking at this?"

"One way of looking at it is that you removed evidence from the scene of a crime that could get you charged with trespassing, obstructing justice, aiding and abetting an arsonist."

Why did this sound familiar?

Comelli rocked on his heels. "What would Detective Greenhouse say about that?"

He'd choke on my spaghetti. "That bottle had nothing to do with the arson!" Well, it did, if the arsonist was also the murderer, which looked more than likely, but Comelli wasn't hearing me anyway.

"I'm glad we think alike on that one," Comelli said, "but don't go thinking Bud Warren was an innocent man. Bud Warren shoved Valium down his wife's throat to make her death look like a suicide, then he held her under until she was dead. If you're all doped up you're not going to put up a fight, therefore no marks on the body." He lifted his sea captain's hat to wipe his forehead. He was bald.

"Shoved?" I asked. "Is that the great revelation in Dick Knight's file? An eyewitness who saw Bud force Valium down his wife's throat?"

"No."

"I find your certainties scary."

Comelli took his time to slip on sunglasses, the mirrored kind. "Polly Warren's autopsy showed traces of Valium still in her stomach." His voice slowed to a sultry tango. I wondered if he spoke to men in those tones. "There was no Valium bottle in her house."

"Polly's killer kept it and used it for Bud."

"Polly Warren's doctor never prescribed Valium for her."

"Her name was neatly typed on the bottle I found."

His chin snapped up. "Got it with you?"

"It was stolen." I explained about being bumped into a tree in Green River Cemetery, how the bottle had disappeared from the glove compartment either that night or while the car sat outside Kirkwood's garage.

"Remember the doctor or the pharmacy?"

"I wish I could."

"Laurie Warren is paying you?"

"She's honoring her father's agreement."

"To find her mother's killer?"

"No, her father's."

"She thinks her mother committed suicide?"

I nodded, wondering what he was getting at.

"The bottle's gone missing?"

"That's right," I said.

Comelli's mouth did an Ex-Lax–craving pucker. "You don't believe me."

"I'm not saying that."

Of course not. He can't insult Detective Greenhouse's girlfriend. "Then what are you saying?"

"I'm not saying anything. Just thinking out loud. Which doesn't have the same weight as making an outright statement, you understand."

He was working hard to keep that NYPD favor he thought he'd earned. "Laurie Warren's insisting her mother's death was a suicide and now she's coming up with this murder theory—"

"She's got good reasons!"

"Sure she does. She wants her famous daddy to come out looking clean. That Laurie is a proud woman." He lifted his hat to air his scalp. "And I'm also thinking it's kind of funny that you should see Polly Warren's name on an empty Valium bottle, 'cause according to Polly Warren's fancy New York City doctor, a doctor she'd been going to for the past thirty years, Polly Warren wouldn't touch the stuff."

"Why not?"

"'Cause it made her sicker than a sailor after a three-day binge."

TWENTY-FIVE

THAT PROVE BUD NOT KILL HIS WIFE," Dmitri said as he angrily punched buttons on the phone. We were back in The Pynes cottage. His attempt to pry information about Dodo out of the old dock fishermen had bombed. "As husband he knows Valium make her throw up."

"That's what I told Comelli." The ironing board wouldn't unfold. One of the legs had slipped out of its track. I was trying to get it unstuck for Dmitri, who wanted to iron his slacks. Who also had three cracked ribs. "He calls that a ploy. Bud used Valium on purpose. Once it came out that Polly was allergic to it, he'd be exonerated. Comelli said enough Valium stayed down to dope up Polly. He's sure that Polly was murdered and that Bud's death was a suicide, but he won't tell me what hard evidence he's got against Bud." I pulled. Nothing doing.

"Dick Knight's phone is busy still," Dmitri announced.

"Keep trying."

Sabrina, belly heaving, waddled over to the screen door and sprawled down with a long, wet sigh. She was probably regretting her five minutes of debauchery with some canine equivalent to Harrison Ford. Dmitri lowered the fan so the mutt could benefit.

We'd taken a break from our preestablished schedule: first, finding Dodo to uncover more about his connection to Polly Pynes; second, confronting Steve and his possible theft of the empty Valium bottle; and third, confronting Laurie the second she got back from Manhattan. The reason for the postponement—a dinner invitation to Lester Kennelly's tony home on Lily Pond Lane. Suddenly Dmitri wanted to iron his slacks, a shirt, his handkerchief, maybe even his underwear. I was low-keying it by wearing my wrinkled linen pantsuit from Sunday night. Okay, I'd wash my hair. Jim was going to be there. Laurie and Rebecca. A dinner to commemorate Bud, Mrs. Kennelly had told Dmitri at Guild Hall. Laurie had asked that we be invited too.

"Beautiful woman, Lester's wife," Dmitri said.

"*Ah, capisco.* That's why all the elaborate preparations." I abandoned the ironing board and headed for the kitchen counter.

"She is married."

"Complications in love are good."

I cut a slice of Italian bread. "Actually, they're in the process of getting a divorce."

"After I meet her I check with my sources."

"They still let you in at FizzEd?" I sliced a plump red tomato that I'd left on the windowsill to ripen.

Dmitri scowled. "I now have beauty parlor source. Lester's wife work hard as lawyer. No children. Forty-five years old. Still very young. Very elegant. She still share Hamptons house with husband because they fight over it." He pulled at his mustache. "If Lester leave such attractive woman, he must love someone else!"

I spread the thick tomato slices on the bread and sprinkled salt. "Dmitri, I do believe you're smitten!" I bit in. "What were you doing at Guild Hall? Still looking for Dodo?" Who seemed to have been swallowed up by some marine monster. "And you owe me twenty dollars. The redhead outside of the American Hotel still had every hair on her scalp when we left."

"No time limit on bet. I canvas Main Street asking about Dodo. I see Rebecca go inside Guild Hall. I follow, maybe to offer tea, talk about Bud, Dodo. Some women, they like to confess to me their hearts."

"And lose their hair." I finished my open sandwich.

"There is no market for gray. Lester's wife stop me at door. She has good hair, but it is dyed. A shade too yellow. She make kind invitation. Then when I go into hall, Rebecca is nowhere. I wait. She finally come out with much paper in her arms. I greet her with open arms. Papers fall, and being gentleman, I pick up."

"You bumped into her on purpose." And here I was worrying about his ribs. I went back to the stubborn ironing board.

"I see what she carry."

"And?"

He snuffled at length. Big news, lots of approval coming up. I didn't play into it. In a partnership it's important to keep a balance of power.

I offered Dmitri his own handkerchief. Unironed. "Blow your nose and give me a hammer."

Dmitri reluctantly obliged. I gave the ironing board a good whack. It worked. I unfolded it, turned it around. "All yours. I don't know why you're always making heat."

Dmitri chuckled. "Slavic passion."

"First the borscht, now the iron." I took over the phone, punched the redial button, and fanned myself with the first available piece of paper. Still busy. I repunched Dick Knight's phone number. This time it rang free. We'd probably been calling the wrong number all along.

"At the sound of the beep, please leave a message for Armored Knights Incorporated."

Armored kni—Dio mamma! "Dear Dick, Captain Comelli has just informed me that you're the one who offered the Bud Warren file to the police. Without solicitation. Which means you lied to me. I don't—"

Dmitri nudged. "Tell him I find Uma."

The iron hissed. "Knight, I don't like to help you under the circumstances," I said into the phone, "but we know where your kidnapped cat can be found. Maybe we can trade information. But no more lying." I hung up. "Okay, so where's the eighty thousand dollar feline?"

"A trick. Now he will call." Dmitri balled his handkerchief under the streaming faucet.

"And get real mad. Look, in America irons can steam. You don't have to do the old wet handkerchief routine."

"I do my way."

It's that balance of power thing.

"Okay, partner, I'm going in the shower. We have twenty minutes to get ready." He stopped me at the bathroom door.

"You not interested in what Rebecca carry?"

I turned around. "Should I be?"

Dmitri's mustache stretched out into a Cheshire cat smile. He handed me a foldout. It was a program from Rebecca's June Guild Hall show. The cover picture was an oil painting of five blue vases half buried in the sand. Inside was an introduction by the director of the Pollock-Krasner Study Center. Four more pictures of Rebecca's paintings.

"Look at back," Dmitri said.

Her bio.

"Rebecca Barnes came to New York City from Colorado in 1948. She studied at Stanley William Hayter's Atelier 17 on Eighth Street and befriended Jackson Pollock, Bill de Kooning, and Franz Kline, artists who strongly influenced her early years as a painter. 'And as a drinker,' Rebecca likes to add jokingly, 'I did find myself wondering if my own art wasn't just a product of an alcohol-blurred mind. I wasn't very good at it, and then certain events in my life made me come to the Hamptons. In Springs I turned back to the reassurance of realism.'"

"She drank too much once," I said. "Is that what you wanted me to know?"

"Now read Bud's bio in *New York Times*."

"Sum it up."

Dmitri reached in his trouser pocket. Half his life fell out onto the floor. Letters, bills, a hank of blond hair, business cards, rubber bands, paper clips, two pencil stubs, money. Sabrina bellied over to check out the goods.

"Don't pick up," Dmitri said to me.

"Not a chance."

He dug deeper into his pocket. "Here." He unfolded the clipping, his eyes dashing down the column until he found what he wanted. "Before becoming an advertising man, Mr. Warren had wanted to be an artist and had studied painting in Greenwich Village in the late 1940s under Stanley Hayter at his Atelier 17. In his acceptance speech for his first Clio, won in 1968, Mr. Warren thanked his 'lousy painting' and his wife, Polly Pynes, for his success in advertising." Dmitri refolded the obit. His eyes floated in gloating.

"Okay, we're even," I admitted. I lifted the hot iron and pointed to the burn mark he'd just left on his handkerchief. He checked the pants underneath. He'd been lucky.

"No, we're not. I find bottle, I find Dodo photo in paper—"

"I find out about Dick Knight and his file"—I headed for the shower—"I find out Polly gets sick from Valium"—I closed the bathroom door. That was it. The extent of my sleuthing.

"I win," Dmitri shouted from behind the door. "I find Rebecca and Bud are in same—"

I turned on the shower full force.

TWENTY-SIX

"B E UP FRONT WITH ME," I told Laurie, "or else I'll return your father's money."

"I'm not big on trust."

"I guessed as much." After my shower, I'd taken the car to look for Dodo, eager to even the score with Dmitri. Laurie's car was parked in Bud's driveway. I'd found her in the master bedroom upstairs. The smell of smoke was still bad.

Laurie got on her knees and looked under the bed. She was in her city clothes, a blue tailored suit, pumps, stockings, her hair combed back. She looked lawyerly and unhappy. "I got the list of phone calls Dad made."

"We'll deal with that later." She was trying to distract me. "Tell me why you lied to us."

"Help me look for a sketchbook. Spiral-bound. Nine-by-twelve." She kicked her shoes off. "I finally remembered Dad always kept one in his bedroom, in case he got any ideas during the night."

"You knew about the empty Valium bottle. You'd seen it Sunday when you walked through the house with the fire marshal. You saw that the label had your mother's name on it. You also must know that your mother would never have had a prescription for Valium. The stuff made her throw up."

Laurie dropped down on her butt. "How did you find out?"

"The 'how' doesn't matter." I opened the bedside table drawer to show I was a good sport. Four black magic markers, one *Complete Poems of Robert Frost*.

"Steve told you."

"No, he didn't. In fact, Dmitri's gone off to talk to him right now." Actually I'd left him combing his mustache in true Hercule Poirot fashion. This detective business was getting to him.

"It's Wednesday night," Laurie said. "Steve's in the city with his Fulton Fish Market pals." She sounded relieved.

"On Monday night Steve took a great interest in the glove compartment of Dmitri's vintage pink Caddie. I think you sent him, Laurie."

"I just told him about the bottle." She tugged at the bedspread furiously. "Where does he get off on being the great savior? I didn't ask him to do anything and I certainly didn't want him to ram you into the cemetery to get it. You've got to believe me!"

I wanted to. "Why is that empty pill bottle so important?" Laurie scrambled up and went over to the bay window. Accabonac Harbor, the Merrill Sanctuary, Gerard Drive, a slice of Gardiners Bay, a stretch of Napeague Bay, you could see it all from that one window. In late afternoon soft splendor.

I sat down at the end of the bed. Something crunched under my thigh. Laurie lifted cushions from the window seat.

"Someone's already been through this room with a fine-tooth comb," I reminded her.

"The thief wasn't looking for a sketchbook. Lester isn't even looking for it." Laurie was angry. "Work has to go on without Dad. Some other art director has taken over. The client won't even wait a couple of days. That's how much Dad mattered to them." She moved over to the closet and ran her fingers down a white tennis sweater. Her shoulders started to shake. "Damn it! The more I think about it, the more I want the campaign to be Dad's. He put Sport4Life on the map. I've got to find that sketchbook."

I stood up, snaked my hand under the cover, the sheets. My fingers hit a spiral, then cardboard. I tugged. I waved the sketchbook in front of me.

Laurie let out a cry of joy and tried to pounce on it.

I pulled the sketchbook back. As Dmitri says, detective ruthless job. "Why is the empty bottle so important? Come on, Laurie, enough with the games. You've hired me to do a job for you. Let me do it."

She sat down on the window seat. She unbuttoned her suit jacket. "You're right. I hired you so that I would know for sure and I'm scared crazy of what you'll find out."

"This has to do with Steve?"

"One of his cousins, Bob King, owns a pharmacy in Riverhead."

"The label on Polly's bottle was from a New York pharmacy."

"I know, a pharmacy right around the corner from Mom's doctor in the city. I called. There's no record of a Valium prescription for Mother."

"Labels can be faked or stolen. I saw my pharmacist throw the end of a roll in the trash. There were at least six or seven labels still on there."

"If Steve asked his cousin, Bob would get him the label, the prescription, everything, without asking questions. A few years back, Steve pulled Bob's kid out of the water just in time."

"You think Steve killed your mother, your father, both?"

"Steve doesn't know what Valium did to Mother."

"Who does?"

"I told Amanda Monday night. I don't think anyone else knows. My mother thought throwing up showed weakness. She'd never admit to that. I only found out about it because I slipped five milligrams in her soup once when I wanted to sneak out to see Steve. I stole them from Rebecca's medicine chest. Mother threw up all night and I cried all night. I was fourteen and I was sure she was going to die. That's when she made me promise I would go to law school."

I'd been lucky. At fourteen, the only promise my tough mother tried to extract from me was to go easy on the salami. "Why would Steve kill your parents? To free you from a difficult mother? To get the land that once belonged to his father?"

"Both maybe."

"Those sixteen acres would be *half* his and *only* if the two of you got married without a prenuptial agreement."

"I'd never want one of those."

"How likely is the marriage once you find out the bridegroom is the killer?"

"What are you trying to say?"

"That Steve as killer doesn't make a lot of sense."

"You don't know all of it."

"Tell me." I dropped the sketchbook on her lap.

Laurie hugged it to her chest. "The day before Mother died, Steve asked me to marry him for maybe the tenth time. That time I said yes. I convinced myself he was in love with me, not waterfront property worth a million dollars. Steve didn't want me to tell anyone. We were going to drive down to New Hope, Pennsylvania, the next day and get married there." She opened and closed the sketchbook. "New Hope sounded like the right place." That thought stopped her for a while.

"Polly found out," I nudged.

"I went home to get my birth certificate. She said she was glad that I finally looked happy, and I wanted to believe her so badly, I told her. She started her usual tirade: I had no sense, I was too bright to throw myself away on a high school dropout, Steve was only after my money, her land; I wouldn't get a cent out of her or Dad—on and on and on. I finally got up enough courage to tell her I didn't give a shit. She slapped me. I slapped back. She'd never laid a hand on me before. I ran out of there, ran all the way to Steve's. He took one look at me and was ready to mow her down with his pickup. I forced myself to stay awake all night. I was scared of what he'd do to her."

"That explains why that same night, on the beach, Bud accused Polly of ruining your life."

Laurie nodded. "Rebecca saw me run out of the house and called Dad. She was worried about me."

"What happened the next morning?"

"I fell asleep and woke up around noon. Steve was out in the middle of the bay and my mother was dead."

"All this time you've pretended to the outside world that her death was a suicide because you're afraid Steve killed her."

"The day after her death I told Steve that I would never marry him. I wanted to put Mother's death and Steve in the past tense."

"But your dad kept hiring detectives."

"Bad ones."

Us included at the rate we were going. "Why were you and Bud so sure it wasn't suicide?"

Laurie got very busy leafing through the pages of her father's notebook. I stood up. My patience had just walked out the door. I was going to follow it. When I got past the bed, with visions of me with a dust mop looking more and more appealing, Laurie started talking again.

"The same day Mother died, Dad and I looked for a suicide note. We didn't believe she'd killed herself, but it was possible. She had suffered from depression when she was younger, so we looked. This is before the police came. We looked everywhere, including that picture frame. It would have been just like my mother to leave her parting shot behind that picture. The guilt game to the end. Polly beaming at dutiful daughter on her law school graduation day. Except there was no note. Three days later, there's a note. 'I'm sorry, I'm sorry, I'm sorry.' As a kid, if I broke something, she used to make me write 'I'm sorry' a thousand times. Two thousand when I didn't clean my room. Fun times." She managed to laugh.

"What is guilt-inducing about your law school graduation picture?"

Laurie turned away from the window. "Mother's big dream. Lawyer daughter she could boast about."

"You did it."

"Wrong. I flunked out after my first year at American. Mother made me pretend I was still going. That's one of the reasons I stayed away from here. Dad went along. The picture is a fake."

Laurie had enough motive to have committed the murder herself.

"The police confirmed that the suicide note was in Polly's handwriting?" I asked.

She nodded. "They also did an ink and paper analysis. The note had been written recently and it had her fingerprints and Rebecca's."

"Rebecca found the note."

"Yes. So now we know the killer wore gloves when he planted the note."

"And you think the killer is Steve?"

"I got back together with him last Saturday night after Jim finally convinced me that Steve would never hurt anyone. That night Steve asked me to marry him again. Again I said yes. The next day Dad died. What am I supposed to think?" Her face scrunched up with anger and unhappiness.

I walked back to the window and gave her shoulder a squeeze. "Maybe Steve's just got lousy timing. You said you got your dad's phone list. What does it tell us?"

Laurie dug into her bag and extracted the NYNEX list. "There's a flurry of phone calls around the time I walked in on Dad last Thursday. He called WSK at 9:49 A.M., Lester's direct office number three times in the next twenty minutes. Jim's Pit. The list is not a great help."

"He didn't call Steve."

Laurie looked up. "I know." Light from the window glinted in her eyes. Or maybe it was hope. Of course, Steve could have done the calling. That applied to anyone and everyone.

"We still have to try to find out who Bud made an appointment with," I said.

"I circled the numbers I knew. WSK, Lester in East Hampton and in the city. Jim's Pit several times. Jim's home once. Rebecca."

"I thought she didn't speak to Bud."

"That's right! If he called her it had to be important!"

"Maybe Bud was calling Dodo? He lives at Rebecca's on and off, doesn't he?"

"Dad consulted him sometimes for his ads because of Dodo's way of looking at things. Off-kilter, backwards, like Alice through the looking glass. The other numbers are service numbers. The garage, Dad's dentist."

"No Monday appointment?"

"No, he scheduled a cleaning for next month. I still have to follow up on the other numbers. I'll do that tomorrow during office hours."

There were at least thirty numbers. "Let's split it. It'll be faster."

Laurie clutched the phone list.

"Trust me," I said, echoing Dmitri's mantra. She reluctantly relinquished the last sheet. Four numbers. Maybe I'd get lucky. Dmitri would be impressed. "Did you meet with the WSK lawyer about the will?"

"At the last minute he had to fly to Los Angeles, but he's coming back tomorrow. I'm meeting him at his place in Amagansett."

"Shouldn't you get your own lawyer? There's a lot of money at stake with Bud's WSK shares. There's a rumor of a possible merger, which means the shares are going to go up in value."

"You're right. I just can't seem to get myself going. I'll worry about it after I read the will."

"Are you expecting any surprises?"

"The lawyer left word that I should bring Rebecca with me."

TWENTY-SEVEN

Y OU STUDIED AT ATELIER 17 at the same time," I whispered in Rebecca's ear as Lester showed off a Martha Keller abstract painting called Summer Dispersion #64. Behind me Dmitri was testing out the upholstery, moving from sofa to sofa, armchair to chair, trying, I thought, to keep his attractive hostess well in view. Amanda Kennelly was talking to Laurie by the wet bar.

"The Metropolitan has just acquired a Keller," Lester boasted. "She's hot."

Rebecca nodded at the large canvas made up of four wide bands of dark grays and reds. "Keller has great clarity of vision."

Something I sure didn't have. "You must be mentioned in Bud's will in a big way," I said.

"This is not the moment," Rebecca whispered back.

"It never is."

Amanda called us to the dining room.

"I'm sorry, I can't stay," Rebecca told her hosts. "Dodo's in Southampton Hospital. Thank you for having me and when you lift a glass to Bud count me in mentally."

Dodo being in the hospital would explain why we hadn't been able to find him, but did I believe her?

Amanda asked, "Is there anything we can do?"

"Bud's death got to him. He went on one of his binges."

Lester gave Rebecca a supportive pat on her back as they moved toward the back door. Dmitri had moved to the dining room to examine the chintz-covered chairs.

"I'll see you tomorrow, Rebecca," Laurie said in a cool voice. "Four o'clock."

Rebecca stopped to give Laurie a hug. "Don't worry, Bud didn't leave me the family fortune. Probably only something to thoroughly enrage me. He had that ability, you know."

"Why?" I asked, feeling like a terrier fighting for a bone. Rebecca ignored me.

"Give me a call in the morning," she told Laurie. "Remind me to bring that envelope of Bud's." Rebecca opened the glass door and slipped out on a deck large enough for a helicopter landing. I followed.

Rebecca waved me away. "Tomorrow."

"Tonight. What envelope?"

"I don't know when I'll be back."

"Is Dodo really in the hospital?"

She didn't answer. "I'll wait up," I shouted as she reached the gnarled sycamores of the street. Jim drove up, scattering a family of wild turkeys. He was forty minutes late.

Laurie and Amanda came out on the deck together. Amanda sent Laurie to greet Jim and called me to the dining room table.

Dinner at the Kennellys' was to be a low-key affair, Amanda had announced. A buffet. No help for added intimacy. She wanted to celebrate Bud, she said. The funeral service was scheduled for Saturday.

Lily Pond Lane is south of the highway, on what once had been grazing lands for the town herd of cows. It is lined with rambling, mostly Victorian mansions built to house large families and even larger staff. Martha Stewart had a place a few doors down. The Kennelly house was a unique Dutch colonial circa 1888, with a sweeping shingled roof, shingled walls, and diamond-paned windows. Cozy wainscoted rooms were stuffed with Mario Buatta chintz and Ming vases. Real flowers and cabbage roses appeared at five-foot intervals. Several of Rebecca's pastels hung on the sponge-painted walls.

"I could get Laurie a job in my law firm at the snap of my fingers," Amanda said as she handed me a gold-and-black dinner plate large enough to pick up airwaves from Mars. "She doesn't want it."

I realized I had seen her before, at The Pynes, when Jim and Steve had brought Laurie home after Bud's life vest was discovered. A robust woman with a deep tan and a pared-down taste in clothing.

Black cotton slacks, a long black sleeveless silk shirt that showed off well-defined muscles from years of tennis. A diamond hat pin on her right shoulder, raisin-sized diamond studs in her ears. She had short hair, dyed a dark blond, an oval face without benefit of makeup, bare feet whose startling whiteness had been the first clue to a tennis passion, and a diamond solitaire that glittered like the thirty-candle chandelier she was standing under. I couldn't decide whether it was her handsome face, her voluptuous figure, or the size of her diamonds that had struck Dmitri's heart. When not looking at upholstery, he was all goo-goo eyed.

Amanda reached over and gently lowered a salmon fillet on my plate. She added crabmeat salad, fluffy greens, grilled Portobello mushrooms, and stilt-long breadsticks. "Lester, don't you think you could find Laurie a job at the agency?"

"Laurie doesn't want a job at the agency." Lester spoke through his teeth as he poured white wine in my glass. "Or in your law firm or anyplace else you think she should be. And now that Bud's dead, she doesn't even need a job. Stop trying to maneuver people. No one appreciates it. What Laurie needs is to be left alone."

Amanda laughed. "You mean stop bugging you, dear? Oh, Lester, speaking the truth makes life much easier." She kissed him lightly on his chin. He turned livid. She moved over to the window. I followed.

"Laurie's a rich girl now," I said.

"Polly was so hard on her." Amanda sighed.

Everyone sighed when Polly's name came up. Very productive.

"You weren't Bud's lawyer?"

"I helped him draft a fair divorce agreement. Polly wouldn't hear of it and he wasn't willing to fight her. I suggested another lawyer."

"I hear Polly got half of Bud's shares in WSK."

Amanda frowned. "Lester, did you hear this?"

"Who fed you that garbage?" Lester asked, serving spoon poised in midair.

I shrugged. "Grapevine gossip. What happens to the shares now that Bud's dead?"

"WSK will buy them from Laurie," Lester said, "assuming she's the main beneficiary. We'll pay fair market value."

"She has to sell?"

"It's in the agreement."

Except Bud's copy had burned with the rest of his papers in his kitchen. Would Bud's partner and friend try to cheat Laurie?

Lester moved away with a drink, back to his Keller painting. I trailed him with my plate.

"Last year the Chass\Dayton–WSK merger fell through about a month before Polly died," I said.

"I was hoping you'd left your *unlicensed* PI hat at The Pynes."

"It's much too drafty in here. Bud thought you might have killed his wife. I'm wondering why."

"The famous suspect list!" He took a long swig of vodka. "I couldn't stand Polly, I'll admit to that. But I didn't kill her. As for what happened with Chass\

Dayton last year, they had a change of heart. If you don't believe me, check the newspapers."

"Don't they look nice together?" Amanda asked from the dining room. I followed her gaze out to the deck. Jim and Laurie were standing close together, talking. In the twilight, lit by the pool's blue aura, they were straight out of a magazine ad for the good life. "That's the coupling I'm hoping for."

"Laurie and Jim?" My voice came out in a pipsqueak. Dmitri opened a door and joined them.

"Jim's an awfully nice man," Amanda said in the brisk voice she probably used to explain paragraph three, clause b. to a perplexed client. "Handsome too. The restaurant is finally making money. That's his food you'll be eating."

"Delicious, I'm sure." The crabmeat salad was definitely runny and the salmon looked drier than desert sand. "Where are we eating?" My plate was getting heavy.

"The table's set up on the porch. It's too hot to eat outside."

I found my place card on the round table in the corner of the glassed-in porch, a modern addition to the house. Lester was on my left, Dmitri on my right. Jim was destined to eat between Laurie and Amanda. I sneaked another look out on the deck. Jim was wearing white linen slacks and a white cotton shirt. With the fading light his tan was turning into milk chocolate. I switched place cards.

I slid open the porch door. "Hi, guys. I think we're supposed to go in to eat."

Jim's white teeth put Amanda's diamonds to shame. I turned into a wet towel. A hot wet towel. Stan, where are you when I need you? Dmitri waved encouragement from the edge of the pool.

"I'm glad you came." Jim leaned over and kissed my cheek. He smelled edible. "I've missed you."

I didn't kiss him back. Too handsome. Too good to be true. "Laurie got us invited," I said.

"Laurie's a pal." The teeth stayed aimed at me. Laurie examined her sandals.

"Hey," I said. "Wait a minute. Is this a setup?"

"It's okay," Laurie said. "You're on friendly territory. Jim even got Amanda to accept the Pinot Grigio. She's more in the Montrachet league."

"I need to talk to you a sec about Rebecca," I said to Laurie.

She swatted at a mosquito. "I found out about the phone call. Dad wanted to give her an envelope."

Jim's eyes crinkled with curiosity. "Is this about Bud's mysterious Monday appointment?"

Laurie looked up. Her face was tired, unhappy. "Rebecca's in Dad's will."

Jim let out a low whistle. "The plot thickens." He gave Laurie his smile. "Relax. No one's going to take The Pynes away from you this time. She's probably getting his childhood crayons."

Laurie gave Jim an edgy smile. "I just miss him, that's all. Look, you two chat." Laurie walked back to the deck. From the pool steps Dmitri grinned at me. He had removed his socks and shoes and rolled up his trousers. His feet sloshed in the water, as if he needed to cool off his new-found passion for Amanda.

"You're not angry I got you invited tonight?" Jim asked.

"First Dmitri, then Laurie. It's feeling like a conspiracy." I sipped from my glass. "I do drink other wines."

"I'm trying too hard, right?"

"Right." Why did I like it so much? I looked away. Amanda was waving for us to come inside. Jim hooked his arm in mine, but we didn't get far.

Dmitri hopped out of the pool, splashing a lot of water. He streaked across the lawn.

"What's wrong?" Amanda called out.

Dmitri whistled. The first notes of Beethoven's Fifth.

I spilled my wine. "Sabrina! We left the windows open in the car. She's jumped out. She's pregnant. She's running away. Excuse me."

I started to run. Jim started to follow. "No, please, Jim. Go to dinner." I pushed my wine glass into his chest. "*Please!* We'll be right back."

He took the wine, but looked annoyed. I didn't care. Beethoven's Fifth meant trouble.

TWENTY-EIGHT

I FOUND DMITRI BEHIND The garden shed at the northern end of the property. He held up a squirming, angry mass of black leather.

"What are you doing here?" I asked.

"Same as you," replied the armored knight without his steed. I tried to arch an eyebrow. Both shot up. "Dinner with the Kennellys?"

"Uma."

"Uma is with Dodo Parsons," Dmitri said, lifting Dick Knight until his feet dangled, which didn't take much doing.

"That's a crock of shit!"

Dmitri lifted higher. "Language!"

"You two are trying to cheat me outta the cat."

"And you're lying. Polly Pynes's divorce settlement didn't include WSK shares."

"That's what I heard. So what if it didn't?" With all that leather, he made a perfect punching bag.

Lucky for him, Dim and Sim are wimps in the violence department.

But Knight didn't know that. "What made you offer your file to the police?" I demanded in my deepest alto. We were far enough away from the house not to be heard.

"Every once in a while a man's gotta do his duty," he answered, turning red. Knight's jacket collar cut into his neck.

"You had that file for a year and you only make a move if someone pays you."

"Or does not pay," Dmitri added, giving Knight a good shake. "You blackmail Bud. He stop payment. You go to police."

Knight was beginning to make funny sounds.

"Ease up, Dmitri. We don't want another body."

Dmitri let go. Knight splattered on the pachysandra then tried to scramble through the bushes. Dmitri placed one foot on Knight's jacket. Dmitri has small feet, but they pack a lot of weight. Knight hesitated. The jacket was open. If he slipped out of four hundred dollars of leather he'd be a free man.

Knight stayed put.

An idea hit me. "Someone put you up to this. You tried to blackmail Bud, but he was too straightforward a guy to stoop to paying you off. Besides, he didn't kill his wife. You decided it was no use going to the police if there was no money in it. So you shoved the file in the back of the drawer. Then you got lucky. Not too long ago someone offered you money to take that file to the police. Who?"

"No one."

"You said a third person asked for the file. Who?" Dmitri's other foot landed on the jacket.

"Aw, come on, it's brand-new." Knight's cheeks sagged.

"Who?" Dmitri thundered.

"Bud."

I dropped down on my haunches. "Bud?"

"Yeah, Bud. You see, I never gave him a copy of the file because Mr. Big Time Advertising Man didn't pay the full bill. Said I was overcharging. All of a sudden he wants to take a look. Then he told me to take it to the police."

"You are lying!" Dmitri declared.

"He wanted the case reopened."

Dmitri's shoe squeaked across the leather. "Why?"

"Hey! I don't have all the answers, okay? Maybe he was a glutton for punishment."

I played good cop. "Come on, Dmitri. That jacket's not a shoe wipe." Dmitri's shoe stopped. I turned my attention to Knight. "What do you mean by 'a glutton for punishment'?"

Knight aimed squinty eyes at Dmitri, then at me. He was mulling something underneath all that gray unwashed hair. "You wanna know what's in the file?"

"That would be extremely nice of you." Bud was dead. There was no case. If Knight talked, the police couldn't charge him and he wouldn't lose his PI license.

"Get the Commie off my jacket!"

Dmitri lifted one foot, a 250-pound flamingo. I stood up. My calves were killing me. "What's the hard evidence that says Polly was murdered and Bud was the murderer?"

Knight twisted around and started cleaning off on the footprint Dmitri had left. "That was no suicide note she wrote." He spit on the leather, then wiped it with his palm. "I found the other sheets. Two of them. She even put on a date. Night before he drowned her. 'Bud—you think I should apologize? Here goes.' Followed by 'I'm sorry' written enough times to cover three sheets. At the bottom of the third sheet she wrote, 'If you think I mean this, you're wrong. You always are.' Signed, 'Polly.'"

In gratitude, Dmitri removed the other foot. Knight wiped the footprint, without spitting this time. When he was through, he squinted up at me. "So what do you think?"

"Definitely not a suicide note."

"I mean the jacket. Looks okay? Clean?"

"Like you just steal from rack," Dmitri said.

I said, "Gorgeous. Where did you find the rest of the letter?"

"That scull of his, with the rowing machine on top. The sheets were folded in a sandwich bag taped underneath the rowing machine seat."

"If Bud was the killer, wouldn't you think he'd destroy the extra sheets?"

Knight bobbed his head. "Killers are mostly dumb. Right? I mean they kill."

Dmitri let him get up, dust himself off again.

Knight cradled his jacket in his arms. "Now about this Uma creature. You see any evidence inside, like grease stains on the upholstery? That breed gotta be wiped down a lot 'cause they have no hair. Maybe Mrs. Kennelly doesn't know that."

Dmitri's chin started twitching, bandage and all. "Dodo has cat."

"Listen, Commie, you're bigger than a Mack truck, but you're not carrying any cargo." Knight tapped his forehead. "Dodo's in Southampton Hospital and it's off-limits to animals and Commies in there. You're out on both counts."

I followed Knight to the street. "What makes you think Mrs. Kennelly has the cat?" A vision of Dmitri jumping from sofa to sofa, armchair to chair, danced before my eyes.

"Ask the truck. He and me share a Hamptons source."

"The beauty parlor owner."

"Where Mrs. Kennelly dyes her hair in the summer months. Along with Mrs. Reed Lawrence III. Mrs. Kennelly is Mrs. Lawrence's divorce lawyer, so what better place to park the contested property."

Which explained my partner's sudden infatuation with our hostess. Eighty thousand dollars' worth of passion.

"Dmiiiitri!"

"Everyone was too hungry to wait," Amanda said as I walked into the enclosed porch.

Dmitri smiled, his mouth full of crabmeat.

"I didn't know you guys had a dog," Laurie said.

Jim stood up and circled the table to hold out my chair. "That's all right, Laurie. Sabrina stays with me." His place was between Laurie and Amanda. Amanda must have switched the cards back.

"Sabrina's fine, thank God." I sat down. "She's very pregnant, though. Anyone want a puppy?"

"She's *my* dog." Dmitri sniffled loudly, as if he'd suddenly developed a cold. A swift kick under the table let him know what I thought of his scheming. He bent over his mound of food. I tackled the salmon. It *was* dry. I covered it with runny crabmeat which helped. The green salad was great, with lemon dressing. The grilled Portobellos moist and chewy like a good steak, without the fat.

"Dmitri is allergic to cats," Amanda announced.

Dmitri stuffed his mouth again.

"He seems to think we've got a cat on the premises," Lester said, a baffled expression on his face. He passed the wine bottle around. "Amanda doesn't like cats."

"Neither do you, Lester," she said.

"He's been sneezing since he came back in here," Laurie said. "I think it might be his dog."

"He's allergic to cats and lies," I said. "If there are no cats around, then someone told a lie. Dmitri?"

"He's allergic to his own lies too?" Jim asked.

"Breaks out in hives all over."

Jim laughed. "He did say the salmon was good, which it wasn't. Sorry about that, Amanda."

"It was heaven," Lester said, "compared to what our cook serves."

Amanda pursed her lips, caught herself doing it, and broke into a hostess smile. "I'm sure we've each told a lie tonight. Even if only a little one. I think we should all confess. We can start a new parlor game."

Lester groaned, "God no, Amanda."

"I'll start," she said. "I told Lester that I agreed to his divorce terms. Who's next?"

Lester banged his fist on the table. "You promised—"

"So did you, darling, 'til death do us part." Amanda's wide hazel eyes swept around the table. "Any other lies?"

Lester poured himself more wine, his face mottled with anger.

I kicked.

Dmitri dumped the last of the food into his mouth.

"You'll have to swallow sooner or later," I told him.

Jim looked at Laurie. "Mine has been a lie of omission."

"What? What? What?" Amanda was all ears. Lester began gathering plates. He didn't like this game. I got up to help. He pushed me back down.

"I just told Laurie tonight on the deck." Jim looked uncomfortable.

"What did you tell Laurie?" I asked, suddenly interested.

Laurie lifted her chin. "Go on. I don't intend to keep it a secret."

Dmitri asked for directions to the bathroom. Which meant he was slipping out of the Tell the Truth game. He was going to look for the cat.

"Get a Kleenex," I warned before turning back to Jim. "What's the big lie of omission?"

Jim flashed me a smile. The wattage was low. "Bud was my silent partner in Jim's Pit."

Amanda clapped her hands. She was enjoying herself. "We should have known. He was always trying to get us to eat there." Jim kept his eyes on me, as though I were judge and jury. "Bud asked me to keep quiet about it. When he signed on, Polly was talking about divorce. He didn't want her to find out. Not that he wanted to cheat her—"

"Bud was a straight shooter," Lester interrupted, handing out dessert plates. "I'm sure he wanted to save something for Laurie."

Amanda stood up, wagging a finger at Jim. "If I'd been Polly's lawyer, I would have found you two out."

"We didn't sign anything until after the divorce. Tomorrow I'm going to show Laurie the books."

Why had Jim waited to tell her until tonight? Because she was supposed to have met this morning with the lawyer?

Amanda brought a big bowl of fruit salad to the table. "Well, I think that's wonderful. The two of you will now have to spend a lot of time together." She dropped a basket of chocolate chip cookies from

Kathleen's Bakery in Southampton in front of me. I think they were meant as my consolation prize.

"Don't worry, Jim," Laurie said. "I won't interfere. Do I get free dinners?"

"Your dad paid for his."

"Then what's the point?"

Jim shrugged. "Modest dividends?"

Laurie laughed. "I've got no lies to confess to, just good news. Lester faxed Dad's sketch to Sport4Life. They love it!"

Lester nodded. His face was now a mask of geniality. "It'll be the campaign's kick-off ad."

"Let's make a toast to Bud," Amanda said, sitting down again. "He was a great man and a great talent."

Lester popped the champagne. We toasted. Dmitri came back in time for the second go-round of bubbly and cookies. And Lester's sudden question.

"What's so important about Bud's Monday appointment?"

"It's just a note I found on one of Dad's Post-its," Laurie said quickly. "He underlined it three times."

"He should have underlined it five times. It was me he was supposed to meet. With the new ad campaign."

Laurie leaned over the table. "This is another appointment. I want to know who it was with."

"Why?" Lester asked.

"It might explain his death."

Lester shifted in his seat. "Well, I don't know about that."

Laurie fixed him with a solemn gaze.

It didn't take long for Lester to give up. "Well, since you're so keen on it, maybe you should know. Amanda, I want you to note that I'm playing along with your parlor game."

Amanda tilted her head. "One notch in your favor."

"This is my confession," Lester said. "Another lie by omission. I know who else Bud had scheduled to see on Monday, although I can't see how it's got anything to do with Bud's death."

"Maybe not," Laurie said quietly.

Lester shifted his weight in his chair. He picked a chocolate chip from a cookie. He offered everyone another round of fruit salad.

"You're the one making a big deal of this, Lester." Laurie's knuckles had turned whiter than her napkin.

"That man you can't seem to give up," Lester finally said. "Steve King."

The brightness in Laurie's eyes flickered, like a lighter running out of fluid.

TWENTY-NINE

JIM PUNCHED IN NUMBERS on his alarm box next to the kitchen door. "Nowadays everybody's wiring out here."

"You should convince Laurie."

The dinner had broken up quickly after Lester's revelation, Laurie claiming exhaustion. She had made a date with Jim to go over the restaurant books after her meeting with the lawyer. "For all we know Dad might have left his share to someone else." She was thinking Rebecca. I decided not to tell her about the missing pages of the suicide note. Not yet.

After driving home, Jim and I had walked Laurie back to the big house. We offered to keep her company. She reminded me of The Pynes' no dogs policy.

Sabrina now traced her nose in nervous concentric swoops across the wide-plank floor of Jim's kitchen. She was going to spend the night. Dmitri had gone to get her a pacifier.

The kitchen was large, with buckling linoleum,

old wood cabinets that needed lemon oil, and the bare, transitory look of a motel room. The only thing modern was a sub-zero refrigerator and the microwave.

"I guess you always eat at the restaurant." I circled the room with Sabrina, feeling awkward.

"I bring stuff back and freeze it sometimes." Jim took my hand. "How about a nightcap and a view of the silver-bathed bay?" He pointed to the porch. Sabrina barked. I peered at the three-quarter moon for a good half minute to make sure it wasn't some man-invented trickery. It was the real thing, a veined bubble swelling with romance.

Stan's forgotten toothbrush rattled in my brain. "Thanks, but I better get some sleep." I tried to retrieve my hand.

He pulled it back. "No, listen. You've got to understand where I come from." His voice was low and earnest. "I don't accept position limits and a trader's always a gambler."

"I heard the Pine Barrens fire is finally out."

"You like to change the subject? I'll play along. Thank God the fire is out, huh? Five thousand acres gone. No casualties. Amazing."

"You warned Laurie about Bud's house burning down."

"Yeah, I ran into Steve burning rubber at seven in the morning. The fire marshal still has no news."

"I didn't see you come to see the damage."

Jim dropped his friendly face and my hand. "For the record, I didn't stand by Laurie on Sunday because one of the restaurant's freezers was out of commission and I can't afford to lose a day's worth of food."

I smiled with relief. "Checking is part of my job. I can't get personal. I'm sorry."

"I'm beginning to think you never get personal."

Before I could answer, Dmitri barreled in with his great sense of timing. He'd brought a heatwave's worth of dirty clothes to anesthetize Sabrina into submission. He settled Sabrina on an armchair, surrounded by a moat of his smell. We waved goodbye. Sabrina's eyes went soggy with disappointment. So did Jim's.

As we touched the screen door to our cottage, Sabrina started howling. After twenty minutes of uninterrupted canine anguish, Dmitri slung a blanket over his shoulder and went to retrieve her.

I changed out of my linen pantsuit into an oversized T-shirt and waited until Dmitri settled back on the sofa with his new beloved. "Why didn't you tell me about Uma?"

"You make trouble." Sabrina nuzzled Dmitri's pocket. He'd stuffed them with Kathleen's chocolate chip cookies. He offered me one as a peace gesture. I took two. They're the best I've tasted.

"Uma is Knight's case. We have to play fair."

"Russian maxim say who gets there first does not wait in line."

"Any trace of the cat?"

"No, and also no red thermos." He seemed strangely pleased by his defeat.

"It's probably bobbing in the Atlantic Ocean by now."

"Yes, and someone pick it up on beach in Portugal or Spain maybe. Maybe it has important message of love or world peace."

"I wish. Thanks for looking, but Comelli is going to stick to his suicide theory no matter how much Valium was in that coffee or in Bud's body."

"I also not find copy of Lester and Bud partnership agreement."

"How did you know—"

"I have long ears." And big fists. He was fishing in his trouser pockets again. And again half the contents spilled out. To Sabrina's delight, two more cookies. He finally dangled a set of keys, his mustache thinning out into a wide grin.

I groaned loudly. "Whose keys?"

"Lester. See, they have initials." Dmitri pointed to the silver medallion on the chain, then threw the keys in my lap. "When you go to Lester's office, try small key first."

"He'll miss these."

"Second set. First set, gold chain, I leave on dresser. Lester not go to office until Monday, so beach is clear. Now you really owe me."

I flung a quarter his way. Sabrina caught it. We reviewed our marching orders for the next day. "While I'm gone, you can call up these four numbers Laurie gave me," I dropped the list on the coffee table, "and try to find out who they belong to."

"Why? We know Monday appointment is with Steve King."

"Any piece of information you get, you've got to

check out. Part of a detective's ruthless job."

"I will check out new information of cat," Dmitri said. He was wresting the quarter from Sabrina's chocolate-smeared jaws.

"You already did. Uma is not in the Kennelly house."

"I bet you not know why some American coins have ridges?"

"I'm not paying money for you to change the subject." I got up to make coffee.

"Free information. When coins were all silver, people shave edges. You shave enough edges you get little mountain of silver and coin no longer half dollar worth of silver. So they put ridge. If ridge shaved off, you know you are cheated. Dick Knight cheat us. With cat we blackmail him for truth."

"I believe he found the other sheets of Polly's letter. That corroborates what Captain Comelli said to Laurie. But he's definitely lying about Bud." Knight at first had told me Bud committed suicide because the police were after him. With Dmitri threatening his wardrobe, he'd changed his story to Bud wanting the police on the case again.

"This is the way I see it," I said. "Polly's murderer suspects Bud is on to him, so he spins Knight some tale about wanting to review the file, pays Knight for the privilege, and makes sure the file contains no evidence that points to him."

"How does murderer know file exist?"

"Bud didn't make a secret of hiring three detectives to find out who killed his wife. What do you

think of this? Knight lets the murderer see Polly's letter to Bud. The fact that a sheet of that letter ended
up as Polly's suicide note makes Bud look guilty as
hell. Which makes the real murderer real happy. He
pays Knight to go to the police so that when the murderer drowns Bud, the police will think he committed suicide because they were about to arrest him for
killing Polly." I grinned with satisfaction. "*Non fa
una piega*. Not a wrinkle."

Dmitri's thick black eyebrows met in a frown. "If
you are right, Knight knows killer."

"I bet that dumbbell thinks it's going to make
him rich." I grabbed my sandals. "Come on, we've
got to warn him."

Dmitri raised his hands slowly, a gesture reminis-
cent of a monarch calming his people. "How?
Where? The Hamptons is big place. Dick Knight is a
licensed detective. He must have gun. If he is black-
mailer, danger is his business."

"That's heartless."

"Practical. Also yours is theory only. Maybe
someone pay to look at evidence in file out of fear for
loved one. Rebecca worried about Bud. Laurie worried about Steve."

"Why did Knight go to the police?"

"Because he was angry Bud not pay him what he
want."

"You think?"

"Trust me."

I shouldn't have.

I called Knight's New York number. I told the

answering machine my theory and warned him to be careful. I then called Gregory, my friend from the office. He was due back from his vacation that Wednesday night or the next morning. I wanted to know more about WSK, and Gregory has contacts.

His sweet voice asked me to leave a message. I told him it was urgent.

Dmitri went to sleep in his bedroom. His ribs felt well enough to risk lowering himself on the bed. I settled myself and my cup of caffeinated coffee on the sofa with the *Independent*, another East Hampton paper put out by well-known Hamptonite Jerry Della Femina, once head of a prestigious ad firm and now a restaurant owner Jim competed with. To be fully awake when I confronted Steve at dawn I'd decided to *passare una notte in bianco*, to spend a white night. That is, not sleep. That way, I'd also catch Rebecca when she came home.

As I glanced over the latest on the beautiful people of the Hamptons, I wondered why straight-shooter Bud had kept his restaurant partnership secret once his ex-wife died. Everyone considered him a paragon of honesty. What if it was another advertising illusion? What if Bud had really killed his wife and then in turn been killed by an avenger? Who? No one seemed to have liked her. Except Dodo perhaps. They'd been friendly, and there was that old "Recover the Past" picture of the two of them in front of the cement mixer.

After a while Sabrina padded out of Dmitri's bedroom and sank down in front of the screen door.

She barked once. She'd quickly learned that barking would get her the world.

"It opens by itself if you nudge it," I told her.

She barked again. I guess she preferred doorman service. Outside, the din from the katydids et al. was strong. So was the lapping of the water. The tide was coming in. No wind. The three-quarter moon had moved behind a cloud. It was humid. All lights were out in the cabins. Even in the big house. If Laurie was sleeping, she was probably having nightmares of Steve holding her father underwater.

Back inside, Sabrina decided to keep me company for a while. I lifted her and her huge belly up on the sofa where she scavanged for crumbs under the pillows. She came back up chewing on something white. Something belonging to Dmitri, I assumed. He'd spilled half the contents of his pockets reaching for Lester's keys. I bargained. Half a cookie for soggy paper. She held out for the entire cookie. One quick snap of her jaws and the cookie was gone. In my palm, a balled-up envelope, one side chewed off. I saw part of the address. West Seventy-seventh Street.

That's where I lived. I smoothed out the envelope. The addressee was familiar too.

Stan Greenhouse.

I turned the envelope around. Sheree Debuskey. She lived on Fort Washington Avenue, up in Washington Heights. What did she have to say to Stan? And what was this letter doing in Dmitri's pocket? None of my business, perhaps, but I extracted the sheet anyway. It was wet, with one side eaten away, but I read more than enough. She'd written the letter three days before we'd come to the Hamptons. For once the post office had been speedy.

> Darling G.,
> I'm so happy. You're the best thing that's ever—— to me. Come soon. Even in the middle of the night. D—— orry. I haven't told a soul.
>
> With all my *corazón*,
> Sheree

Vaffanculo, Stan! I don't need this.

THIRTY

I DEBATED WAKING DMITRI, demanding to know where he'd gotten the letter, why he hadn't shown it to me. But I already knew the answers. I now understood why my loyal friend had been pushing Jim.

I debated waking Jim. "I'm ready for that nightcap now. And maybe something else if you're in the mood." When something like this hits you in the face, you want to play the aggrieved one, the victim, the loyal lover who deserves the world's sympathy to the hilt. God damn it, you *are* the aggrieved one! I felt that instant hot flash of anger that made me want to get Stan where it hurts. But I'd been through this once before. I had some control.

The short length of beach below the cottage was the place to go. I paced, trailing Sabrina. In my stomach, my dinner was pitching in a gale. I tried to shut down my feelings and think. What had happened? Catholic retribution, my mother would call this. I'd entertained lewd thoughts of another man. But wasn't that only because Stan had turned into Robo Cop? Maybe. Forty was looming in my very near future and maybe I wanted to kick up my heels, dance in the moonlight with a stranger, bask in another man's flattery, still marvel at the thought that something new was waiting around the corner. Well, I got my something new. Did it serve me right? No way.

What about honesty?

I sat down in the sand. Sheree? Never heard of her. But Willy had heard of her all right. Stan dreaming sweet dreams of Cherry pie. And maggots. May they eat out his pecker.

Sheree. She sounded like a stripper.

"Any piece of information you get, you've got to check it out." Stan's words.

What was the payoff?

The truth.

If it hurts, who wants it?

Basta, grow up! That was mamma again.

Sabrina dropped down next to me and hooked her head over my thigh. She felt good. I brushed sand off her wavy coat. The moon came out and spilled white light on the beach. Sabrina lifted up her head and growled. A shadow covered her.

"Too hot to sleep?"

I looked up. Jim offered me a tall glass. I took it. Sabrina continued to growl.

Jim dropped down, the edible smell still on him. He stroked her head. "She thinks I'm going to drag her back to my place."

Why not me? I drank. Thank God it was water. Iced, like my insides. Jim continued to stroke. Sabrina turned silent.

"Can I help?" Jim sat down next to me. His knee brushed mine. The moon slipped behind a thick cloud.

"What makes you think I need any?" I couldn't make out his features. He was just a pulsating mass.

"How did I know Microsoft was the stock to buy?" Jim asked, his voice low, lapping at me. "Okay, forget instinct. Let's examine the fact sheet. You're out here in the middle of the night. It's humid. The moon is in and out so fast you've got nothing to look at. The dog's with you, which means you don't care if anyone sees her. Deduction. You've got indigestion from my food or you're upset about something. I don't want to think my food would do that to you, so I prefer to think you're upset. No, that didn't come out right. I meant—"

I put my hand on his arm. "It's okay, Jim. I know what you meant." My hand stayed where it was.

"I brought you water so you wouldn't accuse me of trying to seduce you."

"Thanks."

Jim bent his arm, trapping my hand inside. He felt cool rather than hot. Soothing. "Although that's exactly what I'd like to do. Are you upset? I'm not try-ing to pry or anything. I need to know, because if you are upset, I can't kiss you. The SEC would nail me for insider trading. Unfair advantage and all that."

It didn't take me long to answer. "I'm not in the least bit upset."

Jim tasted salty and soft, like a just-opened oyster.

I kissed him back, sliding my arms up and down his linen shirt. I felt his chest press against my breasts as he nibbled at my ear. Our kisses got wetter and wetter, the salt in the air leaving a spicy residue on our lips. Sand rubbed the back of my thighs as we fell back on the beach and continued to kiss. The tide seemed to rise suddenly. The sound of water rushed in my ears. The katydids and tree frogs screamed. In a moment drunk with anger and self-pity I opened up my thighs to this man's hand and thought of making love on the wet, sandy lip of Gardiners Bay while the moon ran from one cloud to another, as though ashamed.

Jim rolled over me. Sabrina yelped. I sat up and pushed him away. "I'm sorry. This isn't fair."

"You *are* upset."

"Very." As I opened my eyes, sounds shriveled back to reality. The water of the bay lapped lazily; the night animals chattered.

Jim waited for his breath to subside before speaking. "I always did have good instincts. This time I didn't want to listen." He reached over to fondle Sabrina's ear. "Sorry, baby, I didn't mean to kick you."

I wiped my mouth, used my fingers to comb my hair. Pulled the T-shirt down over my knees. "Please forgive me."

" 'Errors of omission are the ones to watch out for.' That's a Warren Buffett quote."

"Who's he?"

"An investor and one of the richest men in America. Look, don't worry. It was a delightful five minutes that I would have enjoyed stretching out for about a week, but to paraphrase Buffett, to go into business with people who have entirely different expectations is crazy."

The moon made another appearance, to point out what a very nice face Jim had. "Bud had the same expectations you did?" I asked.

"Yes, he did, but I was talking about romance."

"I know, but talking business is less embarrassing."

"Why do you think I brought Warren Buffett into it." His hand shoveled his shirt back into his pants. "What are you upset about?"

"I don't want to talk about it."

"Good for you. It would be disloyal to the cop." He peered at me to make sure he was on the right track. I guess he got his answer. "I hope it works out. If he's what you want."

I nodded, not at all sure.

"Okay, then let me help you with your investigation," Jim said, his voice all business. "What more do you want to know from me?"

"Nothing. I think it's time I went to sleep." I got up. Sabrina scrambled to her feet. So did Jim.

"Listen, I want to feel useful here. And I know you have one question for sure. I saw it in your face tonight at dinner. Why did I wait so long to tell Laurie about the partnership? Because I asked myself, 'What if she doesn't inherit his shares?'"

"She would have found out about them anyway. From the will." We were walking back to the cabin, Sabrina leading the way.

"He could have created a revocable trust that included the proceeds of the restaurant. Revocable trusts are not public record."

"Why did you even think of that?"

"Bud brought up the subject recently, in one of our after-dinner conversations. He didn't mention the restaurant specifically, but why bring up revocable trusts in my presence if I'm not going to be involved in some way."

"What made you decide to tell Laurie after all?"

"If I hadn't said anything and the restaurant came up in the will, what would you have thought?"

"That you were trying to hide something."

Jim leaned over and kissed my forehead. "Sleep well. I still would like to show you the hot spots of the Hamptons if you'll let me."

"Thanks, I think you just did. It's going to last me for a while."

"Then I'll leave you with something Buffett likes to quote a lot. For when your cop comes back. 'The chains of habit are too light to be felt until they're too heavy to be broken.'"

"Thanks again. Now I'll really sleep tight."

"A man's got to defend himself." He gave me another kiss. On the cheek. "If you want to talk some more, I'll leave the door unlocked." This time he kissed my mouth and told me his alarm code. "You've got thirty seconds."

To change my life?

THIRTY-ONE

SHOWERED, WHICH MADE ME FEEL CLEAN, but not blameless. I donned a clean oversized T-shirt, tucked Sheree's letter back in the envelope, and slipped it inside my breast pocket, lest my heart forget. I looked in on Dmitri. He was sleeping on his back, looking like a marooned boulder a glacier had left behind. The fan whirred through its semicircle. His snoring had the resonance of a Shostakovich symphony. I decided that being mad at him required too much energy. He'd meant well by hiding the letter. I quietly closed the door to his bedroom and settled back on the sofa. Scarlett O'Hara with her tomorrow bit came to mind and I decided to hell with waiting up for Rebecca. It was past one o'clock. What I needed was to get off the bus for a while. I turned out the light.

Sabrina's growl was deep enough to wake me. She was standing by the door, her snout pressed against the screen.

"Shh," I commanded, desperate to drop back to sleep. I'd been dreaming of swimming at the bottom of the ocean and finding Bud's red thermos. Upon opening it, a genie, who looked very much like Jim, had given me one wish.

"It's supposed to be three," said I.

"You've got thirty seconds." Jim's face turned into Sabrina's. She was angry at my greediness. Her growl lengthened, deepened, was almost a prolonged bark. Much too loud. I shook myself awake again and raised myself up. Sabrina was still at her post by the door. I got up silently. I listened, but I had cuckolding on my mind. That makes a pretty loud sound of its own. I looked out of the kitchen window at Rebecca's cabin. Was she back?

Sabrina's growl swelled into a bark. I rushed to the screen door and wrapped my hands around her snout. "*Zitta*, you'll get us kicked out of here!"

A light arced in the back of the property. From where I sat on my haunches, I couldn't tell if it came from Rebecca's cabin. The alarm clock said two-thirty. Sabrina barked through my fingers. "You're as stubborn as Dmitri!" She lowered herself into a crouch and was quiet.

"Good girl!"

Then she sprang, head aimed at the door. It swung open from her weight. Sabrina leaped out over the steps, her belly flattening out with the stretch. A flash of white spots disappeared across the grass. I leaped after her, Italian curses rinsing my teeth. The moon decided not to cooperate and I lost her in the dark. I circled the back cabins. Rebecca's parking spot was empty. Everyone else's car was there. No lights in any of the cabins. No Sabrina.

I plunged into the woods that she used as a bathroom and that sheltered The Pynes from Fireplace Road. I kept whispering Sabrina's name. I heard traffic and prayed she wouldn't get run over by a car. I passed Rebecca's cabin again. I heard a muffled yelp. Or thought I did. The tree frogs and the katydids hadn't called it a night yet, so I couldn't be sure. I crept up to Rebecca's porch door. Something tickled my leg. I stepped back and reached down. My fingers touched wire. Rebecca's screen door had a hole in it, I remembered. I listened for a few minutes. Was Rebecca in there?

Another yelp. Still muffled. Definitely from inside the cottage. I yanked the screen door open and dropped into a black void. A few more steps and alcohol fumes punched my nose. "Dodo? Don't hurt the dog! She's harmless." The headlights of a car swept across the cabin, startling me. Something rolled underneath my foot. I stumbled and fell on my knees. My hand hit a bottle. Something else hit my head.

Jim was kissing me again. Warm, soggy kisses full of salt. On my cheeks, my lips. His body weighed against my chest. His hair tickled my neck. He'd been drinking. The smell of alcohol was strong. Or was it Stan? No, Stan's kisses were dry. And sweet. An icy hand pressed against the back of my scalp.

I moaned and opened my eyes. A slap of light made me shutter down. The second time my lids lifted only a fraction. The light was now indirect. It shined into one gigantic black, baleful eye staring at me. A tongue, pink as a girl's hair ribbon, washed my nose.

"Sabrina's a good resuscitator," a voice said. "Southampton Hospital should hire her." A cold glass nudged my cheek. "Drink up. It'll make you feel better."

Rebecca! I opened my eyes, lifted my head. Something shattered to the floor. The earth shook. I dropped back down. Sabrina went to work on my face again. I buried my fingers in her fur for reassurance.

"'How are you getting on now, my dear?'" Dodo said, with a worn, lulling voice. Crouched down to my level, he peered at me, the gray of his eyes shining from the lamp behind me. "I am 'burning with curiosity.'" His eyes widened, showing off the whites, washed clean of whiskey.

Sabrina stiffened under my fingers and growled. Dodo jumped.

I scratched behind her ear. "Shh, baby, no one's going to hurt us anymore." My other hand patted around. Linoleum. I was still where I'd fallen, it seemed. "Sabrina's not hurt, is she?" She was trying to burrow herself underneath me, still growling.

"She's had a shock. She's frightened. I would be too." Rebecca's voice was unusually loud. "Would you like to go to the hospital? I hate them myself. So does Dodo. You've been out about five minutes, not much longer. No blood. The skin isn't even broken. We didn't move you, just in case. Open your eyes and tell me how many fingers you see."

I obliged her. "Two. With blue paint on them. And Billy Crystal is president of the United States."

"Phthalo blue to be exact," Rebecca said. She didn't care about presidents. "Used it for the ocean this afternoon. With a touch of rose madder. You'll be fine."

Easy for her to say. "I also see an architect who built The Pynes." He'd moved.

Seconds of silence. Then Dodo grinned from the far corner of the room. "'What a noise they make when they tumble.'"

Sabrina barked once. She was now wedged under my legs.

"Dodo's allergic to dogs," Rebecca explained.

Scared stiff, more likely. "What happened?" I asked.

Rebecca lifted my head gently and stuck something cold behind it. "The ice pack fell on the floor."

"So did I."

"'I vote the young lady tells us a story,'" Dodo said.

I sat up slowly and leaned against the wall. Sabrina settled herself and her load on my lap. Rebecca held the ice pack in place. "Sabrina ran away. I thought I heard her yelp from in here. I opened the screen door, smelled a lot of alcohol, and then tripped over the bottle."

"That's how you hit your head, then," Rebecca said, nudging me with her orange cure-all drink again. I drank.

"The bottle was already on the floor?" Dodo asked.

I nodded. A mistake when you've just been hit on the head. "And open, judging from the reek."

"Broken," Rebecca said. Her voice was still not friendly. "You're lucky you didn't cut yourself when you fell. Dodo swept the floor clean. Are you trying to tell us you weren't the one who broke the bottle or locked the dog under the sink?"

I sat up. "Hey, what are you two thinking?" My head split in half. "Listen, someone was in here. Sabrina found him out. He didn't want her to give him away so he locked her up and then I came in. Since I couldn't fit in a kitchen cabinet, I got bopped." I pulled Sabrina to me and scratched behind her ears. "Why was he here at all? That's what I want to know." Such clear thinking. I should get hit on the head more often.

Rebecca dropped on the floor beside me, her long nose inches away from mine. The smell of oil paint was still on her. "You're the one who's getting paid to nose around. At the Kennellys' tonight I mentioned that Bud had left me an envelope. You wanted to know all about it and then hours later I come home, my cottage has been searched, and you're out cold by the back door. The locked up dog becomes a wonderful excuse."

I looked around the porch. "Searched? First

Bud's place, then Laurie's, now yours." I scrambled to stand up and slowly crossed the room. The jars she used for her still lifes were in a jumble on the table. Her box of paints sat upside-down, spilling gnarled silver tubes. Seashells covered the floor. "Did he take the envelope? Do you know what was in there? Maybe this is the break we need." The room wobbled. I grabbed the closest thing to me. Dodo.

"'If you'll believe in me,'" Dodo said, "'I'll believe in you. Is that a bargain?'"

"Sealed in blood." Rebecca wasn't as easily convinced. Neither was Sabrina, who'd taken refuge in the main room. I leaned against the wall for extra support. "All right, I've been insistent, and I'm not above rummaging through someone's personal belongings while on the job, but I didn't even think of coming in here while you were gone. I should have. Any detective worth her salt would have jumped at the chance."

Rebecca's cheeks folded into a smile. "Maybe Laurie should fire you."

"Maybe." Dick Knight, was he behind this? "You two aren't, by any chance, hiding a hairless cat?"

Dodo gave a whisper of a laugh, the sound of two sticks scraping together in his throat. "'Sometimes I've believed as many as six impossible things before breakfast.' This one no."

"Just a thought. So what about that envelope?"

Rebecca led me into the main room and turned on the light. Sabrina scrambled under the sofa. At least she'd stopped growling.

The prowler had been in a hurry. He'd scattered pots and pans over the floor, flung open all the kitchen cabinets, the oven door, overturned the pillows of the sofa, tossed Rebecca's art books over the area rug. He'd been fast and silent.

"The only thing I've done," Rebecca said, "is shut the refrigerator door and pick up my art."

Dodo stayed by the porch doorway, rocking on his heels, a look of utter desolation on his weathered old face. "'We're all mad here.'"

"Is the envelope gone?"

Rebecca crossed the room with heavy steps and went inside her bedroom. "Bud had put it in here," she said, coming out, a large paint-splattered canvas bag in her hand. "I use it when I paint outdoors. It holds a great deal. Why didn't the thief look in here right away instead of tearing up the place to find it? It would have saved me all this cleaning up." She sank down on a hardbacked chair and kneaded the bag with her long phthalo blue fingers. "It wasn't what he wanted anyway."

I straightened out the sofa and sat down next to her. "How do you know that?"

"'If everyone minded their own business,'" Dodo said, "'the world would go 'round a deal faster than it does.'" He slipped into the spare bedroom and shut the door.

Rebecca's fingers continued to knead. Her posture was ramrod-straight as always, but some strong and unhappy memory dragged across her face. I bent down to put her books in order. My head throbbed.

A simple headache. Nothing more. Rebecca was right. I was going to be fine. I wondered if she was.

Sabrina left her hiding place underneath the sofa and sniffed at each and every pot. A few minutes passed in silence. I moved on to the pots and pans, but lifting up a cast-iron skillet proved too much for my head. I sat back down on the sofa.

Rebecca followed me with her eyes. "You don't have to clean up the place to prove your innocence."

"I'd like to help."

"Dodo would say 'you're enough to try the patience of an oyster.'" Her expression was not unkind.

"I've heard a lot of quotes tonight."

"Dodo claims he doesn't trust his own words. I've been wondering about mine. It's one of the reasons I haven't answered your questions. Besides the fact that I still think it's none of your business. But I do want to help Laurie, and if she wants answers then I suppose I must give them." She didn't look in the least bit convinced.

"What was in the envelope Bud gave you?"

"Love letters."

How familiar.

THIRTY-TWO

I DIDN'T KNOW THEY WERE LOVE letters to start with," Rebecca said. "Last Thursday afternoon Bud called me. I told him I had no time for him and hung up. I went on Gerard Drive in the blistering sun. I'd started a painting of a vase of wild roses against one of the white boulders edging the road. I wanted the heavy shadows. The light moves quickly and I only had about half an hour's time to get the effect I wanted. I didn't pay much attention to Bud when he walked up and slipped a manila envelope into my bag. What with my being on in years and the annual barbecue coming up, which always sets my teeth on edge because everyone pretends to like one another, and then with Bud disappearing, dying . . . I plain forgot about it. Until this afternoon when Laurie called me about meeting Bud's lawyer. I haven't gone out to paint since that day. The bag's been hanging from my bedroom door for a week." She got up and came over to where I was sitting. I moved to make room for her, but she bent down and reached underneath the sofa where Sabrina had gone exploring.

"She's not eating anything up, is she?" My head told me not to bend over to look. "She particularly likes love letters." Sheree's letter was still in my breast pocket.

Sabrina barked in protest as Rebecca extracted a large manila envelope. Intact, thank God. On it, I noticed the WSK logo. Rebecca sank down next to me on the sofa and shook the envelope.

"So our prowler didn't take the love letters," I said.

"What would he do with them?" Her face was red from bending over. From anger too. "Dog food!" she declared. "Letters written over a span of forty years. They might as well have been written on sand. You know what Bud said to me when he dropped this in my bag? 'This will explain everything!' This afternoon I remembered that too when I looked at the envelope, felt it in my hands. Look, it even has some paint on it." She pointed to an arc of smudges in one corner. "I was on my porch, painting the ocean—calm, never-ending—feeling suddenly happy, and this"—she shook the envelope as if trying to rid it of dust—"this was lying in wait for me." She threw the envelope on the coffee table. I caught Sabrina in mid-lunge.

"Why did you think the envelope was for Laurie?"

"Because of what he said when he gave it to me. Laurie was the reason I had stopped speaking to Bud after Polly died. It was horrible and spiteful of Polly not to leave Laurie the Pynes land. I told Bud he should hand the deed over to her. She could then sell the land and be free of it or give it to Steve as a wedding present. Bud, as usual, promised and then did nothing. My old anger came back and I just couldn't open my mouth in his presence. I was afraid of what would come out. Dodo understood me perfectly. He started feeding me Lewis Carroll quotes for all occasions. About the only person I felt like quoting was Lady Macbeth so I refrained. I think I need a drink." She marched over to the refrigerator with Sabrina padding after her. She poured herself the orange drink and gave Sabrina cranberry juice in a skillet that the prowler had left on the floor.

"It helps pass kidney stones," she muttered. "It might do the same for puppies."

I accepted a refill and two aspirin. "Your gills are flapping," she said.

"With curiosity." I waited for her to sit back down. "Bud said, 'This will explain everything'?"

"That's right." She took a long swig. "When I finally remembered this afternoon, I thought, 'Ah, this has something to do with The Pynes, with Laurie.' Tonight, after I left the Kennellys', I drove back here to pick up some clean clothes for Dodo to wear home from the hospital and I thought I'd better look inside that envelope. What if he'd written something cruel about Steve. Or his daughter, for that matter. This is a man who thought his own daughter capable of killing her mother."

"Jim says he liked to be impartial."

"Bud liked to believe that he was ruled by intellect, not by heart." Sadness shadowed her face. "The envelope had nothing to do with Laurie. It had everything to do with me. Half a lifetime of letters."

"You loved him very much."

"I had an affair with him years back when we were both art students. We all had affairs. We made love, we painted, we starved. Except Bud, who had some family money. He liked to pick up the bar bills at the Cedar Tavern. He helped me with the rent. I lived on Eighth Street in Greenwich Village, a block away from Pollock and Krasner. Bud lived uptown, on the Upper East Side of all places. With his parents! We teased him relentlessly.

"Bud had talent, but his was commercial art. Neat. Predictable. Mine was old-fashioned with easy sentimentality. But we both hung on with the innovators. Bud dropped out first and got a job in advertising. After his first raise, he offered to bankroll me. Rent a big studio for me on Union Square, pay for my art supplies. He was going to introduce me to a friend of his father's, who owned an uptown art gallery. Bud wanted nothing in exchange. To prove his point he stopped visiting my bed. I filled it with someone else. What was important to me was that Bud thought my art was valid. He convinced me to stop being imitative, to paint what I truly loved. We were great friends. I treasured that more than anything. We came out here together the summer of 1950 after hearing about Springs from Lee Krasner and Pollock. They'd been here since 1945.

"Bud thought Springs might be the ideal summer place for me too. He was going to be my Peggy Guggenheim. Peggy had lent Pollock the two thousand dollar deposit for the farmhouse they bought. Five acres of land for five thousand dollars. She had a gallery then and she'd put Jack on a stipend. That's what Bud was going to do for me.

"We were looking at property when he met Polly. By the end of the summer he forgot about me and my art. I confronted him. 'Never mind the money!' I yelled. 'What about our friendship?' I was furious. The money did matter—I'd quit my job at a bookshop to have more time to paint—but I'd be damned if I was going to let that show. Bud offered me a check. Five thousand dollars. The price of a house. I tore it up in front of him. In October he married Polly. The next summer I sublet my Greenwich Village apartment and with that money moved to The Pynes, into the first available cottage."

"Did Polly know about your previous relationship with Bud?"

"I told her when I applied for the lease. I think I wanted to rattle her. I certainly wanted to get back at him. She thought it made her husband more interesting."

"Nice."

"That was Polly. All these years I thought she'd been the one to turn him against me, money hungry as she was. And now I discover . . ." She lifted her hand, then let it drop.

I got the queasy feeling I'd misunderstood something and leaned forward to pick up the manila envelope from the coffee table. It was full. "These love letters Bud returned are yours."

Rebecca cooled her cheeks with her hands. "His. Never sent. Rivers of ink on how much he had loved me from the very first. Embarrassing, trite words that make me shake with anger. He only married Polly because he'd finally realized he couldn't buy my love. That's what he wrote. And when she divorced him he was devastated because he'd made another bad choice. On and on like that. The damn fool never said anything to me. He wanted to marry me, he wrote. I never heard a word of love. Ever!" She glared at me, wisps of gray hair quivering around her forehead, her mouth narrowed to a straight line. "Why didn't he speak up? Why?"

"Bud didn't like to lose from what I hear. What if you said no?"

"How stupid men are!"

I thought of Sheree's love letter burning in my chest pocket. "They don't have a monopoly on lack of brains."

"Well, now you know why I was on Bud's suspect list. I did harbor a grudge against Polly, but the one I could have killed was Bud. For taking away a friendship I held very dear."

"After more than forty years?"

"Some things don't go away."

Yes, like love. But she'd be damned if she ever admitted it. "What I want to know is what was the prowler looking for?"

"Evidence that points to him. Maybe something that reveals a motive."

"Did he go through the letters?"

"They were all over the sofa. I stuffed them back in the envelope and threw the envelope under the sofa."

"Bud could have given you something else besides those letters."

"There's a cover letter. He only mentioned the letters. He wrote that he wanted me to have them before he died."

"Who knows Bud left you the envelope?"

"Laurie, of course. Dodo. Lester and Amanda must have overheard me."

"Laurie mentioned the envelope in front of Jim. She might have said something to Steve if they're still speaking." And Dick Knight might have overheard from the bushes. I looked at Sabrina, now fast asleep at my feet, and wondered if she'd been able to sink her teeth into whomever he was. Maybe we'd find a nice strip of torn black leather.

I moved my head slowly from side to side. It didn't break. "You'd better call the police and let them search for evidence."

"I will not have my privacy invaded."

"Rebecca, whoever came in here is also Bud's killer."

"Then we'll search ourselves. I will not have that idiot Captain Comelli asking me questions about my life."

After an hour we came up with a wastepaper basket full of dust motes, lots of gray hairs, countless crayon ends, and another whiskey bottle, untouched. No black leather. From the other room Dodo snored. I had questions for him too, but they would have to wait. It was four-twenty in the morning. Time to wake up Dmitri and take him and his gun for a boat ride.

THIRTY-THREE

B ETWEEN LONG SIPS OF THE blackest coffee I could make, I filled Dmitri in on Rebecca's prowler and Bud's love letters. He grunted mostly, as he drove and ate his breakfast. More boiled potatoes. He'd run out of hot dogs. I said nothing of Sheree. Our headlights cut through pitch-black roads, as we passed thick woods and silent houses. Even the night creatures had gone to sleep. I love the few minutes before dawn, its hush, the expectation of light. When my head doesn't throb and my lover doesn't cheat on me.

We got to the commercial dock of Three Mile Harbor before Steve. Yellow light from the street lamps pooled on a bleak rectangle of concrete and asphalt. Behind the pilings, only five fishing boats bobbed. Steve's trawler, *No Wife*, was among them. A flag on one of its ties flapped, depicting a fish whose fat belly was the American flag. Printed above the fish: U.S. PRISONER OF THE DEC. The Department of

Environmental Conservation and commercial fishermen had been at loggerheads for a long time.

To the left, on the other side of a small inlet, the marina was packed with yachts and sailboats. Jim's Pit was a long dark hulk above the boats. The white flags on its vast deck picked up lamplight. The wind was having an early morning run. Halyards slapped against masts. The sound was bell-like. The air was cool, the water choppy. The horizon was three different shades of dark—water, land, sky. The only other visitor was a red-billed tern balancing on the bow of a motorboat.

We heard the shifting of gears coming from the main road. Dmitri tensed beside me. For all his macho stance, he isn't comfortable carrying a gun.

Steve's pickup swung down onto the dock and parked in front of his thirty-eight-foot trawler. He dropped out, all six feet of muscled hunk, with Tanner right behind him. He was wearing jeans, laced-up boots, a plaid red shirt over a T-shirt, a red baseball cap. The surprise on his face was as deep as his tan.

"What are you doing here?" If Steve had been the one who bopped me on the head, I'd be the last person he expected to see.

"The early worm gets the bird," Dmitri offered.

Steve glanced up at the sky. "Getting rain's more likely."

He started hauling empty cartons from Stuart's Fish Market off the truck bed. Dmitri helped him, which meant his hands weren't free to reach for the gun, should it be needed. Sabrina jumped out of the car and wiggled. Tanner cut air with his tail. They seemed old friends.

Which left me playing the heavy. "What did you do with the empty Valium bottle?"

Steve hesitated for only a second, then continued his work. The cartons got dropped on the deck of his trawler. He jumped onboard, slipped into the cabin, turned on his engine, and whistled. Tanner gave Sabrina a reluctant last sniff and followed his master.

"Come on, Steve, we deserve an answer. Dmitri cracked three ribs in that cemetery!"

"You're crazy if you think that was me." Steve hoisted a rope off one of the piles.

I edged closer to the boat. "The paramedic saw you going through our glove compartment!"

Steve pushed his hands against the concrete slabs to propel the stern of the boat away from the dock.

A pile held one last line. I wrapped my arms around it to give Dmitri time to grab Sabrina and jump onboard. The boat rocked. Tanner barked. Dmitri stretched his hands out toward me. I let go of the pile and jumped, missing his hands. Slipping on the dewy slick of the deck, I landed on my ass. I felt it in my head.

Steve cast off the last line, retreated to the pilot-house, backed the trawler away from the dock, swept it around, and we were off, toward Gardiners Bay. On a fishing trip.

"You have a captive audience," I said, not moving from where I'd fallen. "Come on, Steve, we're all ears." The fish stench was taking care of my nose.

The noise of the engine was loud. From the cabin, there was no way he could hear me. I gave the contents of my head a few minutes to regroup and wedged myself into the cabin. There was no way Dmitri would have fit in there.

"Let's talk." I perched on top of a small refrigerator. Ahead of us the sun began to spill over the horizon, mopping the bottom of a pride of pink-edged clouds. In back of us a purple sky was bleaching to lavender.

"Hope you guys don't get seasick or sunstroke 'cause I'm not comin' back 'til about three."

I should have thought of that before I jumped. "Got any food?"

"Fluke. And butterfish. That's what I'm trawlin' today. Japanese love fluke, use it for sushi. This afternoon I'll take my haul to Stuart's Fish Market, he packs 'em for me. The fluke gets shipped to Japan in six hundred pound coffins."

I didn't like the sound of that.

"They'll bid from thirty dollars up to eighty dollars a pound for fluke," Steve said. "After my first pull I can feed you sushi. Wholesale. Seven dollars a pound. That's what I get paid for it."

I love raw fish, but not carved right off the animal. "Thanks, I'll pass." I readjusted my position on the refrigerator. This wasn't going to be a smooth ride. The water was baring lots of teeth.

"We're on Laurie's payroll. I don't know if she told you that."

A barely perceptible shake of his head. Dark brown eyes, a well-chiseled nose, full lips, a strong, tucked-up chin. His skin looked surprisingly soft for a seaman. Handsome with an honest look in those eyes.

Ted Bundy came to mind.

I checked on Dmitri. He was right behind me, darkening the doorway. "Forget the pill bottle for the moment. Why did Bud want to see you on Monday?"

"I could just as easily chuck you overboard as answer your questions."

I straightened up. "Dmitri's two hundred and fifty pounds of black-belt muscles!" Potato and hot dog was more like it.

One side of Steve's mouth twitched. "Not for long."

I gave Dmitri a closer look. He was holding onto the doorway, legs wide apart, face a pale tinge verging on green.

Bargaining time.

"I'm a lousy swimmer," I said. "Besides, Laurie would hate it if her detective team drowned."

"Laurie can't make up her mind how she feels about anything." He flicked on a switch. Voices crackled over the radio. "What about trust? You love someone, you trust 'em. That's the way it is in my book."

I stored that for later, for when I was going to deal with Sheree. "Both her parents have been killed," I said. "That doesn't make for clear thinking. Your attitude doesn't help."

Over the radio a Bill was complaining to a Pete about some North Carolina fishermen he'd met up with the day before. Steve preferred their conversation to ours. Something about their catching fluke and taking it back to North Carolina.

"How about letting me catch an answer, Steve?"

"I don't know what Bud was after." His tone was flat.

"What did he say over the phone?"

"No phone. He was waiting for me one morning. Just like you two. Saturday it was. I had two buddies with me, the same two who are talkin' now." His thumb indicated the radio. "Bud wanted me to give him fifteen minutes, just the two of us. I said no, he hadn't done anything for Laurie since the day she was born. He said he was going to come back on Monday, that it was something important."

Was he telling the truth? I had no way of knowing. "You don't have any idea what that 'something' might be?"

"Laurie, what else? Maybe he wanted me to know she was outta his will if she married me. That was Polly's favorite threat." Steve cut into the radio's ongoing conversation. "Hey, Bill, Pete, you know we're working to keep the seagulls alive, so quit beefin'. I got two of 'em riding with me on the gallows right this minute."

First coffins. Now gallows?

Steve clicked off the radio, his eyes chuckling. "I wasn't talking about you two."

"Sure."

"If your pal gets out of the way, you can see for yourself."

Dmitri heaved to one side. In the middle of the deck rose a tall metal frame in the shape of an A. It held up a drum around which a net was rolled.

"That's the gallows," Steve said. At the very top, next to an orange plastic basket, two seagulls were trying to keep their balance on one of the cross wires. "Meet Bill and Pete." Tanner and Sabrina aimed their snouts at them. "They got the same mean puss as those two on the radio."

The wake of the boat was a long orange line, as though we were towing the sun.

Dmitri blocked the view again. "What is laundry basket on top for?" He was having a hard time keeping his balance. The green tinge of his face had deepened. We'd left Three Mile Harbor and entered the more open waters of Gardiners Bay. The boat was rocking hard. I wished I'd brought a hunk of salty prosciutto, my mother's preventative cure for seasickness.

"Maybe I can use," Dmitri said.

Steve slipped on sunglasses and turned back to the bow. With the sun behind us, the cabin burst with light. "If you're going to throw up, do it overboard. Leeward." He pointed west. The wind was coming from the east.

Dmitri drew himself up to his maximum pride. "Pshaw! I think of basket maybe to sit on."

"Try the deck, it's clean," Steve said. "The basket lets the other boats know I'm towing, stops them from cutting across my net." Steve checked his loran to determine his geographical location. "Net costs three thousand dollars." Behind him a sign declared ZERO TOLERANCE. NO ILLEGAL DRUGS ONBOARD. Later he would tell me the Coast Guard came by about once a year to check for drugs and illegal fish.

"Bud had no backbone when it came to Polly," he said, "but he was an all-right guy. He wouldn't cut Laurie off. Not on account of me. When I got him in the dory a year ago, the day Polly died, I told him Laurie and I were going off to New Hope to get married. Actually, I asked him for her hand. It seemed right. He gave his blessing. Made me promise I'd put the past behind me. I did, but it sure in hell hasn't done me or Laurie any good."

"What did you do with the pill bottle?"

"I didn't ram into your Caddie and I didn't take the pills. I told Laurie enough times and I'm not repeating it."

"I have a witness."

"Not to me ramming your car, you don't. I wasn't even following you!" His voice got loud. The muscles in his neck stuck out. "I was driving home from delivering my fish and I saw your pink Caddie in the cemetery. I looked in the glove compartment because Laurie was real upset about the damn bottle and she's been upset about one thing or another all her life. If I can, I'll help her, but I won't hurt no one. If I didn't knock her mom's teeth out after what she did to Laurie last year, there's no way I'm going to hurt you two over an empty pill bottle. You got that?"

I nodded.

His neck muscles settled. He lifted his sunglasses up on his forehead and showed me his eyes, as if that would settle any doubts. No sparkle of deception, no glint of evil. They were nice, honest brown eyes. Just like two-timing Stan's.

"Okay, you didn't ram into us, but what happened to the bottle?"

Steve slid his sunglasses back down his nose. "When I looked in that glove compartment, the bottle was gone."

THIRTY-FOUR

I BELIEVED STEVE. There was no reason not to. At least while we were on his boat. Totally at his mercy.

Dmitri admitted he'd left the Caddie unlocked while he'd tried to convince Kelly Klein to give up her locks.

"Then someone stole the bottle while I was asleep in the backseat. They could have stolen my wallet too!" I might have made a big deal of this if Dmitri hadn't looked so miserable. Steve had slowed the boat down to set his net. We rolled like the bottle my mother uses to thin out her pasta dough. Rolled like the drum clanging to release 150 feet of net, its towlines thick with rubber "cookies" and the lead sweep that keeps the net at the bottom of the bay, thirty-seven feet down.

I rolled, remembered swaying in the air on Ferris wheels, and concentrated on how much fun I'd always thought it was. Dmitri rolled and searched heaven for release. Clouds were moving in.

"Fishin's better when it's not so calm," Steve said. He'd put on blue rubber gloves and looked ready to do the dishes. "Expect some rain. Weather's finally cooling off." Two metal doors large enough to shut a bank vault dropped in the water.

"What are those for?" I asked.

"The net's like a real long funnel fifty feet wide. The doors keep the mouth open. They're three hundred pounds each." The boat's wake was now marked by a wide double row of orange balloons.

We trawled for an hour, Steve careful to avoid the clusters of orange balls that floated in the water, signaling lobster pots. It started raining lightly. Dmitri finally threw up—leeward—and felt better. I got too sleepy to think. Steve offered me a Coke. Seagulls flew in, folded themselves on the water, bobbing in wait for Steve to push the switch that would pull in the net. The boat was doing three knots an hour, the speed determined by how fast fluke swim, Steve explained. "For bluefish I'd have to go up a knot."

When the Coke's caffeine kicked in, I asked questions about Polly and Bud and what Steve might have learned in the years he'd known and fought with them. He had seen them through angry eyes, he said, which made for bad sight. He told us how he had started fishing when he was nine years old, how at ten his grandmother bought him his first knee boots. How his great-grandfather taught him about the ocean. How his granddad would pay him ten dollars a day for skinning bottle fish. By the time he was twelve he'd saved up four hundred dollars and bought his first outboard motor.

Steve fished from March through December. To earn some money in the winter months he'd taken up carpentry. "No one has ever come across a rich fisherman, that's a saying. It's also the truth." His mother was still alive and begging him to stop, to get married and have a family. He didn't mention his father or the brother who had died before he was born.

He explained why radio Bill and Pete were complaining. "Nothing wrong with North Carolina. Everything's wrong with the New York DEC. We've got to throw back any fluke that doesn't make fourteen inches. In North Carolina it's twelve inches. They trawl fluke in our waters, take 'em back home where it's legal, then most of 'em end up in New York City sushi bars. Doesn't make sense. Worse with sea bass. The DEC promised they'd ease up on the restrictions once the population was up again. Now the waters are full of 'em and the DEC won't budge. And we got to measure everything. Fourteen inches for fluke, twelve for flounder. Twenty-four minimum, thirty-six max for sea bass. We've become goddamn seamstresses, not fishermen. And by the time you throw 'em back in the water, they're gull bait, so what's the point?" His neck muscles were working again. I took a short walk on the deck. Bill and Pete, the seagulls, were still with us on the gallows, feathers ruffling in the wind.

"This is good," Dmitri said, slicing the horizon

with a thick arm. His green tinge had retreated to his jowls. The rain had stopped. "When I was little I like to be sailor."

"And I wanted to be a ballet dancer, except my knees cracked on every plié."

Dmitri grinned. "Squashed dreams."

"I'm going to die out here," Steve said, coming up behind us.

I hoped not with us.

He'd stopped the engine, was stepping into waders, which he followed with an orange slicker and a thicker pair of rubber gloves. "You get stung by a jelly fish, you remember." He smiled. "Like first love."

Steve opened up the back of the boat and pulled a tall switch on one side of the gallows. The drum rolled. The clanging started. Tanner jumped up from his sleep, his tail erect. Sabrina did a low-bellied snake wiggle. The sky above us was suddenly covered with flapping wings and the squawk of seagulls. *Mangiare* time.

Steve's jaws tensed. My own stomach tightened. The haul. How good? How much money? We were playing roulette with nature. Suddenly I understood Steve and his buddies. They had gambling fever.

The net rolled in, wide bands of kelp trailing like wet packing paper. Seagulls made stabs at the crabs trying to wriggle free. The pocket at the end of the net poured silver ribbons of fish onto the deck.

Once the net was rolled up again, free of all fish, Steve ran to start the engine at a slow pace and came back to pull the switch. The drum noisily unfurled its net again. Meanwhile Sabrina sniffed at a flapping flounder, Tanner nudged her away, the gulls flapped, and the fish began to die. I wanted to throw them all back in the sea, but I also wanted to live. And become a vegetarian.

Steve shoveled the fish on a table screwed into the middle of the deck. He sorted and measured, using the marks etched on the wood surface. What he discarded he dropped in a plastic tub full of sea water. Lots of sea robins, too small flounder, weak fish, and horseshoe crabs that looked like leftover Nazi weapons.

"Couldn't you sort before you set the net again?" I asked.

"Takes too much time. Can't afford it." Steve kept the small, silvery butterfish with their pretty blue and pink cast and their mouths forming a perfect stunned O. He kept squid and one lobster that passed the measuring test. Steve worked fast, reserving his careful attention to the fluke, the flat, pale fish that would fetch the most money. The Japanese want their fish bled and weighing at least two pounds. Only six were large enough. With a small sharp knife, he made two small cuts along the backbone, where the main artery was, and threw them in a low vat of their own. Then he swept the discards out of the back of the boat. The gulls went wild. Sabrina barked. Steve hosed down the deck, removed his outerwear gear, and went back to the cabin.

It was while Steve sorted his second haul, with the seagulls screaming overhead, that he added one small tidbit that I stored away, along with the "love 'em, trust 'em" item. In that two-hour dory ride Bud and he had taken the day Polly died, Bud had talked about his work. He was thinking of getting out.

"Did he say why?" Maybe because the Chass\ Dayton merger hadn't gone through.

"No. He was real bitter, like something had gone bad. He talked a lot about greed. How it was ruining the world. I got mad. His wife was greedy, is what I told him, not me. I'd gotten it into my head he was making some city-slicker remark about my wanting The Pynes back for the money. He straightened me out. Even apologized. He was talking about work. Something wasn't right."

"Very true indeed," Dmitri said, stepping forward. "Mr. King, where you find this?" Dmitri swung out his arm. In his hand, a red thermos, its lid chipped.

"That belongs to Bud!" I gasped. "What's it doing here?"

Steve didn't flex a head muscle. That includes his mouth. Maybe he was concentrating on his work. The fluke were getting their arteries sliced.

"How did you get it, Steve?" I asked in a small voice as blood colored the white-pink flesh of some Japanese person's future lunch. "Why didn't you turn it in?"

"I find in cabin, under wheel," Dmitri volunteered, to keep the conversation going.

"That's evidence the police need," I said. "It'll prove the coffee was drugged. The same coffee that Bud let me drink. It proves his death wasn't suicide. You should have turned that in."

Steve stepped back and pulled the tall switch on one side of the gallows. The drum churned. He was pulling his net in. It had been towing for all of ten minutes.

"What's up?" My throat constricted for some reason—like fear.

"You're going home."

To my maker?

Dmitri moved in closer and rammed his fist down his pocket, where the gun was.

"I don't take 'shoulds.'" Steve's voice glinted in its sharpness. Tanner stood up, at attention, his head shifting from his boss to us. "Not from Polly Pynes, not from Bud, not from Laurie, and least of all from you."

In the thirty minutes it took for *No Wife* to reach Three Mile Harbor, Steve threatened us with only heavy, angry silence. After helping us out of the boat, Sabrina included, he asked Dmitri to hand back the thermos. We were safe on terra firma. We could have run with it. He knew it. We knew it.

"It's not yours to give to anyone," Steve said. His anger had died down with the wind.

"Finders, keepers?" I suggested.

"A man needs to be believed. God damn it, trust! That's all I want. If you think I'm a killer, then keep the damn thing. Call the police. I don't give a shit." He walked back to the pilothouse.

Steve was asking for an act of faith. Something Laurie hadn't given him. Maybe faith is what Stan needed too.

"Give him the thermos, Dmitri." Faith was easier with Steve.

"You crazy?"

"Maybe not." I took the thermos from Dmitri. "Steve, it's yours," I called out. My broken heart wanted to believe Steve loved Laurie too much to harm her parents.

Steve walked back to the side of the trawler. He took his sunglasses off and thanked me. His eyes smiled. They still looked honest. "Now let's see if you two are Jonahs." He pushed himself off.

"What does 'Jonah' mean?" Dmitri asked as the *No Wife* turned around in the harbor.

"Bad luck. Jonah went to the bottom of the sea."

THIRTY-FIVE

I DREAMED ABOUT BAD LUCK all the way into Manhattan: Steve's net hauling up bands of black leather being shredded by an army of horseshoe crabs. Dick Knight floating up as naked and as white as fluke. A dead woman in the last of the haul.

The body was mine. And Stan was waiting by the fish table, knife in rubber-gloved hand, ready to cut arteries.

"A man needs to be believed."

I woke up thrashing in the darkness of the Midtown Tunnel. I smelled the sea. Salt, fish, and water. The half-liter bottle of designer water the Jitney included in its forty-dollar roundtrip fare was dripping off my lap. The salt was in my hair, my skin. The fish smell all over me, like a perfume sprayed from the attacking aisles of Bloomingdale's.

I got out at the first stop, Third Avenue and Thirty-seventh Street, nearest to HH&H Advertising. It had rained heavily during the night. The street gleamed with puddles. I needed to change out of my fishing clothes, but I needed Gregory and his advertising talents even more. Or let's say I wasn't ready to walk into the bedroom I shared with my lover.

I'd called Gregory while Dmitri raced to get me to the nine-thirty Jitney. We'd made a date for a late lunch at Coffee Shop.

In ten years the place had become a favorite with an arty downtown crowd that had barely outgrown pimples. The food ranged from potato latkes to *feijoada*, a thick black-bean stew heaped with sausage, pork, bacon, and beef, which is the national dish of Brazil. I liked the place for its sidewalk tables overlooking the elms and sycamores of Union Square Park, which had been redeemed from the drug pushers and was now boasting the best farmers' market in the city. On market days you can gaze across the street and watch the happy exchange of food and flowers. Thursday isn't a market day, but the all-night rain had cleaned the city trees to spring green. The temperature had dropped to a tolerable eighty-seven degrees. The clouds had gone out to sea and our patch of sky was as blue and shiny as bathroom tiles.

A young waitress in hotpants with a shaved head showed us to our table. Gregory ordered a sugar-rimmed *Cachaça* shooter—a Brazilian version of a daiquiri. I ordered a Diet Coke.

"After I got your message I called Ross in California," Gregory said. "He used to work with us. Travel accounts. 'Come to Jamaica and feel all right,' kind of thing. He's before your time." Gregory squinted at me. He'd chosen the sunny seat. He's in his late forties. Transparent blue eyes, a baby's complexion, fair hair going gray, the body of a jockey, and the best of friends. If I told him about Sheree I'd start crying. Tears for Sale. Hundred Percent Organic Guaranteed. Get 'em by the Liter. I concentrated on the case.

"What's Ross know?"

"He got fired from Chass\Dayton three months ago."

"You know the best people."

Gregory sat back and folded his arms, his subtle way of telling me to shut up. I did. Our waitress brought our drinks. From an oversized menu Gregory ordered *Sopa de Peixe Bahia*, a seafood chowder with tomatoes, garlic, and saffron. I went for *Pastel de Camarao*, dumplings filled with spicy shrimp and seasonings. We would share.

"June a year ago, Chass\Dayton made an offer for WSK." He edged to the rim of his seat and took a lick of sugar from his glass. "They'd buy WSK for sixty million dollars in Chass\Dayton shares, what's more they'd help the company with a twenty million booster shot, the three WSK partners would retain their positions for a guaranteed five years, and the agency would assume the name of Chass\Dayton, WSK East."

"Pity the phone operator." I sank my teeth into a round soft roll with spikes of fragrant dill. "Why didn't the merger go through? Sounds like a great offer."

The waitress served our food.

For the next five minutes Gregory opened his mouth only to eat. My dumplings were moist, the shrimp crunchy. Gregory's chowder was a bowl of sun and sea memories. We let our senses take over.

I finished my plate before he did. "Talk or I'll scream."

"You're back in New York. Who's going to notice?" Gregory smiled. "Am I getting a badge for all this work? Something big with embossed gold letters like the latest bestsellers?" He lifted his chin toward the northern edge of the park, at the newly renovated redbrick building that was now a Barnes & Noble Superstore. A few years back Gregory had thought of leaving the ad business and opening up a bookshop. Now he knew better. "Detective vice president. That's what I want my title to be."

"You've got it. I'll even pay for lunch. Come on, Gregory, what did Ross tell you?"

"Merger didn't go through because Bud Warren nixed it."

I jerked up. "Why would Bud say no?"

"The man has scruples. His fax read 'There has to be an end to greed. For WSK I'm it.'"

"Didn't the other two partners have enough shares between them to outvote Bud?"

"WSK had to deliver all the shares. If one share was missing, no deal. Chass\Dayton was protecting itself from possible lawsuits. What you may find even more interesting is that a week before Ross got fired the acquisition buzz started going again. This time it was East calling West. Kennelly was eager to deal. Either Warren changed his mind—"

"Or he got killed."

I ordered double espresso for both of us. "When I went over to WSK, gold rush fever was palpable. The merger is going through."

"Sunny California is taking over. What do they call the Hamptons now? Hollywood east? Did you schmooze with Spielberg while you were out there?"

I opened my eyes wide. "Didn't I tell you? He's cast me in his most intelligent female role yet. A sexy shower scene with rats for water." The man behind Gregory shivered.

"What did you use for dress rehearsal? Fish?"

"I took a trip on a trawler this morning."

"You okay?" Gregory dropped his credit card on the table.

I substituted it with mine. "I'm off men." Then I grinned. "Except you."

"You need another favor."

I nodded and showed him the drawing pad I'd bought on the way down. After going into a dog shop and spending fifty dollars on a collar, leash, and toys for Sabrina.

"What am I supposed to do with this?" Gregory asked. He was HH&H's in-house illustrator. The nine-by-twelve pad I handed him was a Strathmore, an exact replica of the one I'd found in the bed at Bud's house. The black magic marker was the brand I'd seen in Bud's night table drawer.

"Bud had an idiosyncratic drawing style, I hear."

Gregory smiled. "At Parsons School of Design we called him Slash-Dash-Cash."

"Imitate that style, *per favore*." Gregory can do Picasso when he wants to. "A few sketches. Sport4Life is the client."

"Which product?"

"Do you know their latest? Neither do I. Pick one you like. No cash. Just my undying affection."

"I'll settle for a plate of pasta." He started sketching. What I love about Gregory is that he doesn't ask intrusive questions, such as "Why the hell do you need this?"

THIRTY-SIX

"WHERE DID YOU FIND THIS?" Charlene was leafing through the drawing pad Gregory had half-filled with Bud Warren–like slashes and dashes. She'd let me come up to her office with great reluctance.

"I found it under the picnic table that's in front of the cottage I'm renting. Bud used to come over for coffee in the morning." Stop there, Simona. Too much explaining is the liar's defeat.

"It's got no sun damage." The fists she had for cheekbones sagged at a new thought. "You're not playing detective, are you? I don't have time for a lot of questions again."

"Not a one." God, woman, I need a break. "The pad was in a plastic bag. I thought Mr. Kennelly would want to see it. You know how it is. Maybe that pad's got another Bud Warren winner for the new product. Is he around?"

"That's a question."

I slapped my hand over my mouth. Charlene

slapped the pad shut and dropped it in her drawer. "He's not coming back until Monday." She stood up and tried to hitch a smile. It slipped off.

"You've had a rough week," I said. "That's a statement."

"Yeah, I guess I have." With her boss away in the Hamptons, Charlene had downplayed the Power of Color theme by wearing blue jeans, a plain white cotton sweater, and four-inch black heels. Her hair was still five-alarm-fire red. "Thanks for dropping it by. Now I got work to do."

"Me, too. Keep warm." The temperature of the place was sub-zero. I walked down the corridor, knowing her eyes were following me. Halfway to the elevator I slipped my hand in my pocket and palmed Lester's keys. I turned back. "Excuse the question, but where's the ladies' room?"

I got lucky. Charlene's phone rang. She picked it up and nodded to me. "Good afternoon." She pointed a forefinger down the corridor, then jerked her thumb left. "Mr. Dayton, how can I help you?"

Mr. Dayton of Chass\Dayton? I mouthed a thank-you and rushed down the corridor as though I might not make it to my destination in time. I wanted to get to that copy room while the Olympian God of California Advertising kept Charlene in his thrall.

Most of the offices were empty. It was four o'clock on a Thursday afternoon in August with the boss away. Not too many people around who would need the copier. I walked past the women's bathroom. The file room was empty. The sign still warned me not to copy body parts. I walked in, lifted up the top of the copy machine, and dropped the crossword puzzle page of the *New York Times* facedown on the glass as though I were ready to make a copy. That was my cover should anyone come in. He or she would, I hoped, assume that I belonged here. The copier doesn't work without a code.

My luck held out. The file drawer I was looking for was wedged behind the door. No one would spot me while I searched. The small key on Lester's key chain didn't fit, but the third Yale key did. I looked through the P file drawer for Partners. Nothing. I tried K for Kennelly, W for Warren. No Partners' Agreement file anywhere. My armpits sweated, stomach flipped, heart heaved, and my breath froze in my mouth. I opened the S drawer, riffled through looking for Shepard, the third partner. I found the Shareholders file first. I lifted the file and dropped it in the Pet Dreams bag. No one saw me.

I came up for air next door, in the sanctity of the ladies' room. The smell of soap and the sheen of white tiles greeted me. I have always liked the bathroom. In my family it is known as *il pensatoio*, the thinking parlor. When my marriage got bad it also became a reading room, a refuge. I was going to end up doing a bit of both.

I slipped into the first stall, locked the door, and sat down. I quickly found what I wanted. A Shareholders' Agreement. I flipped through the pages. Bud had gotten special treatment. He owned "four hundred shares of no-par common stock in the Company, representing forty percent (40%) of the total issued and outstanding shares . . ."

That's how Kennelly and Shepard had convinced Bud to leave Doyle Dane Bernbach.

"You okay?"

I jumped. Charlene.

"I'll be out in a minute." I hoped she hadn't heard the rustle of paper.

"You've been in there an awful long time."

"I ate *feijoada*, bean stew."

The bathroom door snapped shut. I went back to thinking. A man who wasn't into greed demanding a bigger share didn't make much sense. Unless it was Polly who had argued for more. She who held such sway over her husband, who probably dictated his every move until she got bored by his passivity and turned him out.

I went back to reading. My eyes started to droop at the legalese until I hit page seven.

"In the case of William Morris Warren's death, the Company shall purchase and the representative of the deceased shall sell to the Company three hundred shares of the stock owned by the deceased. The remaining one hundred shares will be held by William Morris Warren's heirs."

Bud didn't want the merger; the merger fell through. At that point the third partner had sold his interest back to his two partners and gone to worship the sun in the Caribbean. A year later Bud died. The merger was back on. Now Laurie had the power to stop the merger, assuming she was Bud's beneficiary. Was she in danger?

Lester Kennelly stood to make eighteen million dollars plus another nine million from his half of Shepard's share. That wasn't all.

If Lester managed to buy Bud's shares from Laurie before the deal went through, their value would be lower and he'd make more millions!

How about that as a motive for murder?

But why kill Polly?

The bathroom door clicked open. Charlene was back. This time I expected bared fangs. I quickly flushed the toilet and stuffed the file in my Pet Dreams bag.

"It's kind of weird, don't you think?" It was a young, throaty voice, not Charlene.

"Whatcha mean?" Another young voice.

"Look at the ad. Read the copy. I mean the guy died. He must have had some kinda feeling it was gonna happen. So, did Bob call you or what?"

I came out of my stall, bag safely hooked on my shoulder. The talking stopped. The two women peeked at me, one with a lipstick in midair. They were in their early twenties, wearing jeans, T-shirts, had the same winged hair, acrylic nails, and hoop earrings. They probably came from Traffic, the department in charge of walking a print ad through its various approval stages before sending it off to the selected media. I gave them a quick smile as if to say it's okay, I work here too. The comp—a facsimile of the final ad—was leaning against the tiled wall, a four-by-two-foot piece of cardboard covered by a sheet of vellum.

I washed my hands. "That's got to be Bud's ad for Sport4Life?" My voice was brisk. "The client's been screaming for it. Mind if I take a peek?"

The woman with the lipstick nodded. The other woman's eyebrows slowly formed a frown. She wasn't buying.

I dried my hands on my hips, hunched down, and lifted the vellum carefully. "This looks great." The stenciled headline read "Not a Fashion Statement." Below the headline, magazine cutouts of fifteen to twenty people had been pasted onto a blown-up photo of Gardiner's Bay. The white windmill was in full view. Young and old, men and women cutouts in various fashions seemed to be walking on water. The top half of their bodies had been painted over with Sport4Life's latest product: a Day-Glo yellow life vest.

A line of copy ran along the bottom of the ad. "A vest for life. We'd like you to keep yours." Followed by Bud's famous tag line. "Sport4Life Saves Lives."

"Are you a new ad exec?" Doubting Thomasina finally asked.

"New? I wish." I let the vellum drop back over the ad and got up quickly. Advertising is a paranoid business. You don't let strangers see an ad that hasn't run yet. "They're going to love this. Thanks." Time to leave. Time to ask Charlene another question. I swung the door open, but didn't make it out. The guard dog with the red hair had come back.

"You still here?" Her voice could have split a brick. She eyed the covered ad, cheekbones jiggling like fists warming up. The two women disappeared inside the stalls. I pushed past her, hesitating only a fraction of a second when I passed the copy room. I would have to come up with some creative way of returning the Shareholders' Agreement file. *Domani*, as Scarlett would say.

"Don't worry, they wouldn't show it to me." I headed to the elevators with false purpose in my stride.

Charlene hounded at my heels. "You had no business asking." She pushed the button for me. The elevator opened. I didn't take it. "The Sport4Life life vest sample," I said, "where is it?"

She shook her hair, brandishing fire. "I don't have time for this."

"What if Bud was wearing the sample the last morning he went out? Maybe something was wrong with it. That would explain why he took his life vest off."

Charlene's eyes widened in alarm. "Sport4Life had nothing to do with Bud's death! The sample's locked up in Lester's office."

"Could you make sure?"

She hesitated.

"I'll wait here." I decided against a dash to the copy room. I'd never make it.

"No, you come with me," she said.

"More than happy." That way she couldn't lie.

We marched into Lester's California Colors

suite presided over by the David Hockney pool. Charlene jangled keys and opened a long cabinet underneath the VCR. It was empty.

"I put it here myself." There was panic in her voice.

"When?"

"Friday morning, that's when it came. Lester was on his way out to the Hamptons. I showed it to him. I even put it on, then he asked me to lock it up in here."

"He could have moved it."

She tried all the cabinets, the closet, Lester's bathroom. She even opened drawers designed to hold nothing more than a pad and pencil.

The life vest was gone and I had the information I needed.

"He probably took it with him." I took pity on Charlene. "What color is it?"

"Yellow. They're only going to make them in yellow."

I gave her a smile. "Sport4Life is in the clear. Bud's vest was red."

THIRTY-SEVEN

BACK IN MY APARTMENT, I took a long shower, then called Laurie. She'd just come back from the lawyer. "Are you Bud's beneficiary?"

"I am now."

"Don't sell your WSK stock."

"Lester's already called in a guy to assess the value," Laurie said. "He wants to take care of it tomorrow. I told him he can have all of Dad's shares."

"Stall."

"Why?"

"I just want to make sure you get a fair deal." I told her about the merger. "It's just too soon after Bud's death. No one is thinking rationally, including Lester. Let the grief settle. You might want to keep those hundred shares."

"I guess you're right." She sounded relieved.

"Everything else okay?"

"I found out Dad never changed his will after the divorce."

"What?"

"Mother was still the main beneficiary. He didn't want to admit the divorce had happened. That's what Dad had told Lester."

I let that sink in slowly. "What about Rebecca?"

"Dad added one codicil. He left her his house. Isn't that great? Even half burned down it's worth a lot of money. They were old friends, I discovered. She doesn't want to accept the house. Something about it being forty-seven years too late. She wouldn't tell me what that meant. Do you know?"

"Nope."

"Steve wants to talk to me."

About Bud's red thermos, I hoped, among other things. "Hear him out, keep an open mind, and don't worry about having too much money. You can always give it to charity. Does anyone besides the lawyer know that your father hadn't changed his will after the divorce?"

"I don't know. Why?"

I didn't answer her. "I'll be back tomorrow morning. And don't worry. We'll get to the truth." *And you're going to hate it.*

If Bud had never changed his will after the divorce, it meant that if Polly had outlived Bud, she would have been able to keep a hundred WSK shares and foil the Chass\Dayton merger. Lester knew Bud didn't accept his divorce, but did he know about the will?

I walked into the bedroom. It had been a long time since I'd slept. The double bed looked foreign, lumpy. I walked out. The thought of Sheree made me remember that I hadn't picked up the mail. Our downstairs neighbor was doing it while we were away. I went downstairs, mumbled thanks and a few platitudes, turned down a drink, and crawled back upstairs.

I threw the mail on the coffee table in the living room and stretched out on the couch. I tried to sleep. Couldn't do it. Those unopened letters were whispering. I sat up and picked a blue airmail envelope from the pile. I favor those. They mean either old friends or my parents. This time it was Mamma. Her health was fine. My father was complaining about his arthritis, but he was cleaning his lunch and dinner plate so it couldn't be that bad, could it? When was I going to bring Stan to Rome so they could meet him? Was there anything special I wanted for my fortieth birthday? When were we going to get married?

My birthday wasn't for another seven months.

I tossed the letter aside and went hunting. I came up with fistfuls of junk mail and a few bills. No missive from Sheree. Which somehow didn't help. I trudged over to the kitchen and examined cabinets and the refrigerator. Eating would make me sleepy. And happier. My search yielded short pasta, Italian canned tuna fish (tastier than American), a jar of capers, an onion, red pepper flakes, and a can of flat anchovies. I was in business. I'd miss the parsley but I was too tired to go down to the Korean deli to get it.

I cooked. While the pasta water worked up to a

boil, I sautéed chopped onions in half a tablespoon of olive oil, mixed the tuna with a tablespoon of capers and an anchovy fillet, and thought of the missing life vest.

I was pretty sure that I now had the MO of Bud's murder. On Sunday morning Bud had glanced at his watch and said "I gotta go." He was going to exercise in the bay, but also going to meet someone—Lester and the new yellow Sport4Life vest.

Sunday had been the third morning in a row blanketed by a fog. The continued excessive heat had guaranteed it. A perfect time to carry out the murder. The two men met in the water. From his kayak, Lester extended the vest. "Come on, take that old smelly vest off. Try this on. Tell me how it fits."

Bud took off his vest. Lester came closer, as if to help him with it. Instead, he pulled his partner off his rowing machine. Groggy from his spiked coffee, Bud put up little resistance.

Eating had made me sleepy. I lay down on the couch, closed my eyes, and went off for an hour. No dreams. I woke up thirsty. Across the street a row of windows was blazing with the sunset. I thought of the Pine Barrens fire, now thankfully over. I thought of Bud's house burning. Why? Lots of questions had no answers. Why had Polly been killed? Did Lester kill her? Did Bud? Where was I going to get the hard evidence to prove Lester killed Bud? And who the hell was Sheree?

I grabbed the phone and called Stan's precinct. Raf had gone out for pizza.

"You want him to call you back?" asked Tony Chibas, detective second-grade, who'd come to our surprise party and polished off four large pizzas on his own. Mas Tony, he calls himself. More Tony. He likes nicknames. Stan Greenhouse is El Verde. I'm La Romana.

"I don't know, Tony." Did I want to know? I wasn't sure. I needed more sleep. "Maybe you can help with some of this. Blue magnet, that's a code name for one of your cases, right?"

Tony laughed, the kind of laugh that eats the air in a room. "No, blue magnet's cop talk. Stands for a police groupie."

"A groupie?"

"Yeah, someone who's crazy about cops. Ehi, La Romana, you want him to call you back?"

"No." I hung up. Raf knew Stan was having an affair for sure. Had to, Stan being his partner. Did the rest of the precinct know?

I showered again. I studied a city map, then the subway map. I opened my closet and debated between sexy and scary. Chose a combo. My old black cotton jacket with the outdated power shoulders, a real short white skirt. Heavy eyeliner with an upward tilt. Darkened eyebrows. Charlene red lipstick. I teased my hair out, sharpened my nail stubs, licked my teeth clean, and practiced a Samurai scowl. Blue magnet my *culo!* I was ready for war.

When I reached the front door, the phone rang. Probably Raf, getting back to me. Or Stan. I slammed the door shut.

THIRTY-EIGHT

THE NUMBER ONE TRAIN made it to the northern tip of Manhattan, Washington Heights, in twenty-five minutes. Much too fast for the way I felt. My tuna pasta was doing the twist by now. Maybe this wasn't really such a great idea. What was I going to say to Sheree, "Get off my man or I'll chop your head off"? Stan wasn't my possession, was he? I mean, if he wanted to walk, be my guest. But so far he hadn't. Which meant he wanted both appetizer and main course.

Not acceptable.

I stepped out of the heat of the subway onto the street. The day was cooling down. The place looked friendly and thriving—181st Street was crammed with store awnings of all colors and languages. What had once been a predominantly Irish community had become, in the last thirty years, an ethnic mine-strone. The shops were closed, the city lights had been turned on. Kids pooled around the fast food stores. Older folks eddied along the street alone or in couples. Across the street was the 1909 building that housed the Collegiate Church, a reform Protestant Dutch congregation whose members had emigrated to Manhattan when it was still a Dutch colony.

Sheree lived a block and a half away, in a red-brick building across the street from a park. Spotting a marble monument at the entrance to the park, I was seized by a sudden urge for cultural enlightenment. After all, I wasn't likely to come back up here any time soon.

It was called Bennett Park. The monument told me I was standing on what had once been the site of Fort Washington, built in the summer of 1776. "Taken by the British after a heroic defense."

My head nodded. I could relate to "heroic defense."

"Repossessed by the Americans." Hurray!

"Simone?"

I spun around.

A frizzy blonde, thin as a weed, was walking down the steps of the park, her German shepherd aimed at me.

"Simona," I corrected, buying time. Where did I know her from?

"I came to your surprise party for Stan's promotion, remember? It was fun." The dog scanned me for smells, caught Sabrina's behind my knee, and stayed there. His nose was cool. The blonde smiled. Good, straight teeth. A pretty woman who had fine skin that was drying out in tiny lines. She was somewhere in the high end of thirty. Her smile progressed into staccato bursts of laughter, like a violin being plucked. That's when I remembered. She'd laughed when Tina turned down Raf's proposal in front of all his friends. Tina had told her to stick it somewhere private.

"You're Tony Chibas's girlfriend," I said. Linda was her name. She was a nurse at Columbia Presbyterian.

"Yeah, Mas Tony." She wiggled her cute nose. "I was so embarrassed when he ate all the pizza."

"No problem. I ordered more." If she dated Tony, maybe . . . "Do you know Sheree Debuskey? At the precinct they call her a blue magnet. Tony told me that means someone who's really into the NYPD. Did you ever meet her?"

She got busy with her dog's leash. "What if I did?"

Bingo. "What's she like, Linda? I need to talk to her about something important and I have no idea how to handle it."

Linda pointed. "She lives over in that building."

"Nice woman?"

"A kitten." Her gray eyes turned into ice balls. "What do you have to talk to her about?"

I gave her dog a pat on the head. He was back to sniffing. My feet this time. "That's sort of private. Thanks, Linda. Maybe you and Tony can come over for dinner sometime. I'll make sure there's enough food." I waved and crossed the street. The dog was all for going after me. Linda held him back.

"Smits, stay!" she commanded. "You hear me, Smits? Stay, you dumb dog!"

I stopped below the two stone lions guarding the entrance of Sheree's building. Linda was still pulling the dog back.

"Smits like in Jimmy Smits?" I called over. "The star of *NYPD Blue?*"

Linda nodded. The German shepherd barked and yanked at his leash. I waited for a car to pass and crossed back over to the park side. I'd remembered something.

"Linda," I said. "That's a nickname, isn't it?"

She licked her lower lip. "It means 'pretty' in Spanish."

"Your real name's Sheree."

Her face puckered. "In French that means 'dearest.'"

"Wrong spelling." I took the letter out, waved it under her nose, and asked, not too gently, "How long has this been going on?"

She smirked. Women on the defensive can be real jerks. "Since the party."

"Did he say he loved you?"

She lifted her hair, aired her neck out, then let her hair drop. "No, it's a sex thing."

That's how it started out with me too.

"I don't fall in love too easy," she added, as if that would be some consolation. I could help her fall. On that pert little nose of hers.

"Does Tony know?"

"He'd snap me in two like a taco. So don't go

telling him, okay?" Her head bobbed like a nervous knee. "What's this got to do with you anyway?"

"It just so happens I love the bastard!"

Her eyes popped. "You're havin' it on with him too? I can't believe the three-timin'—"

"Three-timing?" I sat her down after that, on the steps to Bennett Park. She explained, I listened. At the end, it made an *Alice Through the Looking Glass* sort of sense.

THIRTY-NINE

I JUMPED TO CONCLUSIONS," I told Stan over the phone. He'd been trying to reach me all day. I was back home, curled up on his side of the bed, on the hard mattress that I'd finally convinced him to accept. Wonderful, welcoming bed. He'd come down from the mountains.

"I love you, Sim, and I miss you." His voice sounded light, cheerful.

"Blue maggots, cherries. You in a three-month sulk, Raf calling, Billie calling. I got very confused. And what does the mayor want?"

"I'll tell you when I get home."

"Promise?"

Stan laughed, reminding me of the rush of a waterfall on a hot day. "I promise I'll open up my heart to you and talk you into sweet dreams. Just stay away from that Jim guy until I get back."

I did not confess.

❂   ❂   ❂

I called Dmitri. "We looked at it the wrong way. The '*corazón*' in Sheree's letter should have tipped me off. Sheree's not Spanish and neither is Stan."

"You are talking what?"

"I'm talking that the man Sheree is bedding on the sly is Raf Garcia."

"Raf in love with Tina! He even propose to her in front of all his buddies."

"Raf's angry and humiliated. He wants to pay Tina back. That's why he's sneaking around with Sheree. Without Tina knowing, of course. Sheree made me call Raf, and he confirmed her story." After which I'd told Raf he was an *idiota* and that Tina's view—that a marriage proposal made out of the blue in front of a peer group presupposes an affirmative answer which in turn makes the proposal another example of male hubris and patronization—was right on.

"Then why Sheree send letter to Stan?" Dmitri's tone was skeptical.

"Both Tina and Tony are jealous." I eyed my bedroom, with its off-white walls. It gleamed, as if newly washed, despite the overdue spring cleaning. I guess my eyes were sparkling. "Sheree thinks letters are sexy, especially if forbidden. Except she couldn't write to Raf at the precinct because of Tony, and Tina has the key to Raf's mailbox so Sheree picked Raf's partner."

"How Stan know love words not for him?"

"Sheree assumed Raf had told Stan about the affair. Besides, she'd put the letter inside a second envelope with Raf's name on it." I remembered Willie in the cottage sweeping up litter from the broken garbage bag. He'd retrieved one envelope, but not the rest. No wonder Stan had looked under the sofa. He didn't want me to find out that Raf was cheating on Tina.

"All is good on personal life." Dmitri sounded miffed, probably because he'd worried about me for nothing. I was feeling foolish myself. And immensely relieved.

"All is good," I repeated. Or soon would be. "I looked into the WSK partners' agreement." I told Dmitri what I'd discovered. "The problem is that we don't have any hard evidence."

"Maybe we get." A loud sniff hit my ear.

"Okay, what do you have?"

"Much informations. First, twelve white roses waiting for you. Card says 'Can we meet again tonight?' From Jim. What happen while I sleep?"

"Let's stick to the case."

"All right." The voice was cool. "Rebecca is back on suspect list. She inherit—"

"Laurie told me already. And there's a good reason for Rebecca inheriting that house. What else?"

"Mike and Phil"—his Russian friends who worked as bodyguards for Ron Perelman—"they come back from cruise. They never meet Mrs. Lawrence III or Uma"—a heavy pause of disappointment, then—"but I do not stop looking." He blew his nose into the phone.

"Before I forget, did you come across a bright yellow life vest at the Kennellys'?"

"In garage. With Jaguar, Volvo, motorboat, two canoes, and five kayaks. Kennellys are two, what they need five for?"

"The guests."

"Not to mind. I have now most important informations. Remember phone numbers you ask me to check that Bud make before he die?"

"Yes, I gave you four numbers. You hit the jackpot?"

"He call Bookhampton store, Lilco, New York State Liquor Authority, and—"

"The State Liquor Authority? Why?"

"No one know, but not important. Fourth call is ball in basket. We are no longer stricken by ignorance. Appointment Bud make with Steve is nothing." Another pause. This one to breathe, to elicit suspense.

I said, "I just read the best Russian joke in the OpEd page of the *Times*. In today's Russia, what's—"

"On last Thursday, Bud make call and set up Monday appointment that change life of killer forever." The source dried up again.

I leaned back on the pillow, stretched out my feet, took a loud sip of my Coke. "What's the difference between an optimist and a pessimist?" I was feeling great.

Dmitri asked, "You want to know who Bud call?"

"You want to get paid?"

"Criminal Investigation Division of Internal Revenue Service."

I snapped up. "Bud was going to report someone!"

"To special agent Weikart. Very nice for IRS man."

"Go on!"

"Bud tell him he have physical evidence of company's fiscal irregularity. Mr. Weikart set up appointment for Monday afternoon. He did not say what company."

"WSK, who else? Lester's in charge of finance; he's been doctoring the books. If Chass\Dayton ever found out, *ciao-ciao* sixty million. What else did Bud tell Weikart?"

"That's it."

"No names?"

"No. I ask if he not get suspicious when Bud Warren not show up. He say it happen all the time. He's too busy to follow up."

"Bud Warren's death was splashed all over the papers!"

"The Warren who made appointment did not give first name or address. There are two hundred and eleven Warrens in Manhattan phone book alone. I count."

"Good job, Dmitri. Now we know why Bud's house was set on fire."

Fingers snapped in my ear. "Physical evidence was inside."

"That's what Lester thought."

"But he not sure. That's why he still is looking."

"As my mother would say, you've hit the nose where it hurts."

"The Russian joke, how does it end?"

"I forgot."

FORTY

By LATE FRIDAY MORNING I was back in the Hamptons along with half the population of Manhattan. Dmitri and I picked up coffee at Dreesen's while Sabrina stayed sprawled across the backseat, belly ready to deliver at any moment. We stored towels next to her, bought her designer water, and headed for Main Beach. The temperature had cooled as promised, the sky was a clear blue dome. The ocean rolled white foam. The beach was blanketed with humans roasting in oil. What was missing was garlic and rosemary. The salt was in the air.

We got out of the car with our coffee and leaned on the hood. "Look at Kat's Eye," I said and tossed *Dan's Paper* at Dmitri. I'd picked it up at my local supermarket to keep me entertained on the ride out. When I'd hit page forty-three I started fuming. "Look at the pictures of the luncheon for the Bide-A-Wee animal shelter."

"Everyone bring pets and funny hats."

I pointed to a photo of a tall woman half hidden by a sombrero. "Look at what she's holding."

"Uma!"

"The furless wonder. That's Mrs. Reed Lawrence III, the caption says so, and that luncheon was last Saturday. Dick Knight told me the cat had disappeared two weeks ago. He's a liar and a fink." I reached inside the car window for the phone.

"Don't tell him we know who killer is," Dmitri said.

I dialed Knight's number in Queens. "That dumb I'm not." His answering machine picked up. I reiterated my earlier message with anger this time. "Listen, Knight, if you're thinking of blackmailing the killer, you're the dumbest dick I ever laid eyes on, and I've seen a lot of dumb—" Dmitri's finger pressed down on the OFF button.

I glared at him, my mouth open and eager to launch more insults. He tilted his great big bearlike head down. At my feet, I had an audience of two. In the five-year-old range. Both girls. I smiled. "I'm rehearsing for a movie."

The smaller of the two frowned. "Not Jane Austen."

I mentioned Disney. They lost interest. I dropped into the car and called Knight's machine back. "This is what I think." I kept my voice low. "The killer hired you to keep a watch on us." I'd walked into Lester's office on Monday and announced my intentions. Lester had let me look at the file, then he'd probably called Knight and set up the Uma story. He probably knew the Lawrences from the Hamptons' party circuit. "Maybe he told you to discourage us a little. So you borrowed a car and bumped us into the cemetery as a gentle reminder of where we might end up if we didn't butt out."

Dmitri nudged me from the backseat. He was giving Sabrina a rubdown. "Valium bottle?"

"You probably stole the bottle too. Under orders or maybe you thought you'd get something on the killer. Please stop being dumb. Go to the police or you'll end up dead." I hung up and gave Sabrina an encouraging pat.

Dmitri moved up into the driver's seat. "We are in same soup with Knight."

"We're no threat to Lester unless we get hard evidence. If we do, we'll be careful." I buckled his seat belt. "Let's find out what happened to Bud's scull contraption."

Dmitri pocketed the car key and crossed his arms.

"Hey, management doesn't go on strike. Come on, that scull could be important. Let's go."

Dmitri didn't budge. "Laurie not want it. Too much reminder of Bud. That's why Steve keep thermos. Not to make Laurie cry."

"Sweet. So where's the scull?"

The Stalin mustache curled at the ends. "I make deal."

I told him the end of the Russian joke.

❂   ❂   ❂

At Bud's house the smell of smoke still lingered. We parked in the shade of an old half-scorched elm. Sabrina decided to stay put. We kept the windows down for air. "Bark if you need us," I said. Dmitri fussed with her ears. She panted without lifting her head, her lips pushed back into a grim smile. I checked the backseat for a large damp spot. Found none. She still had time.

We left Sabrina and walked on a pebble path past the burned-out half of the house. Black licks from the fire fanned out from the boarded-up windows. The bushes along the path were charred skeletons. Beyond the line of fire the garden was crowded by overgrown rhododendrons, azaleas, and wild roses. At the back of the house, a thin blackened trail led to a short concrete dock. The arsonist had come from the water, leaking gasoline along the way. Once the fire had started, it had followed the path back down to the water.

Accabonac Creek opened its sun-filled skirt before our eyes. To the left, the thick trees of the Merrill Sanctuary where Sabrina had been tied and abandoned. To the right, Jackson Pollock's farmhouse, where Polly had drifted up dead. Straight ahead of us the Sad Hatter sat cross-legged at the end of the dock. He was wearing his new jeans and a frayed seersucker jacket. His wool seaman's cap covered his gray head. His feet were bare. His hands were patting down the sides of the scull.

"Looking for something?" I asked.

Dodo jerked around. His watery blue eyes filled

with alarm. "'No admittance until the week after next.'" He slipped his hand into his pocket.

"Hello to you too." I joined him at the end of the dock. "What did you find?"

"'You better not come very close. I generally hit everything I see.'"

"I don't believe you." I sat down beside him, my feet over the dock's edge. "What's this?" I tugged at the tape. It came away from his fingers. "You found this in the scull?" It looked fairly new.

Dodo didn't answer.

Dmitri dropped on his haunches and reached underneath the seat of the rowing machine.

Dodo tugged at Dmitri's belt. "You are trespassing on private property. The scull is mine. Laurie gave it to me."

"I am sorry, old guy," Dmitri said. "We look for clues."

"'Don't talk jabberwocky.'" Dodo's voice was sharp. "There's nothing there. Not anymore, at least. Go ahead, look for yourself."

Dmitri climbed onto Bud's contraption, rocking it wildly.

Dodo glanced at me, his eyes shrewd. "'This conversation is going on a little too fast. Let's go back to the last remark but one.'"

"I thought you had dropped the fey Lewis Carroll routine," I said.

Dodo did his two-sticks-rubbing-together laugh. "You've no idea how useful it is to keep people at bay."

Too much alcohol does the trick too. "You're not going to get rid of us that easily."

Dmitri stuck his head underneath the rowing machine seat and started scratching.

"Anything there?" I asked.

He sat up with a triumphant gleam in his eyes and a face red from leaning down. "Someone wrap something and tape to boat real good." His fingers held up a thin sheet of plastic, the kind that cleaners use, attached to a long strip of black duct tape. "They take away not long ago. Where tape torn off is very clean." He furrowed his thick black eyebrows at Dodo. "You take?"

Dodo patted his pockets, spread out his palms, and rolled up his trousers, a lopsided smile swinging from his mouth. "What are you two looking for?"

"The same thing Rebecca's prowler is looking for." Evidence of interest to the IRS.

"Why here?"

"A hunch," I said. Dick Knight had found Polly's letter to Bud—a sheet of which had been used as her suicide note—taped inside the scull. Knowing that, Bud might have used the same hiding place. "How long has the scull been sitting here?"

"Steve bring it over yesterday afternoon," Dmitri said. "When you in New York."

"Where was it before that?"

"The Dory Squad men, they find it, they lock it up in shack by Asparagus Beach."

"Which probably means no one had access to it until yesterday afternoon." I fingered the piece of plastic. "I think our killer has finally found what he was looking for." And we were empty-handed. And safe. "I think it's time to have another chat with Captain Comelli."

"No," Dodo said sharply.

"Why not?"

"'When you've once said a thing, that fixes it.'"

"Pshaw," Dmitri huffed. "Communism. Berlin Wall. Marriage. Today, nothing fixed."

"'You don't know much and that's a fact,'" Dodo said. Dmitri and I nodded. Dodo was working up to something. It was only a matter of time, like for Sabrina.

Dodo stretched one leg over the rowing machine seat. He rocked the boat. "'It's a poor sort of memory that only works backwards.'"

"But it help solve murders," Dmitri said.

"Then my advice to you is 'begin at the beginning and go on till you come to the end, then stop.'"

I said, "That's what we'd like you to do."

"In my own slow way, I'm trying." He grinned, his eyes picking up the sunlit blue of the bay. "'"But wait a bit," the Oysters cried, "before we have our chat; for some of us are out of breath, and all of us are fat."'" Two sticks rubbed together in his throat again. "It's taken me years to perfect my act. You can't expect me to stop at the drop of the Madhatter's hat." He rubbed his mouth with the back of his hand. "Being sober doesn't help either." His foot stopped rocking. "'I'm very brave generally, only today I happen to have a headache.'"

He was giving me one.

"But 'the time has come to talk of many things,'" Dodo admitted. "'The sea is boiling hot. Pigs have wings.' And Polly was my love ten minutes after I set eyes on her, back in '49. She'd come for the summer. A slip of a girl with the fire of ninety-proof alcohol and a brave man's strength and will. Of which I had none. She claimed she had no use for the man who thought he was king. She loved me, she said, and proved it by setting out to help me. That winter she bought The Pynes from Steve's father, made me her architect. I was barely out of architecture school, looking for a job, already blacking out on weekends. Polly thought she could make me stop drinking by sheer force of will. I did.

"The next summer, after I'd completed the first two cottages, I went over to my buddy Jackson Pollock who was living in my grandfather's house." He pointed in the direction of the farmhouse. "Jack cooked up his favorite dinner—spaghetti and meatballs. He'd been on the wagon for two years. I was safe from temptation. I hadn't touched a drop in six months.

"After dinner Jack took me back to his shed to show me what he was working on. I didn't understand his art, but I could feel he was great, that he was a force of nature. Nineteen-fifty, that was his most prolific year. The greatest living painter in the United States was showing me his genius, canvas after canvas, as easily as if leafing through an old photo album. And what did I have to show him? Two miserable shacks that would blow down with the first hurricane. I left Jack, got myself a bottle of whiskey, and when I'd finished that, I went back to The Pynes, climbed on a bulldozer, and rammed it into both cottages until they were as flat as the bay." He stared out at the satin-smooth water. "That night the white rabbit caught up with me and hasn't let go. That fall he caught up with Jack too."

All I could do was wrap my arms around him.

FORTY-ONE

Sabrina barked.

Dmitri ran back to the car.

Dodo stood up quickly, breaking my embrace. "'Trees bark. Bough, wough.'" He seemed happy with the interruption.

I got up too. "Why were you looking inside the scull?"

"'I really must be getting home. The night air doesn't suit my throat.'"

I squinted at the sun.

Dodo swung his lopsided smile again. "'I'm older than you and must know better.'" He looked down the path. No sound from the dog or Dmitri. If Sabrina were giving birth, Dmitri would be yelling.

I linked my arm in Dodo's arm and we slowly walked toward the house. "Polly stayed close to you, even after her marriage."

"We were friends. My misery relieved her own."

"The night before she died, Polly had a fight

with Laurie. Bud went over after Laurie left, and they started yelling at each other. Everyone heard them."

Dodo stopped in front of a blackened stone bench half hidden by azalea bushes. "Language is worth a thousand tears a word." He sat down.

"After Bud left, you must have run over to calm Polly down."

Dodo's eyes flickered. His teeth chewed at something. He understood where I was leading him.

I joined him in the dirt. "Did you go over to the big house that night?"

"Yes." His voice made a ping sound, like a drop of water falling into an empty glass.

"After the fight she wrote Bud a letter. Did she show it to you?"

"Yes." Another drop.

"Three sheets of 'I'm sorry,' plus a nasty last line that could have gotten Bud arrested for the murder of his wife."

"Polly's life had not turned out as she'd planned. It angered her very much."

"Did she ask you to deliver that letter?" Mother's errand boy, Laurie had called him.

"She was going to mail it."

"You took the envelope, didn't you?"

"Why would I?"

"Because it was a cruel letter and I think you're kind."

Dodo's eyes turned back to the water. "I regret his passing. 'His look was mild, his speech was slow, his hair was whiter than the snow.'"

"What happened with the letter?"

"She left it in the kitchen. Later I snuck back in, the door was never locked. I didn't like Polly much that night. I felt justified in taking the letter and getting drunk. Next morning I found myself being walked up and down Gerard Drive like a dog by Rebecca. I took refuge at my grandfather's farm and slept it off. When I woke up Polly was floating head down." He rubbed his face with both his hands, as if he were removing the soot of memory. "By nightfall, the rumors had started. Bud had killed her. I fought them. 'Bud is a good man. He didn't kill her!' But my words are written in whiskey."

"So you put on gloves, not to leave fingerprints, and planted one sheet of the letter behind Laurie's law school graduation picture." An appropriate spot. Suicide note and photo, both fakes.

"It took me three days and a few more bottles to work up to it."

"Then you taped the remaining sheets underneath Bud's rowing machine seat." Where Knight had found them. "Why?"

"I couldn't burn them. Polly's words, nasty or not, they were the last thing she wrote. I kept the letter in my pocket until Bud came home from the hospital. When he rigged up the rowing machine onto his kayack, he told me the exercise would keep him healthy. That's when I got the idea what to do with Polly's anger. Put it under the seat that was keeping him alive." Dodo rubbed his eyes. "Looking back it makes as much sense as the White Queen's rule. 'Jam

tomorrow and jam yesterday, but never jam today.'
Maybe she liked whiskey too."

"Does Rebecca know about the suicide note?"

"We're both good at Alice's favorite phrase:
'Let's pretend.'"

I touched his hand, as rough as bark. "Thank you
for telling—"

The azalea behind me growled. Dodo started. I
twisted and looked down. A pregnant mass of white-
and-black fur had wedged itself underneath the bush.

"Sabrina, what are you doing there?"

The growl persisted.

Dmitri turned the corner, flashing the leash and
his annoyance. "Pregnancy make this dog crazy.
Where is she?"

I pointed. "Maybe she wants to have the puppies
in private."

"Sabrina!"

The dog ignored him.

"Sabrina, come here at once!"

Sabrina bared her teeth at Dodo and lunged.

FORTY-TWO

DODO JUMPED UP AND RAN, with Sabrina snipping at his heels. By the time Dmitri and I scrambled on their trail, they were fifty feet ahead of us. *Nessun problema*, I thought, a seventy-year-old man and a very pregnant dog—we'd easily catch up with them.

Dodo, it turned out, ran like that old Greek who raised dust all the way to Marathon. And Sabrina had the wind of a wronged female in her sails. Dmitri and I careened after them across the Merrill Sanctuary. We dodged tree trunks, low branches, and holes in the ground, yelling useless commands like "Stop, you're killing me!"

After about a hundred miles, Sabrina dropped down on a soft patch of shaded grass. Dodo kept running. Dmitri and I stopped. Sabrina's tongue lolled, her lungs heaved for breath. Her water broke.

Dmitri got on his knees, with an awed expression on his face, as Sabrina went into labor. I stroked her head.

She pushed, she whimpered. First one, then another, puppy slipped out, five minutes apart. Lots of black and curly wet fur. Sabrina started to wash them, then lifted her head, bending to reach between her legs. Another head appeared. Sabrina pushed. The puppy's forelegs appeared. Sabrina pushed again. The other two pups were crawling over her stomach, mewling for breakfast and a good wash. I massaged her flank in long downward strokes. She pushed some more, whimpering as she did. Then she fell back, exhausted. The puppy was stuck.

Dmitri clutched his mouth. "She will die."

"Get her some water."

He took off one shoe and charged to the creek.

The new pup had a black curly head, with a big white spot between his eyes like his mom. I rubbed my finger over him. He was as delicate as a bird. I muttered, "*Che Dio ce la mandi buona*"—may God send it good, the "it" being luck—and circled my hand under the pup's forelegs. Sabrina reached up to lick my hand.

"You'll kill her!" Dmitri cried from behind a cedar. His shoe dripped water. So did his eyes.

I pulled.

One heart-wrenching yelp.

A pop.

And Sabrina was the proud mother of three.

"Champanski!" Dmitri yelled. The name would stick. The other two would have to live with the names Caviar and Borscht.

FORTY-THREE

WITH THE FAMILY SETTLED in the backseat—Sabrina grooming and Dmitri munching a dog biscuit and prattling on about "new responsibilities," I drove us toward home and called Rebecca's cottage.

"Is he there?"

"He ran in here, trailing his lungs. What happened? He's locked himself in his room."

"Keep him there. I'll be over."

At the turnoff for The Pynes, I saw a flash of chrome and metal. I screeched to a halt. Dmitri slammed into the front seat with a yell. I took a quick look over my shoulder. The pups had held on to Mom's teats. Sabrina was too exhausted to notice. I jumped out of the car.

I had almost run into Dick Knight's Silver, Trigger, Rocinante, his Harley-Davidson Bad Boy. It was lying on its flank on the side of the road in a pool of gasoline, shimmering green oil and what looked like blood. The front wheel was climbing an oak.

The gasoline tank had a crack along its flank. Tied to the right sideview mirror, a limp red cowboy kerchief. The other mirror was bare.

"What happened?" I asked. Lester Kennelly, in blue Bermudas, a WSK T-shirt, and a baseball cap, was pouring sand onto the slick. Laurie watched, a man's shirt covering her bathing suit.

"We don't know," she said. "About twenty minutes ago I was watering the plants by the garage when I heard a car zooming by, then a cracking sound. I ran back to the house to turn off the hose, then by the time I came here, no one was around. Look," she pointed to the smashed taillight and the dented rear fender, "he must have been hit from behind, lost control, and rammed into the tree."

"A hit and run," I said.

"Can't be." Lester straightened up. He was through pouring sand. "Where's the motorcycle driver? Whoever hit him must have stopped and taken him to a hospital. There are no bloody tracks. That means the car picked him up."

Or Knight had stanched the wound with the missing red kerchief. I shaded my eyes with my hand. There were no tire marks on the asphalt that I could pick up. I turned to Lester. "You just happened to come by?"

He met my gaze and smiled. Who was I trying to intimidate? "I had a delivery to make."

"Yeah," Laurie corroborated. "He found me standing here with my mouth catching flies. He brought me an Iacono chicken and then he got the sand while I called the police."

"Any idea who owns this bike?" I looked straight at Bud's partner.

"No idea." He turned to Laurie. "Do you know?"

Laurie ran both hands across her curly brown hair. "I don't think it's a local or even a regular summer resident. I would have noticed a flashy bike like this one."

"What about the car?" I asked.

"Didn't see it," Laurie said.

Lester dropped the bucket. It clanged a quarter of an inch from my sandaled foot. It was still heavy with sand. He didn't apologize. "What's this about you finding an empty Valium bottle in Bud's bathroom with Polly's name on it?"

I turned to Laurie. "You told him?"

"No, she didn't tell me. For the good reason that it's not true!" His tan was picking up a cooked lobster hue. "Comelli said that's something you cooked up with your pal. Now he's asking a lot of stupid questions."

I looked at Laurie again.

She rubbed her elbows. "The toxicology report came in this morning. Comelli pushed the lab to hurry up after all. Dad was full of Valium and he didn't have another heart attack, although the medical examiner said he couldn't swear to that on the witness stand."

Lester leaned against his car, a green vintage Jaguar parked beyond the gouged tree. "He killed himself then."

I grabbed Laurie's arm before she could speak. "That's what it looks like."

"That's why he took off his vest." Lester couldn't hide his relief.

"Guess so," I said. Laurie started shaking. I squeezed harder. "Dmitri! Come take a look at this Jaguar. It's a beauty."

He rose out of the car slowly. He'd been listening all along.

"Dmitri's got a vintage Cadillac," I explained while I handed Laurie over to Dmitri and joined Lester next to his car. The open windows had given me an idea. "His car's not quite in this good a shape." I leaned against the back door. "In fact, it's full of dents, getting fixed over at Kirkwood. We hit a tree."

Lester didn't care. He was busy watching Dmitri circle the Jaguar with Laurie in tow.

"Car for czar!" Dmitri declared.

I reached into my skirt pocket, found a Kleenex, and started wiping. "In fact," I said, "the Valium bottle with Polly's name on it, which you don't think exists, was stolen right out of Dmitri's Caddie the night we got rammed into Green River Cemetery." My clenched hand dropped out of my pocket. "Can you believe anyone would take something as stupid as that?"

"No."

"Ouch!" I slapped my arm. "Damn horsefly!" My clenched hand reached the open back window. Lester's office keys dropped without a sound on the floor rug. The Kleenex went down too. No matter. At least the keys were clean. Lester might suspect I'd taken them, but he could never prove it. Now the only thing I had to return was the WSK shareholders' file.

I scratched my supposed bite. "Why don't you think the Valium bottle exists, Lester?"

He faced me. Relief had been replaced by what I took for weariness. "Polly had a violent reaction to Valium."

Laurie joined us. "How do you know that?" Her voice was crisp, like the first hint of frost.

Lester looked surprised. "I've always known, Laurie. I don't remember how." He rubbed his eyes. The day was getting to be too much for him. "Maybe Bud told me when I suggested he put a tranquilizer into Polly's morning coffee." He straightened up, opened the car door. I stepped out of his way. "Sorry, Laurie, but your mother could be a real pain in the butt." He got into the driver's seat. "If you need me, you'll find me at home."

"Lester's lying, isn't he?" Laurie said, as we watched the Jaguar make a U-turn and purr off toward East Hampton. "He didn't know before Dad's death, not before Monday night. That's why you pretended Dad committed suicide. You think Lester killed Dad!" She sank down on her haunches and buried her face in her hands. "Oh God, I can't believe it. That's why he had to get rid of the pills."

Dmitri gave her one of his bear-paw pats that leaves dents.

As soon as I'd told the police what I knew about Knight, Dmitri and I slipped away.

"Not one dent on Jaguar," Dmitri reported, as I

parked our car behind the cottage. "He could have used other car, park nearby, then arrive with Jaguar."

"A little complicated, but doable."

"You think Knight dead?"

"Why remove the body and not the bike?"

"Kidnapped?"

"Maybe he got away." I stepped out of the car. "Okay, this is what we do. You call the Southampton Hospital and check if anyone fitting Knight's description has been admitted."

Dmitri's mustache twitched. "The police will do."

"If Knight managed to get away we want to get to him first. He knows who the killer is and he's probably got the evidence to prove it. Otherwise why ram him into a tree?"

"To warn him like he did with us."

"In broad daylight? That's a pretty desperate act. I'm afraid our killer wants another body. If Knight's not at Southampton, try all the Long Island hospitals. Then canvass the neighborhood and ask if anyone's seen any black leather wandering around."

Dmitri's eyes fogged over. It was lunchtime.

"You can eat between phone calls. Maybe we'll get lucky and Knight's still alive. Save me a hot dog."

"What you going to do?"

"The easy part. Fall into the rabbit hole."

FORTY-FOUR

DODO PERCHED ON A STOOL. A swatch of sunlight from the window made him look like an old seabird sunning himself on a pile. Rebecca, sheathed in her blue painting coat, sat erect on the sofa. This time she wasn't offering any sunrise drink.

"You're the one who locked Sabrina under the sink. That's why she wanted to take a chunk out of your calf." We were back in Rebecca's cottage. She'd straightened the place up. All traces of the prowler's handiwork were gone. We sat in a semicircle in her living room.

"When I came along," I continued, "you bopped me over the head."

Dodo slowly shook his head. "'There's no sort of use in knocking because I'm on the same side of the door as you are.'"

"What's that supposed to mean?"

Rebecca leaned bony elbows on her knees. "He's on your side."

"I didn't do it." Dodo's voice strengthened the minute he dropped his Carroll act. "Why should I? I was in the hospital."

"Maybe you got out before Rebecca arrived. Or she dropped you off and ran an errand. You'd been dry for a while. You wanted your whiskey bottle. Sabrina comes along yapping away, you're scared of dogs, you panic. I come along, fall over your bottle, you panic even more."

Dodo wagged a finger at me. "'Speak roughly to your Dodo boy and beat him when he drinks. He only does it to annoy because he knows it stinks.'"

"Tell her," Rebecca said, "in your own words."

Knees cracking, Dodo unfurled from his stool. "I'm not afraid of dogs. I like animals. It's humans I have trouble with." He slipped his hand in his pocket, rustling cellophane. "Last Saturday, the day of the barbecue, Sabrina found me on the beach. One lost dog meeting another. She was hungry and thirsty. I fed her the sandwiches Rebecca kindly prepared for me. I gave her fresh water out of my pail. I wished her goodbye and set off. She followed. I explained I couldn't keep her. My only home is this cottage and no dogs are allowed. Besides, I have no money to feed her and her brood. The dog wouldn't listen. At sunset I left her at the beach and hitched a ride with a tourist." He licked his lips. Rebecca got up, opened the refrigerator door, and took out a bottle of Tiepolo colors.

I took my glass gladly. "Sabrina followed you."

He nodded as he gulped down the health drink.

"Sunday morning she showed up at my grandfather's house. I like to sleep by those boulders Jack brought in. Gives me strength, sitting against that force of nature and looking out on the creek. If I've had enough to drink young Polly comes to visit. The dog, she woke me up. Licked me all over." In his pocket cellophane crinkled again. "You're a dumb dog, I told her. Picked the wrong man." Anger flashed across his eyes. "She picked the god damn worst man!" He turned and headed for his bedroom. The door clicked shut.

I turned to Rebecca. "Why didn't he call the animal rescue people?"

"He called the *Star*. An anonymous tip. The ARF is always full of homeless dogs. Dodo wanted Sabrina to make the papers. Pregnant mixed breed tied to a tree and abandoned! She was sure to find a home then. These days hearts get stirred up only if there's good media coverage."

"Can't you get him to go to AA?" I whispered.

"I'm trying, but it's hard to convince a seventy-year-old man there is still a life to lead." Rebecca brushed her hand against Dodo's door. "He has something else to tell you. Something related to Bud's death. He won't talk unless you promise not to go to the police."

"How can I promise without knowing what it is?"

Rebecca leaned her head against Dodo's door, her mouth close to the crack. "Simona can't promise, but she'll do the best she can."

Two, three minutes went by. Rebecca finished a half-eaten tuna sandwich.

"There's a thousand dollar fine for endangering the life of a dog!" I shouted.

The bedroom door opened a crack. "That's why I can't call the police." The whites of Dodo's eyes looked bleached. "No matter how bad it is, I can't do that to Rebecca. She'd pay, you know. She would and that's not right."

"Once I sell that monstrosity Bud left me, there's going to be plenty of money." Rebecca's voice was soothing. "The police won't hurt you."

"They threw me in jail."

"You destroyed Manny, the mannequin."

The door opened wider. "He had a dumb grin on his face." Dodo's smile was sly. "Reminded me of Nixon even when I was sober."

Rebecca looked away not to show her own smile. "You did what you thought best. Now tell Simona and get it over with."

Dodo shook his head. "Not if she won't promise."

"You saw something that morning at the sanctuary?"

He swiped his cap from his head and stepped out into the room. "Promise."

"Okay. I promise."

He narrowed his eyes. "What?"

I was going to regret this. "I promise I won't go to the police."

Dodo slowly nodded his approval, saying nothing.

"I did my part," I said, my patience long gone.

Dodo took two more steps into the room, swung his head to Rebecca and back to me. "I saw who killed Bud."

"You witnessed the murder?"

"I saw what led up to it. Inland, the fog wasn't bad. I was coming back from tying up the dog. I was going to cut through Bud's property and go back to sleeping next to my boulders. It was around six o'clock in the morning. The sun was still low."

"What *did* you see?"

"I saw a canoe with two gasoline cans tied to Bud's dock. I could smell the stuff. And then I saw him come out of Bud's kitchen, holding some papers and looking like a man down to his last swig. He stole the papers, burned the house to cover it up, and then he went and killed my friend. And he probably killed Polly too, and I didn't have the guts to go to the police." He covered his face and started crying.

Rebecca wrapped him in her arms. I stroked his back. "Who did you see?" I asked.

"The young guy," Dodo said in a muffled voice, "the one who owns the restaurant."

FORTY-FIVE

"No Knight anywhere," Dmitri announced, walking into our cottage. "You owe me twenty dollars."

"Never mind Knight." I was on my third can of water-packed tuna fish. "We've got a job to do. Why do I owe you?"

"Redhead from Sag Harbor surrender hair to one fearsome Dmitri K." He waved a hank of flaming hair at me.

"That's how you were looking for Knight?"

Dmitri raised hands that could cradle a pound of pasta. "I have entrepreneurial spirit."

I looked at the dozen white roses Jim had sent and told Dmitri about Dodo's news.

Dmitri's face sagged. "Pshaw. I don't believe. I like Jim!"

"So did I."

"He is not murderer!"

"Why did he try to burn the house down? Because Bud had something Jim wanted. Maybe something the IRS wanted too. Remember, those two were partners in the restaurant."

"Time to talk to police." He rinsed out my tuna fish cans.

"Time for Italian revenge."

One heavy black eyebrow shot up. "Garlic?"

I called Jim at the restaurant. I had to wait. Friday at lunchtime is busy. A lot of the Manhattanites head out Thursday evening or early Friday morning.

It took him five interminable minutes to come to the phone. I thanked him for the flowers. "I'd love to meet again tonight."

"Great. My place?"

No! "You mentioned wanting to show me the Hamptons' hot spots."

"That's right." He sounded less pleased. "How about Della Femina's? I want to check out their new menu. I know someone who's about to cancel his reservation."

"I hope it's a late one." After dark.

"Hold on, I'll ask." He lowered the receiver and picked it up again after a couple of seconds. "Don't go away."

I listened to half a minute of murmuring voices and clinking ice cubes while Sabrina covered her master's mustache with a wet tongue. Champanski, Caviar, and Borscht slept in sunlight on Dmitri's precious purple shirt. Dmitri gave each a pat, tears coming to his eyes. Fatherhood overwhelmed him.

Jim came back on the phone. "Nine-thirty?"

"Perfect. See you then." I hung up.

328 CAMILLA T. CRESPI

"So what is Italian revenge?" Dmitri asked.
"I seduce. You steal."

We spent the afternoon scouring the neighborhood for Knight and taking Sabrina and family to
the vet. All was well with the dogs. Knight had
disappeared. Thirty-eight Suffolk and Nassau
county hospitals denied that anyone by that name
or fitting that description had sought medical
help. We debated calling New York hospitals and
decided it would be a waste of time. Either Knight
was dead, kidnapped, or he didn't want to be
found.

Just as I was deciding what to wear for my gourmet
dinner, Jim called. Our night on the town was off.
Two prospective buyers for the restaurant had shown
up. They were staying at Gurney's Inn in Montauk.

"I'm sorry, Simona. They want to talk over dinner. They're flying back to Europe tomorrow. I think
they're French."

"I didn't know the restaurant was for sale."

"It isn't, but I'm a trader at heart. They dropped
a big figure. Listen, I'll see you at the funeral in the
morning, and tomorrow afternoon, come to the
Writers and Artists softball game. I need you to cheer
me up. I'm playing for the Writers. We always lose.
Afterward you and I can go off on my boat. We'll
compare notes over lobster, Pinot Grigio, and chocolate ganache cake. Sound good?"

"Compare notes about what?"

"Your investigation. I've got an idea why Polly was killed."

"What idea?"

"There's no way you're going to get it out of me over the phone. Consider it blackmail. Besides, I need to check something with an old buddy of mine. Sorry about tonight."

I opened the bathroom door. Dmitri was blow-drying his mustache. He likes the full look. "Our plan is off," I yelled. "Jim knows what we're up to."

Dmitri went right back to blowing. "Good, you come with me. It go faster. Dress is black."

I pulled the plug. I didn't feel like shouting. "It's too risky." I explained about the sudden appearance of potential buyers. Frenchmen yet. "He's even come up with a reason why Polly was killed. Which naturally he wouldn't tell me. He's stalling for time or laying a trap."

Dmitri sniffed. "He tell the truth. You come with me. Trust me."

"I'm through with that." Then it dawned on me. I poked his chest and nearly cracked my finger. "You set him up!"

"*Da.*"

"Why? My plan was going to work beautifully. While we ate at Della Femina's, you'd ransack his house and find whatever he stole from the scull."

"And after your gourmet dinner and too much wine, what? Maybe he wants intimacy? What do you do? Jim very attractive. Stan would never forgive me." He plumped his mustache with his fingers, then checked his watch. "Twenty minutes after sun goes, we go."

"I still say it's risky." Once Jim got to Montauk and found out there were no buyers, there was no way of knowing how long it would take him to come back.

"Tonight," Dmitri said, running a comb through his thick hair, "Jim eat lobster and steamers dripping in butter and drink ice vodka until he sees sun and thinks it is still moon."

I poked him again, this time with my fist. "Those guys aren't French!"

"You bet. Hundred-proof Russian."

"Mike and Phil?"

Dmitri beamed. "The Brodders K. are on the case."

May God send it good.

FORTY-SIX

W E LEFT THE COTTAGE AT 9:15 P.M. on empty, nervous stomachs. The moon, fat but still weak, did a bad job of lighting up the bay and its surroundings. We tiptoed in single file, both of us in black pants, T-shirts, and pink rubber gloves, the last item being an A&P special. Dmitri had done the shopping.

Up on the redwood deck, Dmitri checked the barbecue grill. Nothing there except coal ash. I stopped in front of Jim's kitchen door, which faced the water. Only the fish, the birds, and moonlight sailors could spot us. And maybe Leon Gardiner, if Leon had a NASA-strength telescope on his island. I looked east. Our cottage blocked the view to the rest of The Pynes. On the western side, a stand of red cedars protected us.

I pulled at the round handle. The door was locked.

"Where are your tools?" I whispered. Dmitri had claimed he was an ace at B&E. He would jimmy the lock and stand back. I then had thirty seconds to walk in, take two steps to the alarm box, and punch in the code Jim had given me on the beach.

Dmitri flipped a card up from his pants pocket and held it between fat pink fingers. "Visa. AA Advantage. Yours." He slipped it in the crack just above the lock. "You get bonus miles for each lock you open." He wiggled his wrist, pushed down on the card. Click. The latch slipped back. That easy.

Dmitri opened the door and started counting. "One and two"—

I rushed in, crashed into the screen door, stepped back, opened it, and turned to the left.

—"ten, eleven"—

The alarm box. There it was, next to a World Wildlife Calendar. Two-by-four inches with rows of lit numbers. Tiny numbers.

—"fifteen, sixteen"—

Mouse droppings is what they looked like. I squinted, pushed my head back. Took two steps in reverse. It was no good.

—"twenty-two"—

Dio, blind at thirty-nine!

—"twenty-three"—

"You're counting too fast!" I breathed in. Air and logic. I remembered that numbers are placed in order.

One. Top left.

Slowly. The gloves were way too big for me. I could end up pushing two buttons at the same time.

Zero. Zero was bottom right.

—"twenty-six"—

One, top left again. Nine, left of zero.

—"twenty-nine"—

"I did it!" October nineteenth. The stock market's Black Monday. Thank God Jim had left out the year.

I waved Dmitri inside. He swung open the screen door.

The alarm went off.

My heart hit the ceiling. My brain went numb.

The alarm kept on blasting.

Dmitri pushed me aside. "What is number!"

"October nineteenth."

"Number!"

"Ten. Ten, nineteen."

He punched quickly, with perfect sight. The alarm stopped midnote. My ears sagged with relief.

The phone rang.

"Don't answer," Dmitri commanded.

The phone went on ringing.

"I have to." I strode over to the counter. "It's the alarm company. All I need is the password and we'll be fine."

Password. Or I'll shoot.

Sweat beaded on my forehead.

What would an ex-trader use for a password? Wall Street, Solomon Brothers, NASDAQ, quotron. Pork bellies?

I picked up.

"Hamptons' Security." An older, polite voice.

Next to the phone, a blueprint of a house. Four

bedrooms. "Sorry. I thought I was too young to need glasses."

"The password?" Bored.

A name loomed large on the blueprint. A famous name. The password as a statement of desire? Why not?

"Richard Meier," I said in a firm voice.

A pause through which you could drive a heart attack.

Hamptons' Security finally said, "You're lucky it's only glasses you need." He hung up, downright friendly. I lunged to kiss the blueprint.

Dmitri swiped it from under my lips. "No saliva. DNA!"

I kissed him instead. "*Ho un gran culo*. I've got a big butt." That means lucky.

We pulled down the blinds. We'd brought flashlights but overhead lamps were going to make our work faster. The house was small, thank God. At deck level, the biggest room was the kitchen, which opened onto a living\dining room overlooking the deck, the bay beyond and the cedars to the west. Next to the entrance hallway, a tiny bathroom with a window onto the driveway.

Downstairs a master bedroom, a smaller guest room, and two bathrooms. Every room was minimally furnished, as if Jim were waiting to make it back to the top, to a south-of-the-highway house with a Richard Meier exterior and a Mark Hampton interior.

Dmitri wanted the kitchen. "Pavel's wife hide

my letters in oven." He winked. "Hot place for hot prose."

I started with the master bathroom downstairs. The bathroom is where I keep my valuables—my grandmother's antique enamel earrings, the gold Pisces pin Stan gave me for Christmas. Never hide anything in a bedroom. That's the first place thieves look. Did Jim know that?

The bathroom only revealed that Jim worried about hair loss. He'd stocked a year's supply of Rogaine in there. I moved into the bedroom.

I riffled through books. A lot of thrillers, *Den of Thieves*, *Free to Trade*, Ridley Pearson's latest. On the bed, with a Jim's Pit paper napkin for a bookmark, was *Liar's Poker*, about Wall Street. I opened the book to the marked page and found an apt quote from Samuel Johnson: "He who makes a beast of himself gets rid of the pain of being a man."

I checked out Jim's dresser, moved to his closet. I was getting tired. Mostly I was having a hard time thinking of Jim as an arsonist—or a killer. At one end of his closet hung an old dirty orange life preserver that looked like it hadn't been used in a long time. I checked the label. It wasn't a Sport4Life item.

An ominous buzz filled the room. I spun around. It wasn't the alarm clock. I checked the bathroom radio. Nothing. While I was still out in the corridor the buzz suddenly stopped. Something soothingly tempting caressed my nose. I ran to the bottom of the stairs.

"Dmitri! Are you cooking?" My legs swallowed the stairs two at a time.

My partner was standing in front of the microwave, a beatific glow on his face. The door was ajar. "Perfectissimo!"

I peered under his armpit. A plastic plate brimmed with cannelloni—six of them, covered in bubbling white sauce with a delicate marbling of tomato. One bare corner revealed paper-thin pasta. The smell told me lobster stuffing with a hint of tarragon.

"Not a good idea." My mouth was watering. "And you splattered sauce all over."

"I look for hard evidence in freezer. I see packet from Jim's Pit. I also see microwave. I surprise you with good food."

I grabbed a wet sponge, then started opening drawers. "Even if Jim doesn't miss his food, he's going to walk in here and smell it."

"You know why Russian woman don't buy microwave oven?"

"This isn't the moment." I opened the last drawer, closest to the stove, and found a red pot holder. I tossed it to Dmitri along with the sponge.

He lifted the cannelloni out of the microwave as if they were his firstborn. "Microwave oven remind Russian woman of husband with vodka. Thirty seconds, he's cooked. Jim, after a night with Mike and Phil, he will be barbecued. Only thing he will smell is vodka." He started sponging the oven.

"What's this?" I pushed another pot holder aside

in the drawer and dug out a file. Bud's name was written on the upper-right-hand corner in his slash-dash style. Inside was Bud's copy of the WSK partnership agreement. "That's probably what Jim was holding when Dodo—"

"Stalingrad!" Dmitri announced. "We defeat the enemy."

I ran over. He carefully removed a plastic package, taped to the back of the broom closet.

Just as carefully I opened the package and found thirty to forty individually folded copies of invoices. The Bear & Bull Distributors of Long Island City, suppliers of fine liquor. The invoices were all made out to Jim's Pit. Jim's patrons had guzzled a sea of alcohol just in the last few months.

"What is need to hide this?" Dmitri asked.

"Pazienza."

The last invoice rewarded us. Folded inside was one statement from a bank in Riverhead, Long Island. In the month of July, the Bear & Bull Distributors had deposited $35,000 and withdrawn $28,000.

Dmitri grabbed the check and turned it around. His face fell. I guess he'd been hoping too. But there was no mistaking that name. I looked over the other checks.

Every single one was endorsed by Jim Molton.

FORTY-SEVEN

W E ATE THE CANNELLONI by candlelight, on our own porch, looking out at the silvery bay. It was almost midnight. We'd put the invoices back, kept one check, and the addresses of the Riverhead bank and the Bear & Bull Distributors. I'd put Bud's file back in the drawer.

"Excellentissimo," Dmitri declared after his last bite, not putting a lot of punch behind his word. The food was good, but the only one enjoying it was Sabrina.

"Jim set up a dummy company as a supplier to the restaurant," I said. "He picked liquor because that's where a restaurant makes the most money. Something about the Bull & Bear invoices must have made Bud suspicious. If nothing else the name. Jim can't seem to get away from the stock market."

Dmitri snapped his fingers. "State Liquor Authority. One of four phone calls you ask me to check."

"Bud called and discovered that Bull & Bear Distributors wasn't registered. Jim's betrayal made Bud so angry he was willing to ruin the restaurant and lose his investment."

"He make appointment with IRS."

I nodded. "And then he called Jim to let him know what he was doing. Bud was giving him a chance to turn himself in."

"Phone call Laurie overhear," Dmitri said. "But why kill Polly?"

I had no answer.

Jim crashed into a bush at four in the morning. Sabrina barked. Dmitri went out to help him. In Jim's state, he would never have been able to punch in his alarm code. I fell back asleep before Dmitri closed the door.

La notte porta consiglio. The night brings counsel. Sometimes in dreams.

A school of Day-Glo yellow life vests bob in the bay. Bud bobs with them in his scull. His torso is naked. He drinks from his thermos and reads his suspect list. Behind him, his house burns and Dodo's voice quotes, "'Through the looking glass, things go the other way.'"

I woke up with a start. It was morning, the air heavy with the smell of coffee and donuts. I shuffled out of bed to look at the view of the bay. The day was clear with pink and orange streaks in the sky. Gulls swooped in pairs. A sailboat crossed the window. The paddles of the Gardiner's Island windmill were back in their X position.

All seemed well in this corner of heaven.

"I find out about Knight," Dmitri said, offering me coffee. "Woman across street see man fall out of oak in her garden last night. Black leather, big helmet, and red bandanna on his knee. Has to be Knight."

"Where'd he go?"

"He limp to water. Bonacker report boat stolen."

That's when I got an idea.

The First Presbyterian Church, somber in its puritan starkness, filled up by 9:45. Half of the New York advertising community was there, including my boss, to pay their last respects to William Morris Warren. In the front pews, Laurie sat fighting tears between Lester and Amanda. On the other side, Steve—his tan face craggy with yearning—listed toward Laurie. Rebecca and Dodo sat stiffly next to flame-headed Charlene. Jim stooped, his head hung low. From remorse or a hangover I couldn't tell.

Standing in the light of a soaring window, Captain Comelli watched through sunglasses.

While Lester Kennelly spoke of the many great ads his dear friend and partner had created, Dmitri sneaked out on an errand and I wrote a note.

Later, at the big house, while the mourners clustered around the drinks table and Dmitri shoveled lobster rolls under his mustache, I left to do some shopping for the softball game. But not before slipping a note into a deep pocket.

The solution to Bud and Polly's murder had come down to a matter of trust.

FORTY-EIGHT

"THE ARTISTS AND WRITERS softball game has been an annual East Hampton event since 1962," Lester informed me. "All the proceeds go to charity." We were sitting together on the grass in Herrick Park, on the edge of a dusty sandlot baseball field behind the A&P.

"It used to be a real contest between the artists and writers of the community," Lester said. "Then about ten years ago Hollywood came knocking. You should have heard Bud on the subject of that one."

A thick crowd of fans and celebrity watchers talked, ate, drank, and bumped one another for a better view. The sun had started to drop and was glaring straight in our eyes. Despite the comfortable eighty-six degrees, sweat pooled at the back of my neck.

"He wasn't pleased," I said, to keep up my end of the conversation.

"Sodom and Gomorrah moving east." Lester

lowered the bill of his baseball cap against the sun. "Sour grapes, in my opinion. A bad shoulder forced him to quit. Bud used to pitch for the Artists. That was when the Writers used to win. Fourteen in a row." Lester seemed to enjoy that.

The British announcer had just finished telling us to hold on to our tickets for the raffle. The lucky third-prize winner would win two weeks at the Citadel. A new inning started, the ninety-ninth inning—that's what it felt like. Hitting a perfectly innocent ball is not my idea of fun. Watching it is boring. Watching it while waiting for Bud and Polly's killer to make a move is deadly.

Second prize was *one* week at the Citadel.

George Plimpton got ready to pitch to Alec Baldwin. *Dan's Paper* Rattiner and his strawhat were umpiring. Ken Auletta was manning first base, Ben Bradlee was on second, and Jim was on third, closest to me. He waved, looking like hell. I nodded back.

First prize was a romantic weekend for two in the royal suite at the New York Mayfair Hotel with a champagne lunch at Le Cirque.

I started to scratch my knees to keep my hands away from my chest. I'd taped a brand-new two-inch tape recorder between my breasts in an effort to scrape up some hard evidence, like a full confession at the bottom of the ninth, with bases loaded and two outs. The tape was itching.

The mike was hidden behind a 1940s sunflower pin I'd picked up, along with a black bomber jacket, that afternoon at the Ladies Village Improvement Society. What could go wrong?

Dodo and Rebecca were sitting two people over from Lester. Laurie and Steve stood behind the left-field wall, which was only a series of metal stakes connected by a rope. They were deep in conversation.

Charlene with her sunset hair was busy buying a commemorative T-shirt. Captain Comelli was busy studying her thighs. She'd put on shorts after the funeral.

Mike, Dmitri's pal who likes to crack coconuts with his armpits, was sitting on the other side of me, disguised in wraparound sunglasses and a black cowboy hat. We couldn't take the chance of Jim spotting him as last night's restaurant buyer. Mike was whispering last-minute instructions on his cellular phone to Phil, the third man on the Brothers K. team.

Behind me, Dmitri stood by the food stand not ten feet away, a gym bag at his feet. Next to him Amanda looked crispy cool in diamond studs and a lettuce green linen pantsuit. Dmitri had promised not to eat, drink, or go to the bathroom. I needed him to keep his hands free. I also needed him to look at me. Instead he was telling a joke. Loudly.

"In Russia today, you know difference between pessimist and optimist?"

My joke.

"Pessimist believes in Russia nothing can get worse. Optimist believes everything can."

Alec Baldwin smacked the ball. It arced high. Got caught by Jim, dropped. Alec made it to second. The audience cheered.

Lester inched closer to me. "What the hell do you know about my business dealings?"

The note I'd dropped in his pocket read, "The merger won't go through."

"And why the hell talk here?" His voice was low.

"I like crowds," I replied. "I know about Bud and Polly's dying. How and why. Once it's out in the open, Chass\Dayton will pull out or risk losing a lot of high-profile clients."

"What are you blabbering about?" He knew all right. His eyes had gone bullet hard. Lester Kennelly stood to lose everything he'd worked for because of what Bud had referred to as the "ugly clichés." Greed and vanity.

Lester grasped my arm. "Would you mind filling me in?" I winced. Behind me Mike rose slowly. The crowd let out a collective moan. Chevy Chase had struck out.

I explained. About Bud nixing the lucrative merger with Chass\Dayton the year before, how therefore he had to be eliminated. "But unpleasant, difficult Polly was also against the merger and she stood to inherit a hundred of Bud's shares, despite the fact that they were divorced. Bud had told you he wasn't going to change his will, that he didn't want to admit the divorce had happened."

Lester's grip got tighter. "You took the share-holders' file that Charlene can't find! You're going to be out of a job, Simona, and I'll see you never work in advertising again." He caught his breath.

"It won't work, Lester. You can't save that merger."

"I don't have to listen to this garbage!" He let go of my arm, but did not move.

"If Polly stood to inherit," I said, "why not kill her first and get rid of any future problems? Laurie as heir would be much easier to handle. So why not fill Polly up with Valium, drown her, and make it look like suicide."

"The whole town thought Bud killed her!"

"Except he knew Polly was allergic to Valium." From the corner of my eye I checked on Dmitri. Amanda was hand-feeding him a hot dog. "Bud and Polly had fought horribly the night before. You heard it from your Jaguar. That fight probably shortened Polly's life by a week or two. And then lady luck almost gave an extra hand. Bud had a heart attack after Polly's death. Maybe he was going to die on his own. No more risky killing."

The crowd cheered again. This time Roy Scheider made it to third base. I raised my voice. "Instead Bud recovered against all odds. You must have tried to convince Bud to go for the merger. You stood to make an awful lot of money. Your marriage was in trouble, you wanted out. With Amanda's tastes, that was going to cost you plenty. Four or five months ago, you made overtures to Chass\Dayton again. You were sure you'd turn Bud around. If he didn't, Bud would be dead."

"He didn't care anymore! 'Sell the company to the Japanese for all I care,' he said."

"Too bad no one else heard him say it."

"We were trying to keep the merger under wraps."

"Saturday night," I said, "while Bud was hosting his annual barbecue at The Pynes, someone slipped inside his house and poured ground Valium in his coffee machine. Thanks to the great heat, two mornings in a row had been foggy. We could all count on fog again."

"Lower your voice!" He didn't tell me to shut up.

"That someone had the new Sport4Life sample life vest and caught up with Bud in the bay. Knowing his habits, it was easy to find him even in the fog. Or maybe the two had made an appointment to meet at Hog Creek Point or Lion's Head Rock to exercise together. And when he was sure that no one else was around, the killer glided next to Bud, lifted the paddle, and said, 'Hey, take that old life vest off, friend. Try the new product. You can't come up with an ad if you don't test your product. Let's see how far we can see it in this pea soup.' Bud took off his old red vest, stretched out to grab the new one, and got pulled down. If this were an ad, the tag line would be 'Sport4Life ends lives.'"

"What proof do you have?" Lester's eyes had narrowed with revulsion, as if the rot of the two deaths was working up his nose.

I stood up and made my way between laps and shoulders to the food stand. Lester followed. Dmitri left Amanda holding a half-eaten hot dog and reached down into his gym bag.

He dangled the yellow life preserver.

Amanda's eyes widened. "You stole that from our house! I'll have you in jail—"

"Shut up, Amanda!" Lester knocked the hot dog out of her hand.

No one was paying attention to us. Alec Baldwin and Kim Basinger were kissing behind home plate.

So much for the protection of crowds.

"What proof?" Lester's voice was a terrified croak.

"Someone see yellow vest in bay!" Dmitri declared, lying. "Sunday morning."

"In your dreams!" said the lawyer of the family. "Honey, don't say a word." Amanda wiped mustard off her hands.

"Not even to a friend?" I asked.

Dmitri whistled the first notes of Beethoven's Fifth and reached in his pocket. Mike rocked on the balls of his feet.

From behind the popcorn machine, an apparition: a black helmet with visor down, followed by a well-filled black leather bomber jacket, black chino pants, and a red kerchief dripping red paint.

We waited to see if our trick would work.

"Knight's coming with us or Simona's dead." Something hard poked my right rib before Mike could move and Dmitri could find the handle of his gun.

"The gun is real." Amanda's voice was as crispy as her clothes. "Tell them, Lester. Give them your truth in advertising line."

"Believe her." His face had turned into a defeated mass of wrinkles. "It's a twenty-two caliber. I bought it for her."

"When he still cared whether I lived or died. You shouldn't have asked for a divorce, honey. None of this would have happened."

"You killed Polly and Bud to make the merger go through." I shut my eyes against the possibility that she'd pull the trigger. "To get a bigger slice of the pie in divorce court."

"Aren't you the clever little sleuth. Now let's take a walk. You'll need your eyes for that." I opened them and breathed. I glanced over at Dmitri. He looked blitzed. So did Mike. We'd all expected Amanda to go for Knight only. She'd tried to kill him. He was the hard evidence.

Amanda wiggled fingers. "Move, Knight. You're not getting away this time."

Phil, his identity hidden behind the helmet, did as he was told, limping as he lined up next to Lester. He was a couple of inches taller than Knight, but just as stocky. He had the bowlegs down pat.

Mike ventured a step toward Amanda, chuckling. "You're going to shoot in front of all these celebs?"

"I'll get Cochran to defend me." Her diamond studs gleamed red from the sunset. I thought of blood. Mine. Ours. Amanda poked me with her .22. Dmitri clutched his mustache. Phil and I walked.

Why wasn't anyone catching on to the big *merda* we were in? Because Regis Philbin had just whacked a fly ball to the left-field wall. Paul Simon was running for it.

"How did you know it was me?" Amanda asked. Killers are vain.

"Lester had the best motive: the upcoming merger. And the best means: the vest. Then I realized both fit you just as well."

"Why pick me?"

"It boiled down to a matter of trust," I said. "My other two options were on Bud's suspect list. He would have seen what was coming if either of them had asked him to remove his vest. He trusted you."

Amanda smiled. "And him so down on greed too."

We were halfway to the end of the field, walking crab style, with me trying to catch Phil's eye inside that helmet. I wanted him to jump her. She couldn't shoot at both of us at the same time. One of us would get lucky. Otherwise we were both dead.

Paul Simon was still running backward to the left-field wall, his glove grasping air. A long fly ball.

He hit the rope and spun around. His face smacked into the sharp metal post. A spraying of gasps. He bent over and grabbed his mouth. People ran.

"Now!" I shouted and yanked Amanda's gun arm. A Tarzan yell came out of the sky. Before my eyes a flash of red, then black. A heavy weight hit my shoulder. My knees buckled under. A tree branch landed on the top of my head. The gun went off. I fell.

Flat on my stomach, I chewed dust. A kick sent me rolling.

Groans. A half-smothered scream. The squeak of leather. By the time I'd wiped the dust out of my eyes and could see, it was all over.

Amanda lay on her back. Phil had her by the feet. The real Dick Knight had her by the throat.

Over the speaker, the announcer declared the winner of the romantic weekend.

Dmitri K.

EPILOGUE

I'M BACK AT HH&H, dealing with shoot deadlines and skimpy budgets. Dmitri is back on the streets of the city in his cousin's cab with Sabrina and the puppies on the seat beside him. He still brakes for long hair. Stan has offered to sponsor him for a resident alien card. Dmitri has refused. Once you've applied, the State Department does not allow you to leave the country. The process can take more than a year. Dmitri says he cannot live without seeing Pavel's wife for that long.

Mike and Phil are back in the city too. Their summer job with Ron Perelman is over. They are currently looking for anyone who wants coconuts cracked and waiting for Borscht and Caviar to be old enough to leave their mother.

Willy will be sharing Champanski with Stan and me.

Knight has moved to Florida. His knee and his Harley-Davidson Bad Boy are as good as new, his postcard states. He looks forward to the trial, where he'll be the star witness.

Bud's Sport4Life campaign is splashing across billboards and magazines all over the country. I look at the Gardiner's Island windmill in the ad and remember fog. It makes me sad. Last week *The Wall Street Journal* announced the merger of WSK and Chass\Dayton. Charlene tells me that Lester's never been happier and his shoulder—which caught the bullet when Amanda's gun went off—has healed. Amanda has been indicted and goes on trial in December.

Dmitri presented the Writers and Artists romantic weekend prize to Steve and Laurie. During the champagne lunch at Le Cirque, Steve proposed again. The wedding is in October. We're all invited to New Hope, Pennsylvania.

Steve has learned that Bud set up a sizable trust for him to compensate for Polly's treatment of his father. It was to tell him about the trust that Bud had made that Monday appointment. Steve is sharing the money with the East Hampton Baymen Association.

Laurie has turned out to be money-wise. She wants to protect her investment in Jim's Pit. In exchange for not turning him in, Jim is selling her his share. She's already come up with a new name for the place: Faith's Landing.

The IRS will survive.

Jim has disappeared. Someone else bought the Richard Meier house.

Rebecca has put Bud's home up for sale. She's going to use the money for her and Dodo's old age. "Still a long way off," she says. With the money Laurie paid me, I've bought Rebecca's pastel of the white peonies in a blue bowl. It's still at the framer's.

Dodo has gone to his fourth AA meeting. He likes having a new audience for his Carroll quotes. His current favorite is "I do wish I hadn't drunk quite so much."

He has sent Dmitri and me a poem.

> You are sweet, said the drunk, one would
>   hardly suppose
> that detecting would be your endeavor,
> yet you captured a killer by the tip of
>   her nose.
> What made you so awfully clever?

And Stan?

Stan came home that Monday night. He brought back maple syrup, maple sugar candy, and a maple-cured ham, as if to sweeten me up. He also brought a week's gray growth on his chin and a need to explain.

We sat down on the sofa, holding hands. I listened.

"Two days after I got promoted, the Mayor's office called me to head a new task force for youth crime prevention."

"That's a great honor."

Stan leaned back, taking me with him. I bent my

head on his chest and heard his heart beat. "It is an honor, Sim, but it meant taking a leave of absence. And if it worked out they wanted a promise that I'd leave the force. How could I? Detective first-grade. That's a really big deal."

"You've served twenty-two years. Maybe that's long enough."

At first he felt that accepting meant he was a traitor to his colleagues, to his father, whose unsolved murder had brought him into the force in the first place. Then he felt like a coward because he realized that he wanted out. He was tired of looking at dead people, looking for killers.

"I love kids. This is my chance to work with them, to deal with beginnings."

"You've made up your mind."

"If you agree."

"I think it's a great idea. I wish I'd known about it before."

He hugged me hard. "God, Sim, I've brooded over this all summer long. I'm sorry. I've been awful company."

I inhaled his warm smell. "I might have helped."

He rubbed his beard against my forehead. It was silky. "You'd have smoothed over my bad feelings, encouraged me, kissed away my doubts, fed me until I couldn't think straight."

"Sounds awful."

He clasped my hands. "Wonderful, but I'm still not used to having you. I've spent the better part of forty-four years thinking things out by myself."

I rubbed my fingers against his chapped lips. "We're going to have to work on that."

"Next time it happens, just kick me."

"You'll be out the door."

Stan relaxed into a long laugh. I kissed him, his mouth still open. This was the man I loved, no other.

Stan pulled me down on the sofa, our mouths attached. Three months of worries fell away like loose change from a dark pocket.

I started unbuttoning his shirt.

And now, as Dodo might say, "'The tale is done.'"

COOL PASTA

(serves four)

4 ears of corn
4 large ripe tomatoes
2 bunches of scallions
4 tbsp. olive oil
1 cup loosely packed fresh basil leaves
5 large fresh mint leaves
1 lb. pasta shells
salt and pepper to taste

Cut corn off the cobs with a serrated knife. Reserve the cobs. Seed and dice the tomatoes. Trim and thinly slice the scallions, including the light green part.

Heat olive oil in a skillet. Add the scallions and sauté over medium heat for 3 minutes. Mix in corn. Cook for 2 minutes. Add tomatoes and season vegetables well with salt and pepper. Cook for 5 minutes more.

Tear basil and mint leaves. Remove skillet from heat and add leaves. Allow to cool to room temperature in a large bowl.

Add the reserved cobs to a large pot of salted water and bring to a boil. Add pasta shells.

When shells are *al dente* (approx. 12 mins.), drain and remove cobs. Add pasta to vegetables in bowl. Mix well, check for seasoning, and serve.

Buon appetito!

ACKNOWLEDGMENTS

Many have helped me with this book. Great thanks to: Joan Meisel for her friendship, generosity, and that great view of Gardiner's Bay; Alberta, Maud, and Rick Salter for "lending" me their property for my own nefarious purposes; Bill and Kathy Kromer for sharing the lore of the hardworking bonackers; Leslie and Barbara Segal for their knowledge of Springs; Helen Harrison, director of the Pollock–Krasner Study Center, Captain William E. Segelken of the East Hampton Town Police Department, and Larry Goldenberg for their time; Ben and Nathaniel Spencer for showing me how young boys are; Judy Keller, Barbara Lane, Maria Nella Masullo, and Sharon Villines for their perceptive comments; Jason Kaufman for his hard work; and Ellen Geiger for her never-flagging spirit.

I ask pardon of the East End Parsons for borrowing their history-laden name.

To my editors, Larry Ashmead and Carolyn Marino, thanks for their faith and encouragement.

To Stuart, my love and trust.